SHERLOCK HOLMES
& The
BEAST
OF THE
STAPLETONS

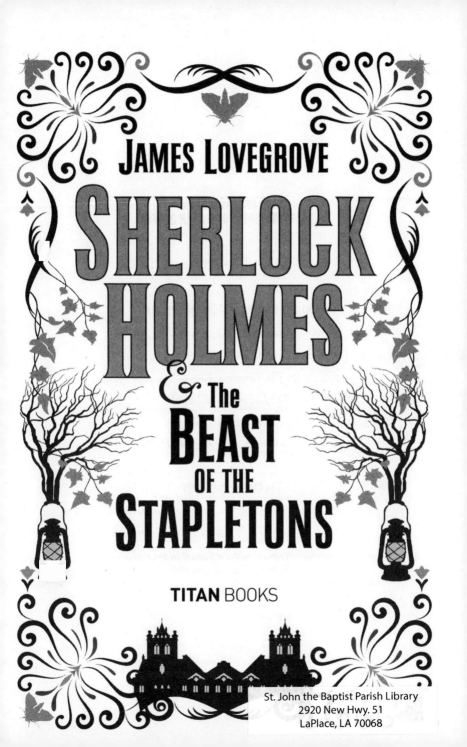

JAMES LOVEGROVE

SHERLOCK HOLMES

& The BEAST OF THE STAPLETONS

TITAN BOOKS

Sherlock Holmes and the Beast of the Stapletons
Hardback edition ISBN: 9781789094695
E-book edition ISBN: 9781789094701

Published by Titan Books
A division of Titan Publishing Group Ltd
144 Southwark St, London SE1 0UP
www.titanbooks.com

First hardback edition: October 2020
2 4 6 8 10 9 7 5 3 1

A CIP catalogue record for this title is available from the British Library.

Printed and bound in Great Britain by CPI Group Ltd

This book is respectfully dedicated to

HOLMESIANS AND SHERLOCKIANS EVERYWHERE

in recognition of their passionate admiration and enduring support
for the deeds of the Great Detective and his ally

SHERLOCK HOLMES

& The
BEAST
OF THE
STAPLETONS

FOREWORD

by John H. Watson MD

The friends of Mr Sherlock Holmes – and these days they are many and multifarious – are liable to know well the events that took place on Dartmoor in the autumn of 1889. Such, at least, may be inferred from the reception of my account of the affair, titled *The Hound of the Baskervilles*, which saw print last year.

Sales of the book were anything but modest – if it is not *im*modest of me to say so. This and, more importantly, the clamour of critical approbation attending its publication have compelled me now to retrieve my notes on another case, one that occurred almost exactly five years later and upon which Holmes's earlier investigation had a direct bearing, and turn them into a narrative.

Here, in the pages that follow, you will find the unfortunate Sir Henry Baskerville who, having narrowly avoided death in the prior instance, was again plagued by a lethal, eerie nemesis and obliged to look to Sherlock Holmes as his saviour.

If anything, the episode is even more garish and perturbing than its predecessor, as you shall see. It is with pride and no small amount of caution that I invite you to peruse this chronicle, which I have dubbed *The Beast of the Stapletons*.

J.H.W., LONDON, 1903

PART ONE

Chapter One

A CANINE CONTRETEMPS

Having finished my rounds for the morning, I decided to pay a visit to my great friend Mr Sherlock Holmes. It was early autumn, with the warmth of summer still lingering in the London air, and the prospect of strolling across Hyde Park on such a clement afternoon to get from Kensington to Baker Street was a highly pleasant one. In that regard, fate had other plans.

Having crossed the Serpentine Bridge, I was proceeding northward along West Carriage Drive, lost in thought. Principally I was musing upon the fact that since Holmes had reappeared in my life a few months earlier, subsequent to that dismal three-year hiatus when I and the rest of the world presumed him dead, my visits to his rooms were becoming ever more frequent. My own home, bereft of the dearly departed Mary and the brightness she had brought to it, seemed increasingly dreary. Every furnishing, every piece of crockery, every curtain and rug reminded me of my late wife, for it was she who had chosen these domestic items. It struck me that reinstating myself in the old accommodation of my bachelor days, sharing once again those well-appointed if rather cramped quarters with Holmes, might be the fillip I needed. I resolved to ask my friend if he would be willing to consider my moving back in.

At that moment, a huge black dog came charging towards me along the path, snarling ferociously.

Sight of the animal filled me with utter, all-consuming dread. I was rooted to the spot, every hair on my head standing on end. The dog was making straight for me, as an arrow flies to its target, and I could do nothing but stare, helpless, unable to move or even think.

Such paralysing terror may perhaps seem strange to my readers unless they recall that not five years prior I had encountered a hound of gigantic proportions upon the moor of Devon, one that caused the deaths of two men and nearly proved the undoing of another. Even though Holmes had killed it stone dead with five shots to its flank, Jack Stapleton's terrible bloodhound-mastiff cross continued to haunt my dreams. Often I would awaken in bed, soaked in sweat, my heart pounding, having been quite convinced that I was back on fog-shrouded Dartmoor and that the beast was chasing me, its phosphorus-accented features glowing, its fang-filled maw agape and slavering, hell-bent on savaging me to death.

So it was that this dog in Hyde Park seemed like a nightmare come to life, my greatest fear made real. It was hurtling towards me with the clear intent of mauling me. In mere seconds I was going to meet a hideous end.

The dog was less than a couple of yards away, easy leaping distance for so sizeable a creature travelling at so great a speed, when all at once a sharp, shrill whistle resounded from the trees nearby. The dog came skidding to a halt, so close to me now that I could have reached down and petted it, in the unlikely event I should have wished to do so. It stood with its ears erect, its fangs bared, gazing up with dark, acquisitive eyes, regarding me much as it might have a juicy hambone or a cornered rabbit.

"Lucy!" came a gruff voice. "Lucy! Come back here. Lucy! This instant!"

The dog, hearing its name, twitched its head but seemed loath to obey the command.

"Lucy…" said the voice, this time with an unmistakable note of menace.

Now the dog turned about, albeit with a show of great reluctance, as though it could not bear to be drawn away from the human into whose flesh it was so apparently keen to sink its teeth.

A man came into view, brandishing a dog lead. Lucy

slouched over to him, aiming the occasional avaricious look back at me. The man grabbed the animal by the scruff of the neck and reattached the lead. Then he strode towards me at a brisk pace, with Lucy trotting at his side.

"Sorry about that," said this fellow. "Hope she didn't give you a fright. She's as meek as a lamb, normally. Just gets a bit excited sometimes."

My mouth was dry, but I managed to frame words. "A bit excited? The wretched thing was coming to attack me. If you hadn't called her off, who knows what would have happened!"

"There's no need to get so hot under the collar about it. You're all right, aren't you? She didn't bite you, did she?"

"Well, yes. I mean, no. Yes, I am all right. No, she didn't bite me."

"Then what is the problem?"

Lucy's owner looked, to all appearances, like a reasonable, respectable gentleman. He was in early middle age and spoke well, and I adjudged him to be some kind of urban professional, a solicitor perhaps or a chartered accountant. He seemed genuinely surprised that I should take offence at his dog's behaviour.

"The problem," I said, "is that if your Lucy really is 'as meek as a lamb', as you put it, I could not have known that. Certainly not from the way she came at me."

"You must have acted aggressively towards her. Dogs are

known to put on angry displays when somebody threatens or intimidates them."

"I assure you I did nothing to spark an adverse reaction in her. I was merely minding my own business."

"You don't need to *do* anything," the man said. "Some people simply give off an aura of hostility towards dogs. That's all it takes."

"An aura of…?" I spluttered. My fear was, as if through some process of emotional alchemy, subliming into indignation. "How dare you, sir! It comes to something when a man can't walk through the park without being assaulted for no good reason by a vicious, undisciplined mongrel."

"And how dare *you*!" the other retorted, his voice rising just as mine had. "I'll have you know that Lucy is a purebred German Shepherd and, what's more, is as well trained a hound as you could hope to find. You saw how she answered when I called. Like that." He snapped his fingers.

"Hardly. It wasn't until the third or fourth time you used her name that she responded. I've a good mind to report you to the authorities. What if you had not been around to curb Lucy? And what if I had been not a grown man but a woman, or a child?"

"But I was, and you aren't," came the reply, accompanied by an insolent sneer. "So your hypothetical proposition is meaningless."

"I have friends at Scotland Yard, you know. One word

from me and you'd be clapped in irons so fast your head would spin."

This was an empty threat and we both knew it. Indeed, I felt instantly ashamed to have brought up my police connections, such as they were. Yet Lucy's owner irked me so greatly that I could not help myself.

"Hah!" he snorted. "Hiding behind the skirts of the law, just because you were scared by a dog. You pathetic, lily-livered weakling."

"What did you call me? Scoundrel! I've seen and done things more hair-raising than an office-bound milksop like you could ever imagine."

"Milksop, eh? You'll regret that. I have a boxing blue from Camford." My antagonist looped the end of Lucy's lead around the arm of an adjacent bench and began removing his jacket. "It may have been a while ago, but there's not much about the noble art that I've forgotten."

Tempted as I was to roll up my sleeves and dish out a drubbing to the fellow, or at least give as good as I got, our altercation was drawing a small crowd. To indulge in a public bout of fisticuffs would be unseemly and, worse, liable to result in arrest by a passing constable and charges of affray, which would do little for my standing as a general practitioner. With a deep, self-steadying breath, I elected to be the bigger man.

"I have no wish to get into a brawl over this," I relented. "Just keep your dog on the lead in future, that's all I ask."

So saying, I set off past the man. My blood was still up, and it wasn't until I emerged from Cumberland Gate into the hurly-burly of Marble Arch that I began to calm down. At that point, I found myself wondering whether the dog really was called Lucy. It seemed altogether too decorous a name for such a brute. Unless, of course, it was short for Lucifer.

I was still chuckling over this little witticism of mine as I crossed the threshold to 221B Baker Street where, it transpired, the beginning of another adventure awaited, one considerably more remarkable and perilous than my canine contretemps in the park.

Chapter Two

BUFFALO SOLDIER

" Ah, Watson!" declared Sherlock Holmes as I entered his rooms. "Your timing could not be more fortuitous."

"You have a guest," I said, motioning at the person who occupied the chair opposite Holmes. "Or is it by any chance a client?" I added, hopeful that this was so, for I could think of nothing more appealing than to join my friend on another of his remarkable investigations.

"The latter," Holmes confirmed.

The stranger rose and offered me a formal bow, which I reciprocated.

"Corporal Benjamin Grier, at your service," said he, extending a hand. He was a Negro gentleman, large and imposing-looking. Yet, for all that he stood a head taller than me and his shoulders were half as broad again as mine – not to mention that he possessed a voice whose low, rumbling timbre resembled a peal of thunder – there was a marked gentleness and gentility about him. As for his smile, it carried a warmth that could only put one at ease.

All the same, I could not help but notice a certain agitation in Grier's bearing. This, as far as I was concerned, cemented his status as a client of Holmes's, for few called upon my friend who were not in need of his services as a consulting detective and thus, for one reason or another, in a state of some anxiety.

"Dr John Watson," I replied, taking the offered hand. Grier's grip was powerful, but I sensed restraint in it. He was withholding his full strength and could, so I thought, have crushed every bone in my hand had he wanted.

"It is an honour to meet you, sir. I am a great admirer of your works. I read avidly, Hawthorne and Poe being my favourite authors. You, sir, run them a close third."

"You are too kind. It is an honour to be numbered in such company, especially since my literary career is still in its infancy. An American?"

"You have me there," Grier said, letting slip a small laugh. "What gave it away?"

"Watson's perspicacity is second to none," Holmes said with an ironical lift of an eyebrow. "Nothing escapes him, least of all a pronounced Yankee accent. Watson, Corporal Grier arrived scarcely two minutes before you. So far I have gleaned a little about him, albeit nothing whatsoever about his reasons for visiting me. He is a soldier, of course. He introduced himself to me by his rank, as he did to you. He is an American, too. That much we have both established. Aside from those two rather obvious inferences, I can hazard a few further."

"Pray do," I said, taking a seat.

"If it's all the same to you, I would prefer that we got down to business, Mr Holmes," Grier said. "I am here on an errand of some urgency and I feel that every second is crucial."

"Naturally, Corporal Grier." Holmes gave an obliging wave of the hand. "Let us delay no further. What, I wonder, has compelled you – a Freemason, who has seen service with the 25th Infantry Regiment during these so-called Indian Wars – to journey to London from the West Country by train, in a forward-facing seat beside the window, and seek me out with some haste?"

Grier's eyes widened and his jaw dropped. It was a shift in expression familiar to me from the countless other occasions when Holmes would deduce intimate details of someone's life and habits based upon that person's appearance alone.

"Very well, Mr Holmes," said he. "I cannot resist. You have earned yourself a minute of my time to explain how you came by those facts, every one of which is as true as I'm sitting here."

"A minute will more than suffice. Really all I have done is play the odds, tendering the most likely conjecture in each instance. So often the commonest interpretation of evidence is the correct one. Firstly, an American soldier of your race must perforce belong to one of only four regiments, namely the 9th and 10th Cavalry and the 24th and 25th Infantry. No regiment in the US army will accept black enlisted men save those four. Collectively, the troops in your regiments are known as Buffalo Soldiers."

"Yes. The name was given to us by the Apaches. Our skin tone and curly hair remind them, it seems, of a buffalo's hide and topknot. Even if it is perhaps not meant as a compliment, I choose to take it as one. The buffalo is a mighty, noble beast, docile unless provoked, dangerous when it is. But how can you be so sure I am infantry, not cavalry?"

"Simple. You are far too big to be a cavalryman."

Grier nodded at that with some amusement. "I pity the horse that would have to carry anyone of my bulk for long distances."

"That makes you, by default, an infantryman," Holmes continued, "and hence, given that there are only two foot regiments to decide between, I had an even chance of choosing the right one. Happily, the gamble paid off."

"Fine, but what prompted you to suggest I am a Freemason?"

"It is a fact – not a well-known one, maybe – that the vast majority of Buffalo Soldiers are also Freemasons. The balance of probabilities that this would be true of you was, therefore, significantly in my favour."

"You have played your hand excellently," said Grier, "but I am still mystified as to how you could know I have come here today by train from the West Country."

"The ticket stub," said Holmes, gesturing towards the other's chest. "The one tucked into your breast pocket. Enough of it is projecting for me to discern the words 'at', 'stern' and 'way', from which it is easy to extrapolate the longer words 'Great', 'Western' and 'Railway'."

Grier glanced down at the stub. "The answer was in plain sight all along."

"The same may be said for proof that you sat in a forward-facing seat. I imagine, with the weather being warm, that it was rather stuffy in the compartment in which you rode and that the window was at least partially open. This would admit smoke from the locomotive's chimney, and smuts from said smoke have adhered to your left shirt cuff."

Grier inspected said shirt cuff, observing – as I did – the few tiny dark speckles that besmirched it.

"Compartments on Great Western Railway trains are on the left-hand side of the carriage, with the corridor on the right," Holmes said. "The location of the smuts thus reveals that you must have been seated facing forward and, moreover, adjacent to the window. It is quite straightforward." He threw a glance at the mantel clock. "And with that, I believe my allotted minute is up."

"I will grant you a brief extension to the time so that you can explain how you knew I have come in haste."

"Oh, as to that," said Holmes airily, "had your journey been a leisurely one, you would surely have taken the opportunity to neaten yourself up between disembarking from the train at Paddington and making your way to my door. The carelessly neglected ticket stub implies otherwise. So, too, does the rapidity with which you took the stairs to my rooms. Indeed, your general mood is one of impatience and preoccupation. To that end, let us prevaricate no further. How, Corporal Grier, may I be of assistance to you?"

Grier composed himself. "It is not I, Mr Holmes, who require your assistance. At least, not directly. Rather, it is an old friend of mine, a man who is already known to both you and Dr Watson."

Holmes steepled his fingers and leaned forward. "Go on."

"The gentleman in question is a Masonic brother of mine. We met in Chicago at the Hesperia Lodge in the mid-eighties, struck up a close comradeship, and have remained in touch ever since, reuniting whenever circumstances allow, although our paths in life have taken us in very different directions. He is Canadian by birth but spent much of his adulthood in America, until providence took him to the shores of your own land some five years ago, where he has remained ever since."

"A-ha. From that thumbnail description, I believe I can identify the fellow in question."

"I had a feeling you might. He has told me how you once aided him in his hour of need, when death loomed and all seemed hopeless. Regrettably, sir, a similar evil situation has befallen him again. However, the crisis, I would submit, is far more acute this time than last."

"I must confess I am in the dark," I interjected.

"A perennial condition with you, Watson," Holmes quipped.

"Come now. That is unfair."

"I apologise. Yet it surprises me, old fellow, that you have failed to interpret the clues Corporal Grier has provided. Can it be that you have forgotten our adventures on Dartmoor back in 'eighty-nine? I know full well that you made copious notes about the case, and by your own admission you have every intention of turning them into one of your published chronicles at some point."

"My goodness," I breathed. It seemed an uncanny coincidence that, a mere half hour earlier, I had been forcibly reminded of Stapleton's grim hound and its predations.

"Yes," said Holmes. "I see it is all coming back to you."

"The man I am referring to," said Grier, "is Henry Baskerville. And I have to tell you, gentlemen," he went on sombrely, "it is not just Henry's life that is at stake on this occasion but his very sanity."

Chapter Three

THE BASKERVILLE CURSE STRIKES AGAIN

"But to begin at the beginning…" said Corporal Benjamin Grier.

"If you wouldn't mind," said Holmes.

Sitting back, the American commenced his narrative. "I was owed several weeks' leave by the army, and got it into my head that I should visit with my old pal Henry all the way across the Atlantic. I was keen to see his home and get an idea of how life as a baronet was treating him. He had a wife now, too."

"Lady Audrey."

"That is she. You know her?"

"Know *of* her. A Devonshire lass, and by all accounts a great beauty."

"He also had sired a son, and I had yet to make the acquaintance of either. I wrote him, expressing my intentions, with the proviso that if he was too grand now to consort with commoners such as myself, naturally I would not come. In his reply, Henry matched my joshing tone. 'Normally I send peasants packing with my shotgun when they come to my house, but for you, Benjamin, I shall make an exception.'" Grier heaved a deep sigh. "Those words proved, in the event, to be horribly prophetic.

"Throughout the ocean voyage my prevailing mood was one of joyous anticipation. Everything I knew about Henry's present circumstances, from the correspondence he and I had exchanged over the years since he came to England, suggested that he had found happiness. He was deeply in love with Audrey, and she had provided him with a healthy heir, name of Harry, who had lately turned three and upon whom Henry clearly doted. He was settling into the ways of Dartmoor, befriending neighbours and enjoying an active social life. It seemed he had put behind him the whole episode involving the hound and Jack Stapleton, or whatever the man's name was. About this his letters had furnished only a sketchy account, but from what I could gather, it was a horrendous ordeal. By the way, regarding you, Mr Holmes, Henry was fulsome in his praise. The same goes for you, Dr Watson. It is quite apparent that he owes you two his life. But how much can change in a single moment! How easily can disaster strike when least expected!" Grier nodded towards the whisky decanter on the sideboard with an importunate air. "I realise it is barely gone noon, sirs, but might I…?"

I stood up, charged a glass and handed it to him. With appreciation, he drank deep.

"That's better," said he, and resumed his account. "Of my arrival at Southampton and my subsequent journey to Devon, there is little to say, other than to mention a strange foreboding that came over me, its intensity increasing the further inland I travelled. At first my inexperienced eye roved with delight over the hills, rivers and quaint villages I passed in a succession of trains. Yet, as I crossed into Devon, the terrain grew not only wilder but in some weird way darker: small towns interspersed with solitary stone hovels, all huddling beneath a low, grey sky. An oppression settled over my spirits, and I ascribed it to the bleakness of my surroundings, and also to exhaustion. I had been a week at sea and am no sailor; nor had my accommodation helped, for all I could afford was a cabin in steerage. There was a part of me, however, that seemed convinced somehow that disaster lay ahead – and in this, alas, it was proved accurate."

"Yes, yes, enough of the hors d'oeuvres," said Holmes, somewhat curtly. "Please, I beg you, Grier, the entrée."

One might deem this remark rude, and I fear his interlocutor took it as such. I, on the other hand, who knew Holmes's ways intimately, understood that he was excited by Grier's story and anxious to get to the heart of the matter.

"You are right," the American said, a little stiffly. "Here I am, insisting that time is of the essence, and what do I go and do but get lost in digression? I shall henceforth do my best to be concise."

"But at the same time, you must omit no salient fact."

"Agreed. Well, eventually I alighted at a place called Bartonhighstock, a tiny, out-of-the-way village with an inn and a train halt to its name and not much else."

I knew Bartonhighstock, for it was there, at a little rural wayside railway station, that I had fetched up, along with Dr James Mortimer and Sir Henry himself, on the way to my memorable sojourn at Baskerville Hall.

"By prior agreement, Henry was to have laid on a wagonette to collect me," said Grier. "None, though, was to be seen. I waited a full hour, and still no wagonette appeared. This struck me as odd but explicable. Maybe there had been some kind of miscommunication. Maybe Henry had got his dates muddled up, or I had. So I assured myself, even as my misgivings mounted.

"In the end I decided to walk, and duly went to ask for directions to Baskerville Hall. There was no station master – the station was too small for that – but there was a booking clerk. Upon hearing my destination, the fellow's face turned grim.

"'You have heard about the recent tragedy there,' said he. I shan't attempt to replicate his thick rural burr.

"'Tragedy?' I enquired.

"'The death of Lady Audrey.'

"At that, my heart sank like a stone. All at once, my feelings of foreboding were justified.

"'Her Ladyship was killed,' the clerk said, 'just a short distance from the Hall.'

"'Killed? How?'

"Now his expression became not just grim but evasive. 'Well, it's not for me to say one way or another what might have been responsible. Nobody knows for certain. But a terrible bad death it was. And there are rumours...'

"'What sort of rumours?'

"'That some monster did it. Nothing else could account for the awful state of her body.'

"'Monster,' I echoed wonderingly. I pressed him for more detail, but none was forthcoming. All he would tell me was that Baskerville Hall was not somewhere I, or anyone, should go. He advised me to take the next train out of Bartonhighstock.

"He still had not vouchsafed the Hall's whereabouts. However, I managed to extract that morsel of information from him, if nothing else. I can be quite... persuasive when I put my mind to it. What is the good of being built so sturdily if one cannot take advantage of it from time to time?

"I was told it was a distance of some seven miles to the Hall, and it was anything but an easy journey. Yet to a soldier who has marched, day upon day, across desert, mountain and prairie, seven miles is nothing. Having double-checked the route with the booking clerk – for there were many junctions where I would have to make turns, and few signposts for guidance – I hefted my suitcase and set off at a fast lick. A couple of hours of daylight remained, I estimated, and it would not do to get caught out in the open, somewhere remote and uninhabited, as darkness fell.

"Along narrow lanes and up and down hillocky slopes I strode. A wind stirred, bringing enough of a chill to the air that I felt obliged to button my coat up to the neck. The overcast sky darkened. All the while, as I walked, I felt a profound pang of sorrow for my friend Henry. A widower now, after a mere four years of marriage – and his wife taken from him in circumstances which, judging by the clerk's hints, were as violent as they were mysterious. I recalled Henry saying once, in a letter, that there was a widely held belief that the Baskervilles were cursed. The wicked antics of an ancestor of his, name of Hugo, had seen to it that the family would never know happiness. Successive generations would pay the price for their forebear's sins. He had mentioned this laughingly, and doubtless when the supposedly spectral hound that killed his uncle was revealed to be no more than a flesh-and-blood dog, it did put Henry's mind at rest, convincing him that he was not the victim of some supernatural legacy of suffering.

"But now it occurred to me that perhaps, after all, the Baskerville curse was real, and Audrey was just the latest in line to fall to it.

"Night was fast approaching when at long last I spied what could only have been the Hall. As you yourselves know, gentlemen, it is a huge, stark edifice built of black granite and dominated by a pair of twin towers, its walls covered in ivy and inset with meanly small mullioned windows. All Henry had told me about his home was that it was large and rambling, and up until that moment, in my New World ignorance, I had had in my mind's eye some grand, porticoed mansion in the American style. I had not thought that the place would be quite so ancient, nor quite so austere.

"The Hall sits in a natural depression in the landscape fringed with ragged trees. As I headed downhill towards it, I met a man and a woman coming the other way. He was tall, with a square black beard and a lugubrious air, while she was large and broad and similarly had a very serious look about her. They were carrying luggage, and from their stooped shoulders and repeated backward glances I could see they were in a state of some consternation. I hailed them, and soon enough, after they had overcome their initial wariness, we fell to talking. I swiftly ascertained that these two were the Barrymores, Henry's butler and housekeeper."

"The Barrymores?" I said. "They are still working for

Sir Henry? That is somewhat surprising, given everything that—"

"Hush, Watson," Holmes interrupted, wagging an admonitory finger at me. "Let Corporal Grier tell his tale."

"Mr Barrymore was quick to inform me that he and Mrs Barrymore had handed in their notice that very afternoon and were leaving Baskerville Hall with no intention ever to return. 'The master's behaviour,' he said, 'has become unconscionable.'

"'Since Lady Audrey's death,' said his wife, 'he has been quite out of his mind.'

"'Grief may do that to a man,' I pointed out.

"'Grief?' said Mr Barrymore. 'Oh, this is not grief, sir. This is something far worse. I would not go so far as to call it madness, but the word is as good a description as any for Sir Henry's mental state. The fits of rage. The shouting and raving at all hours of day and night. The smashing of plates, the defacing of portraits...'

"'Nine days we have endured it,' said Mrs Barrymore, who seemed a woman of some fortitude, if her stolid features were anything to go by. 'What happened to Her Ladyship shocked us all, but nothing could have prepared us for Sir Henry's reaction. At the funeral he scarce spoke a word, save for a few combative grunts, and it has only got worse since. This morning he even brandished a gun at my husband! Said he would shoot him, or himself, one or the other, he didn't much mind. That was the last straw as far as we were concerned. We have quit, and good riddance.'

"'It is the lad I feel sorry for,' said Mr Barrymore.

"'You mean Harry, Sir Henry's son,' I said.

"'We only bore it as long as we did for that poor little mite's sake,' said Mrs Barrymore. 'I had half a mind to make off with him, just to preserve him from his father's fury. But, if we had attempted to take Harry with us and Sir Henry had caught us in the act, I cannot say what would have happened. I doubt we would have survived, and maybe not Harry either. That is a mark of just how far beyond reason Sir Henry has gone.'

"'You say you are a friend of his, sir,' said Mr Barrymore.

"'A good and, I hope, trusted friend.'

"'Then perhaps you may talk some sense into him, where my wife and I could not. I tell you, though, the way he is now, he is a danger to all and sundry, not least himself. To enter Baskerville Hall is to take your life into your hands.'

"'Consider me warned,' I said. 'Good luck to you both.'

"'And to you,' said Mr Barrymore. 'I fear you shall need it more than we.'

"With that, they trudged off into the night, while I squared my shoulders and, with perhaps pardonable trepidation, covered the last quarter-mile of ground to the Hall."

Chapter Four

NO WAY TO WELCOME AN OLD FRIEND

"I cannot say for certain what I thought might happen to me as I opened the lodge gates and made my way up the drive," Grier continued. "I *can* say that the last thing I expected was to be shot at."

"The very event Sir Henry joked about in his letter," said I.

Grier nodded. "Yet it was no laughing matter. There was the booming report of a shotgun, and I swear to you, gentlemen, the cluster of pellets flew past my head *this* close." He held up a finger an inch from his left cheek. "I felt it go by. A hand's breadth to the right, and I would not be here now to talk about it.

"'Ho there, Brother Henry!' I called out, presuming the unseen sniper to be the house's sole adult occupant. 'It is I, Brother Benjamin. I see you have travelled to the east.' I was using one of the standard Masonic greetings in order to establish my *bona fides* beyond any question. I might equally have said, 'Have you seen my dog, Hiram?', but I imagined the topic of dogs might be a sensitive one for Henry."

"He is not alone in that," I muttered.

"To my astonishment, there came no verbal reply. Rather, the shotgun boomed again. This time a small divot was blasted out of the grass just to the side of the drive. I had spied the flash of the gun's discharge in an upstairs window, and now, focusing upon that window, I could just about make out the weapon itself and the person holding it. Even at a distance and in poor light, I was able to confirm that it was Henry.

"'Henry!' I declared. 'This is no way to welcome an old friend after so long an absence.' It may seem remarkable to you, gentlemen, but I felt no great fear. I know Henry to be an excellent shot, and if he had wished to hit me, he could have. His goal was to deter me, no more than that, and thus I felt safe standing my ground. My main emotion, aside from a sense of shock, was affront.

"At last my friend spoke. 'Go away, Brother Benjamin. You are not needed here. Go and save yourself. Leave me be.'

"'I shall not budge from this spot,' I said, 'until you tell me why you are acting so out of character. I know about your wife, and you have my deepest condolences. But if this is how you are mourning Audrey, it is inappropriate, to say the least.'

"'I am under no obligation to explain myself,' said Henry.

'All I need tell you is that while you are in my company, you are in peril. I appreciate that you have travelled far to be here, but please just do as I ask, Benjamin, and go.'

"'I have braved many dangers in the past,' I said. 'If there is further danger here, I am quite prepared to face it. Let us confront it together, indeed, side by side, as friends and brothers of the square should.'

"'You do me a great honour, and yourself great credit, with that offer,' came the reply. 'But I am adamant. Every minute you remain on my property, you expose yourself to hazard. The sooner you leave, the sooner all will be well for you.'

"'And the boy? Young Harry? What about him? Surely all is *not* well for him while he is on the premises.'

"'I shall protect him,' said Henry. 'I shall defend him to my dying breath. I trust no one but myself to keep him safe.'

"'I beg you, one last time,' said I, 'let me in. Whatever has gotten you so in fear of your own and your son's lives, surely it is better if there are two of us to guard against it.'

"I heard, then, the distinctive click of a breech being snapped shut. Quite clearly Henry had just loaded his shotgun with fresh cartridges.

"'I have no desire to injure you, Benjamin,' my friend said. 'Yet if the threat of bodily harm is not enough, I may yet have to resort to the reality. Go. There is a smallholding half a mile due south of here, where the farmer, Mr Wonnacott, will be willing to put you up for the night for a small consideration.

You may reach it before full dark if you start now. Farewell. I am sorry that you did not come at a more propitious time.'

"He closed the window, and I was left standing there on the drive with a dilemma. Should I persist? Or should I do as bidden and depart? The former option seemed futile. Could I break into the house? Force Henry to accept my assistance against his will? On present showing it was unimaginable. More than likely I would end up with a peppering of buckshot for my trouble. The latter option meant abandoning him – him and of course innocent, vulnerable Harry, who I could only assume was living in terror of his desperate, gun-wielding papa – and such an act would weigh sorely upon my conscience. Yet if Henry did not want me there, whatever his reasons, I had no choice but to respect his wishes.

"I lugged my suitcase all the way to the smallholding Henry had described. The owner, the aforementioned Wonnacott, grudgingly offered me a bed, at the cost of three pence. I hardly slept a wink, and the next morning I returned on foot to Bartonhighstock, my thoughts all awhirl. I fervently wished to help my friend but could not think how. It was as I was approaching the village that a certain name suddenly sprang to mind. Yours, Mr Holmes. Not only are you renowned worldwide as an unraveller of knotty conundrums, but you have had prior dealings with Henry and Baskerville Hall. All at once it was obvious to me that you were the man to see.

"The next London train was not due until midmorning. I was famished, so I went to the village inn and ordered breakfast. The landlord there seemed to find me as fascinatingly exotic as a hothouse orchid. Hence, while I ate, he sat with me and engaged me in conversation. He asked me about my homeland. Was it really so huge? Were all us former colonials as brash as our reputation would have it? And so on.

"When the cause of my visit to Devon came up and I told the landlord about my abortive expedition to Baskerville Hall, a similar look stole over him as had over the booking clerk the previous afternoon.

"'Oh my word,' said he, shaking his head sorrowfully. 'You know, of course, what has happened at the Hall lately. An awful business. And the condition of Lady Audrey's body – ghastly.'

"'How so?' I said, reckoning I was going to get more out of this garrulous fellow than I had out of the tight-lipped booking clerk.

"'Bereft of blood, she was. Scarcely a drop left in her veins. And there was a hole in her neck, through which the stuff must have been drained. Drained or...'

"He hesitated. I made an encouraging gesture, and the landlord, with some circumspection, resumed.

"'Sucked out of her,' he said. 'Sucked out of her by some kind of vampiric animal!'"

Chapter Five

SKINWALKER

S herlock Holmes was unable to suppress his disdain.

"Pooh!" he said. "Vampiric animal indeed."

"You do not know of any beast that drinks the blood of others to sustain itself?" said Grier. "Why, I could list you a dozen, from the humble mosquito to the freshwater leech and onwards."

"And I could list you a dozen more. However, I would be hard pressed to name one which is so large it could consume practically the entire blood supply of a human at a single sitting in order to sate its appetite, as this creature reputedly has done with Lady Audrey. How many pints is that, Watson?"

"In an adult, somewhere between nine and twelve."

"You see? Impossible! The thing would have to be as big as an elephant, if not bigger, with a stomach capacity to match.

No haemophagic entity of such gargantuan proportions exists or has ever existed."

"Your scepticism jibes with my own, Mr Holmes," said Grier, "if somewhat amplified. But listen. The landlord had more to say. When I queried his remark, he responded with a wry, knowing nod. The manner of Audrey's demise, you see, was not wholly unprecedented. He told me that over the past few weeks there had been reports of sheep in the region being molested in much the same way as she had been, the blood extracted from them by means of a hole in the neck. A fair few had died more or less straight away from blood loss, while the rest had been left so deathly ill that they had to be slaughtered just to put them out of their misery. Farmers were understandably very worried about their flocks and had taken to bringing them indoors at night or standing guard over them in the field, armed.

"'Nobody has caught the being responsible for the bloodsucking,' the landlord said. 'Its attacks have all taken place under cover of darkness and well away from human habitation. But there have been definite sightings of... something.'

"'Something...?' I prompted.

"The landlord lowered his voice and leaned a little closer. 'More than once it has been spotted flying across the moon,' he said. 'A fearsome thing, even in silhouette.'

"'Flying?' I said. 'So we are talking about some kind of bird?'

"'No. Not bird. Insect, sir. To be precise, a moth.'

"'Moth!' I exclaimed."

"Moth!" Holmes said, echoing Grier's ejaculation, but in this case with a mixture of derision and glee. "Really, now I have heard everything! And yet…" A contemplative gleam entered my friend's eyes, and he stroked his chin with a forefinger. An idea had occurred to him, that much I could tell. In the deeps of his vast brain, something had snagged, like a bite on a fishing line.

Grier continued. "'A big one, too,' the landlord said, 'in as much as anyone can judge. Wings wider than a man is tall, and a body as thick around as a tree trunk. Just three nights ago, when the moon was at its fullest, the moth was seen, and its outline covered the moon's disc almost completely.'"

"A matter of perspective, surely," said Holmes. "I may hold up a thumb before my eye and blot out the moon with it."

"I believe I lodged a similar objection," said Grier, "but the landlord claimed that the witnesses concerned were, in every case, reliable sources. Each saw the moth at a distance and was able to estimate its size accurately from context. Each swore, too, that the moth's wings were fluttering and that the looping, swirling pattern of its flight was consistent with that of a member of the species. What distinguished it from every other moth was its sheer excessive scale. That," he added, "and the fact that its eyes glowed bright red in the darkness."

"And this same exceptionally large moth with the glowing red eyes, having first feasted upon unsuspecting sheep, graduated thence to human prey in the shape of Lady Audrey Baskerville," said Holmes. "Was that the presumption among the good people of Dartmoor?"

"According to the landlord, yes."

"Well now," my friend said, musing. "There is, to my knowledge, at least one genus of moth that feeds off the blood of vertebrates. Watson, would you do me a favour? You see that slipcased edition of Kirby and Spence's *Introduction to Entomology* on the shelf behind you? Take down volume three and pass it over. Thank you."

He leafed through the book until he came to the page he sought.

"Yes, here we are. *Calyptra*. Common name: the vampire moth. A lepidopteran gifted with an unusually strong, hollow proboscis with which it is able to pierce any fleshy integument, even cattle hide, and thus suck blood, much as its non-carnivorous equivalents suck nectar from the flower." He closed the book and laid it aside. "However, there is no known member of the species possessing a wingspan greater than an inch or so, let alone a six-foot-wide behemoth such as you are describing. Nor is it anywhere stated that *Calyptra*'s eyes glow red."

"If you ask me," said Grier, "you are looking at this the wrong way by treating the beast as though it is part of the natural order."

"You are asserting that it is *un*natural? Or, for that matter, *super*natural?"

"I am asserting just that. Earlier, Mr Holmes, you correctly intuited that I have seen action in the Indian Wars with the 25th. I served on the Great Plains, in the Dakota Territory, although I was not part of the regimental detachment that took part in the Battle of Wounded Knee, and I thank the Lord for that. I was also posted on the Mexican border. There I came into contact with members of the Apache and Navajo nations. We skirmished with war parties and carried out police actions against bands of raiders, but I may say the circumstances were not always hostile. Some Navajo, indeed, were army recruits, serving as scouts and trackers. It was from just such an individual, attached to our regiment, that I learned about skinwalkers."

"Skinwalkers?" I said.

"According to the scout, whose name was High-Backed Wolf, skinwalkers are evil witches who can transform themselves, through ritual magic, into animals. In the Navajo tongue the word for them is *yee naagloshii*, meaning 'he who goes on all fours'. Skinwalkers can adopt almost any animal form and are known to suck the blood of their prey. Their distinguishing characteristic, aside from inhuman speed and the uncanny ability to disappear from view in an instant, is their lambent red eyes.

"Now, Indians lay claim to all manner of miraculous powers. Their shamans are able to commune with the spirits of their tribal ancestors and use mystical totems either to heal or to cause death. It isn't for me to say whether any of that is genuine or not. High-Backed Wolf, however, was utterly sincere when he described skinwalkers to me. His voice was hushed and his eyes darted nervously around, exactly the behaviour of one who, against his better judgement, was speaking the unspeakable. He told me he had even met a skinwalker himself. It swooped down upon him one day while he was on a hunting expedition near the Colorado River. It had taken the shape of a large white eagle, and High-Backed Wolf knew that he must not look the creature in the eye, else it would absorb his soul and he would become its hapless thrall. He realised he had strayed unwittingly into the skinwalker's hunting grounds, and with various signs of apology and obeisance he departed the area in some haste. I could see the terror he had felt at the time reflected in his face as he confided in me about the incident. I did not have the slightest doubt that what he said was true."

"True to him, perhaps," said Holmes, "but objectively true? I wonder. You seem to be implying, Corporal Grier, that this monstrous Devonshire moth may itself be one of these so-called skinwalkers. You mean to say that a Navajo witch has taken up residence on Dartmoor and is using black magic to bring terror and death to the region?"

"I advance it as a possibility."

"I am sure that you can see, as well as I do, the arrant preposterousness of the notion. For a start, assuming an American Indian has exchanged the western provinces of his country for the western provinces of ours, would the natives not remark upon this alien's presence in their midst? Would it not be a matter of such surpassing interest that it merited an article in the national papers? Yet no such report has appeared in recent months, to my knowledge, and I make a point of perusing the press thoroughly every day. But if we accept nonetheless that this migrant has managed to keep a low profile thus far, his attacks upon livestock and now Lady Audrey Baskerville risk bringing unwanted attention. He is even showing himself at night, in moth form. Can hunger have made him reckless? Is it a kind of arrogance? Is he taunting Dartmoor's denizens, boldly inviting them to form search parties and hunt him down? If so, what does he hope to gain from it all?"

Holmes enumerated these objections in an arch manner. Not for a moment was he giving Grier's skinwalker idea credence.

"What if there is some local equivalent of the skinwalker, though?" Grier said. "Your country has a long history of witchcraft and the dark arts. Might there not still be those who embrace those old customs to this day, in the less civilised corners of the land?"

"Modern witches?" said Holmes. "Ones capable of turning themselves into animals? Well, if such folk exist, I would very much like to meet them and see these magical metamorphoses with my own eyes. Until then, however, I am content to believe that an empirical explanation may be found for all the phenomena you have reported, and that whatever took the life of Lady Audrey, no supernatural agency was involved."

"I prefer to keep an open mind, myself," said Grier.

"Mine is far from closed," Holmes rejoined. "I merely make it my habit to exclude the paranormal from consideration when investigating a case. It removes a layer of unnecessary complication. All said and done, this remains a fascinating state of affairs. Sir Henry is quite certain that his life and his son's are in jeopardy, and in light of his harrowing experiences of five years ago and the more recent trauma of his wife's death, he could well be forgiven for thinking that the stars are indeed aligned against him and his kin. It may be, moreover, that there lies in the Baskerville bloodline a streak of insanity, one which runs all the way back to Hugo Baskerville, that wretched rake and libertine, and perhaps further still. It has been latent in Sir Henry until now, when, under the strain imposed on him by grief, it has risen to the fore. Regardless of the cause, the man is clearly in crisis and requires help."

"Help which you are prepared to give?" said Grier hopefully.

"More than willing to."

"Oh, thank goodness!" the American sighed. "How soon can you make the journey down to Dartmoor?"

"A glance at *Bradshaw's* will confirm my supposition that there is a Totnes-bound train departing from Paddington shortly after three."

"You mean you can leave immediately?"

"I can and shall. You, I take it, will accompany me?"

"Gladly," said Grier.

"Excellent. And you, Watson? How about it? Are you ready to return to Dartmoor to confront another murderous marauding beast of seemingly unearthly origin?"

"No," said I.

Holmes blinked, aghast. "Did I hear you right? 'No'?"

"I'm afraid, Holmes, I shall not be going with you. I wish you well, but sorry, I am staying in London."

Chapter Six

A NOT UNCOURAGEOUS MAN

As I walked glumly away from Baker Street, I asked myself again and again why I had given the answer I did. When pressed by Holmes for a reason, I had cited pressure of work. I was swamped with patients, I told him. My two usual locums were both out of town, and I knew of no one else whom I trusted to handle the practice in my absence.

All of which was true enough, but if I had really wanted to, I could have freed myself up for at least a couple of days, with some effort and a good deal of judicious rearranging.

Holmes had said that it pained him to imagine tackling this case without his trusty Watson by his side. He had complained in strenuous terms that I was professionally overstretched and could do with shedding some or all of the burden of my vocation. He had even ventured that he knew a young doctor called Verner who was looking to buy a general practice and that I should consider selling mine to the fellow.

"But that is a long-term solution," he had said. "Is there really nothing that can be done, in the short term, which might enable you to join me and Corporal Grier on our undertaking? Nothing at all? You shake your head. Oh, my dear fellow. How very sad. If it is any consolation, you may be assured that when I return, I shall furnish you with a full account of my deeds so that you may, as is your custom, take copious notes. I shall not skimp on a single detail."

It wasn't until I was near home that I could bring myself to admit the real reason for my refusal to go.

It was fear, plain and simple.

I am a not uncourageous man, even if I say so myself. My service in Afghanistan should attest to that, as does my participation in various adventures with Holmes, during the course of which he and I have opposed many a malefactor with deadly designs and frequently found ourselves in predicaments that constitute a threat to life and limb. I have seldom been deemed deficient when it comes to valour.

On this occasion, however, I could not bring myself to revisit the scene of perhaps our most terrifying exploit. However hard I tried, I could not overcome the pusillanimity that had taken hold of me.

How well I remembered those events of October 1889. It had begun with the young country doctor, James Mortimer, calling at our rooms at Baker Street. He came with news of the death of his friend Sir Charles Baskerville from an apparent heart attack. Mortimer averred that what in fact had killed Sir Charles was terror – terror brought on by an encounter with a hellhound, the same beast that, according to family legend, had been responsible for the grisly demise of his impious ancestor Hugo some 250 years earlier. Sir Charles was a superstitious man and had a weak heart. These two factors, and a panicked flight to escape the clutches of a ravening demonic dog, conspired to cause his premature end.

It wasn't long before we made the acquaintance of Sir Charles's nephew and sole living heir Sir Henry, who showed us an anonymous note that had been sent to him at his hotel in London, warning him to stay away from the moor. The note consisted of words clipped from the previous day's *Times* and glued to the sheet of foolscap, so as to conceal the author's identity. Even more curiously, Sir Henry was being trailed through the capital by a mysterious, bearded stranger, and one of his boots had been stolen from outside his hotel room.

Holmes charged me with escorting Sir Henry down to Dartmoor, saying that he himself was too busy with a particularly thorny blackmail case to attend to the matter in person. Arriving in Devon, I learned that a dangerous convict, the Notting Hill murderer Selden, had escaped prison and was believed to be at large on the moor.

Soon after that I met the naturalist Jack Stapleton, out netting butterflies. He showed me the great Grimpen Mire, an expanse of bog notorious for the risk it posed to the unwary. I saw evidence of this myself when, before my very eyes, a moor pony was sucked writhing and whinnying down into the swamp's remorseless depths.

I then, separately, met Stapleton's beautiful, dark-eyed sister Beryl. She, mistaking me for Sir Henry, advised me in no uncertain terms to leave Dartmoor and go back to London, for my own good. Sir Henry himself came across the lady later, and an attraction between the two was born, much to her brother's disapproval. Yet another neighbour of Sir Henry's, a Mr Frankland, wandered into my orbit, he turning out to be a wealthy elderly eccentric who filed lawsuits for his own amusement.

Late one night at Baskerville Hall, Sir Henry and I surprised his manservant Barrymore in the act of signalling from a window with a candle. We discovered that the convict Selden was Mrs Barrymore's brother and that the Barrymores were aiding him in his evasion of the law by leaving out food and clothing for him on the moor. Sir Henry and I set off in pursuit of the fugitive criminal, in vain, although we did spy an elusive solitary figure atop one of the tors which dot Dartmoor. Not only that but during the chase we heard a sinister, blood-curdling howl coming from the direction of the Grimpen Mire, the cry of some large canine.

At Barrymore's insistence, Sir Henry generously agreed not to report Selden's whereabouts to the police. He gave permission for Barrymore and his wife to arrange passage out of the country for her brother, on the assurance of the felon's continued good behaviour. In return, Barrymore informed us about a letter that had been sent to Sir Charles on the morning of his death from a certain "L.L.", requesting an assignation at the gates of the Hall that night. We swiftly established that the sender was Mrs Laura Lyons, daughter of Frankland. She was in the midst of a difficult divorce from her bully of a husband and had written to Sir Charles to secure a financial contribution from him towards her legal expenses.

Frankland, her father, had another passion besides frivolous lawsuits, and that was astronomy. Through the telescope mounted upon the roof of his house, Lafter Hall, he had spied a young boy furtively ferrying provisions to someone else, not Selden, who was hiding out on the moor. I, presuming this second person to be the figure whom Sir Henry and I had spotted a few nights earlier and thinking him perhaps germane to the case, followed the route the boy had taken. It led me to a crude stone hut, which showed signs of occupancy. The meagre dwelling turned out to be the temporary residence of none other than Sherlock Holmes.

Holmes had secretly been staying in the area all along, conducting researches in tandem with mine. He had fathomed that Beryl Stapleton was actually Jack Stapleton's wife, not his sister, which better explained her supposed brother's censorious attitude towards the mutual romantic interest she and Sir Henry had developed. Holmes said, too, that Stapleton had dictated the letter from Mrs Lyons, gaining the woman's cooperation by deceitfully promising to marry her, and that he was the fellow who had dogged Sir Henry's footsteps in London, disguised by a false beard. It was clear to Holmes that Stapleton was not only a scoundrel of the highest order and a cynical manipulator of women but someone who would stop at nothing, not even murder, to achieve his ends.

The ultimate object of Stapleton's deadly machinations was Sir Henry and, briefly, it seemed that he had succeeded, for the howling of a hound and a series of agonised human screams drew Holmes and me to what appeared at first glance to be the baronet's lifeless body. However, the corpse was Selden's. The convict was dressed in Sir Henry's tweeds, these having been supplied to him by the Barrymores, and had perished of a broken neck, sustained after a fall from a high rocky ridge. Stapleton arrived at the scene with suspicious alacrity and was patently crestfallen upon being informed that the deceased was not Sir Henry.

At the Hall, Holmes remarked upon the close facial resemblance between Jack Stapleton and Hugo Baskerville, the latter as seen in a portrait on the wall. A visit to Mrs

Lyons confirmed that Stapleton had coerced her into penning the letter which lured Sir Charles to his doom. She, naturally, was appalled to learn that her wooer was already wed. Holmes furnished proof in the shape of a photograph of the Stapletons taken four years earlier and endorsed with the words "Mr and Mrs Vandeleur", that being the name by which the couple had previously gone. At the time the photograph was taken, Stapleton had been a schoolmaster in Yorkshire. He had subsequently lost his position when the school closed owing to an atrocious scandal.

Everything came to a head that very night, as Holmes and I lay in wait outside the Stapletons' isolated cottage, Merripit House. With us was that doughty Scotland Yarder, Inspector Lestrade, who had journeyed down from London to lend assistance. Sir Henry was a dinner guest of the Stapletons and, at Holmes's instruction, left their company after dark to walk home. The baronet was, unbeknownst to him, bait in a trap which my friend had laid.

What transpired on that foggy night on Dartmoor is etched indelibly in my memory, and it was this part of the adventure, more than anything, that made the idea of revisiting the region impossible for me. Stapleton unleashed his gigantic hound, which had obtained Sir Henry's scent from the boot its master had stolen – the very scent that had led it to mistake Selden, in Sir Henry's suit, for prey and chase him to his death. The beast pursued its true quarry through the ever-thickening fog. Happily, we three sentinels – that is Holmes, Lestrade and I – were able to intercept it in the nick of time, before its jaws closed fatally around Sir Henry's throat.

Yet the sight of the dog bounding towards us, its eyes incandescent, its muzzle, hackles and dewlap seemingly aflame... The size of it. The coal-blackness of its pelt. The long, loping bounds with which it closed the distance between itself and Sir Henry. The savagery with which it pounced upon him. My God! It was nightmarish beyond belief, the kind of experience which could make a man irrevocably lose his reason.

In the end, a grand imposture stood revealed. The hound's origins did not lie in some pit of Hades. It was merely a dog of unusual size and ferocity, tricked out with streaks of a phosphorus preparation and trained to kill. As for its master, he fell foul of the Grimpen Mire. The fog caused him to lose his way as he traversed the only safe path through the bog, and he drowned in that rank, miasmatic ooze. A more fitting fate for so callous and immoral a villain it is hard to imagine.

From Holmes, I afterwards learned of Stapleton's origins. He was the son of Rodger Baskerville, wayward younger brother of Sir Charles, and was born and raised in Costa Rica, whither Rodger had flown after certain grievous misconduct made remaining in England impossible for him.

When the adult Jack Baskerville was caught embezzling public money, he fled South America with his wife Beryl, née Garcia, a local beauty. Upon arrival in England, he changed his name to Vandeleur and opened the school in Yorkshire, St Oliver's, which failed in infamous circumstances. Changing his name yet again to Stapleton, he moved south to the West Country and hatched his scheme to claim the valuable Baskerville estate, worth just shy of a million pounds, which he felt was rightly his. In order to realise that goal, all he had to do was despatch the two relatives who stood between him and his inheritance: Sir Charles and Sir Henry. The legend of the Baskerville hound gave him the inspiration for a grotesque method of murder that would, in all likelihood, have no unwarranted repercussions for him. As long as he kept the hound's existence hidden, nobody was likely to connect it to him. Presumably, once he was done with its services, he would have despatched the creature and disposed of the carcass in the mire, where it would never be found.

Beryl Stapleton had been his more or less willing accomplice at first, until her fondness for Sir Henry grew to outweigh her uxorial fidelity. It was she who had composed the note of warning to Sir Henry. The scent of white jessamine adhering to the notepaper had alerted Holmes to the possibility that the sender was a woman. That in turn had directed his early suspicions towards the Stapletons.

A secondary accomplice of Stapleton's was his aged manservant, Anthony, whose real name was Antonio and whom the Stapletons had brought with them to England from his native Costa Rica. It was Antonio's job to care for the hound when his master was otherwise engaged. What had since become of him, and for that matter of Beryl Stapleton, was not known to me or to Holmes. The general view was that both of them had returned to their homeland, driven from these shores by the ignominy and opprobrium arising from their association with Jack Stapleton.

Again and again my thoughts kept returning to that vision of the hound homing in on Sir Henry through the fog, all aglow like some phantasmagorical spectre. I recalled Holmes emptying his revolver into the creature, and the hound rolling onto its back and falling limp. I recalled pressing the barrel of my own gun against the hound's skull, thinking to finish it off, but there was no need, for it was already gone. I knew then that it had been, after all, not ghost, nor demon, just dog.

For all that, I could not go back to Dartmoor. I simply could not. Even the idea of it gave me palpitations and brought me out in a cold sweat. As I said, I am a not uncourageous man, but bravery has its limits, and I had just discovered mine.

I assured myself that Holmes would fare perfectly well without me. He did not necessarily need me on his investigations. My contribution to his intellectual efforts was always negligible. What I offered was moral support, a sounding board and a strong right arm, and he could get all that from Benjamin Grier just as readily as from me. I had formed a good opinion of the American, despite having been in his company for a little under half an hour. He was no mean proposition, mentally and physically, and would on this one occasion be a more than creditable substitute for Sherlock Holmes's usual collaborator.

Or so I hoped.

PART TWO

Chapter Seven

THE RETURN OF SHERLOCK HOLMES

olmes was gone from London for a week, all told. I received no communication from him in the interim. I knew he was back only when a telegram arrived summoning me to Baker Street at my earliest convenience.

"You are eager to know," Holmes said as I made myself comfortable in my old chair, "whether my time spent in the West Country has borne fruit."

"Naturally."

A smile played about his lips. "Then let me, in an almost literal sense, take a leaf out of your book. Rather than reveal all at a stroke, which would be the simplest thing, I shall emulate the style of your stories and dole out the information piecemeal and in chronological order. Turnabout is fair play, is it not?"

I may have harrumphed somewhat at this, but my curiosity to hear his tale overrode any finer feelings.

"Why not help yourself to some shag?" my friend said. "That's it. And I shall do likewise. This is, at the very least, a three-pipe recitation."

With tobacco smoke drifting about the both of us, Holmes embarked upon a brief sketch of his and Benjamin Grier's train journey to Devon, which was uneventful. He impressed his travelling companion with his trick of calculating the train's speed by means of timing the passing telegraph poles. In return, Grier amused Holmes with soldiering anecdotes, one of which was a rather bawdy escapade involving a drunken captain, a kitbag and a malevolent skunk. Life on the American frontier was tough and filled with challenges but it seemed it had its lighter moments. In that respect it was not dissimilar to life on the North-West Frontier as I remembered it from my Afghanistan days. Camaraderie and hearty humour made up, to some extent, for the constant deprivations and dangers.

At Bartonhighstock a dog-cart and driver were hired, and on the way to Baskerville Hall, Holmes broached the subject of gaining safe ingress into the house.

"We cannot simply walk up to the front door," said he to Grier. "You yourself have shown the inefficacy of that approach. We could well end up on the receiving end of a load from Sir Henry's shotgun, and it is an experience I am sure you have no wish to repeat and I know I do not crave. We must instead be wilier."

"What do you have in mind?" Grier enquired.

Holmes outlined his plan, to which the other's response was a low whistle.

"Are you certain?" the American said. "It sounds risky."

"It is," Holmes acknowledged. "I am putting my life entirely in your hands. I trust that you are up to the task."

Grier responded with a stalwart nod of the head. "You shall not find me wanting, sir."

"Good man."

"But it would be remiss of me not to sound a note of caution."

"Do you have a better idea?"

"I must admit I do not."

"Therefore mine is the stratagem we must deploy. If you are half the soldier I think you are, Grier, then I need have no concerns."

"I only hope your faith in me is well placed."

Holmes halted the dog-cart with still a mile to go to the Hall and sent the driver back. He and Grier then continued the rest of the way on foot. Night was falling fast and a miserable, chilly drizzle set in, fine rain gusting into their faces like waves of clammy cobwebs. It was the kind of weather the Scots call "dreich", a word that sounds as dismal as the conditions it describes. Holmes was glad of the Inverness cape and the ear-flapped travelling cap he was wearing, while Grier, in a greatcoat and broad-brimmed felt hat that were less well suited to the weather, was palpably jealous of them.

For all that, Holmes's mood was ebullient. "I am never more content than when a mystery beckons," he commented to me, "and will tolerate any inconvenience, endure any hardship, in its pursuit."

At last the Hall came into view. Lights burned in a handful of windows, dispelling any question that someone was at home. Then again, this was hardly unexpected. Sir Henry was in terror of his life, and Baskerville Hall, it seemed, had become his fortress. Why abandon the place when it afforded shelter and a readily defensible position?

Holmes tapped Grier on the shoulder and, putting forefinger to lips, indicated that from here on stealth was the priority. He gestured towards the two structures that flanked the Hall's gates. One was the original lodge, which I remembered as being a blackened ruin and which Holmes confirmed was still in that state of neglect, even more dilapidated now. The other, opposite it, was the newer lodge that Sir Charles Baskerville had begun building but which was left unfinished when he died. Work had resumed on it since, doubtless under the auspices of Sir Henry or perhaps the late Lady Audrey, but it remained incomplete. A skeleton of wooden scaffolding offered a foretaste of how the edifice might look when eventually constructed, while squares of tarpaulin were secured over its open end to protect against the elements.

Holmes pointed to this latter building, and Grier gave a sign conveying acknowledgement. Then the American moved off to the side, hunching low and following a course that ran parallel to the perimeter of the Hall, while Holmes stole directly towards the newer lodge.

The sky was overcast and moonless, meaning the darkness was almost total. The glow from the windows of the main house, a couple of hundred yards distant, lent just enough illumination to see by. Gaining on the half-built lodge, Holmes stepped around a few small piles of stone that at some point would become walls and entered via a hollow doorway.

Inside, he took out and lit a pocket lantern, then shone the beam around the premises. This he did in as ostentatious a manner as possible, taking special care to aim at the empty window sockets that faced towards the Hall. After five minutes or so he set down the lantern, then picked up an offcut of timber that was lying on the floor and tossed it against a wall. He repeated the action several times, eliciting a satisfyingly loud clatter each time.

"My God," I declared. "Were you *trying* to draw attention to yourself?"

"Precisely that," replied he.

At a sudden soft sound from outside, just audible above

the hiss of the rain and the sough of the wind, Holmes snatched up the lantern and hastily extinguished it. In pitch darkness he waited, standing stock-still, scarcely daring to draw breath.

His alert ears detected a surreptitious footfall. Someone had come in through the doorway. He glimpsed the silhouette of a man, limned by the faint illumination from without. The fellow was carrying a double-barrelled shotgun.

Slowly and very deliberately, Holmes shuffled his foot across the bare, unsanded floorboards.

The man pivoted in the direction of the noise. "You there!" he barked. "I see you! Don't you dare move, you rascal. Not a muscle! Or I'll give it to you with both barrels."

"Sir Henry..." Holmes began, for the voice and profile were unmistakably those of the baronet.

"Silence!" Sir Henry Baskerville hissed. "Come here to rob me, eh? You picked the wrong house, let me tell you. Or is it something worse? First Audrey, now it's me you're after. Me and my Harry. Well, by God, you won't get either of us, I swear. Whether you be man or monster, this gun will take your head clean off. I don't see *anything* surviving that, not even a creature spawned in the lowest circle of Hell."

The words ran together, more spat than spoken, in such a way that they were only just intelligible. What was clear, beyond a shadow of a doubt, was that the threat they expressed was no idle one. The shotgun was trained straight at Holmes, at point-blank range, and Sir Henry's tone and stance betokened someone at the very limit of his reason. In that moment, it occurred to Holmes that he had gravely miscalculated.

Chapter Eight

MR SCARECROW AND MR CHIMNEYSWEEP

I shook my head despairingly at my friend. "Sometimes," I said, "I have to ask myself if your reputation as one of the cleverest men in England is really warranted. It sounds as though Sir Henry came within a hair's breadth of killing you."

"It was, I will allow, a high-stakes gambit," Holmes said, with an insouciant little shrug. "Rest assured, I had taken precautions."

Said precautions manifested as a large shadow, which loomed up silently behind Sir Henry. A hand seized the shotgun, wresting it from the baronet's grasp and hurling it aside. At the same time, an arm snaked around his neck. The other arm came to join it, while a leg hooked itself about Sir Henry's ankles and swept his feet from under him.

By this means, Sir Henry was brought precipitately to the

floor, prone. His assailant bore down on him, maintaining the two-armed chokehold around his neck. Sir Henry strained furiously, but the other's strength and bulk were too great. For all his efforts, he might as well have been fending off a grizzly bear. Soon the baronet was gasping for breath, his resistance growing ever more feeble. A few seconds further and he would lapse into unconsciousness.

At that point, Holmes said, "He is subdued, Grier. You may slacken your grip."

Corporal Grier did as bidden. Air wheezed into Sir Henry's lungs.

"Let him up."

The American clambered off, enabling Sir Henry to rise to all fours. The baronet remained in that position for the best part of a minute, panting hard, dazed, with Grier hulking over him. In the meantime, Holmes relit his lantern.

Blinking in its light, Sir Henry looked around. "Sherlock Holmes," he said in a hoarse, quavering voice. "And it's you again, Benjamin. I see it now. This was all a ruse to lure me out of the house."

"Just so," said Holmes.

"But are you mad? I nearly shot you, Holmes. I had my finger around both triggers."

"Come, come." Holmes plucked the shotgun off the floor, thumbed the latch that operated the break action, and ejected the two cartridges, secreting them in his pocket.

"It was not nearly so bad as that. My guardian angel was there all along, poised to intervene. Weren't you, Grier?"

"More or less," said Grier. "I must say it wasn't as easy as I'd thought, climbing through a rear window. I am not built for furtive movement. I feared the creak of a floorboard might give me away at any moment."

"Well, you have the advantage over me," said Sir Henry, a touch ruefully. "But in doing so, you have most likely damned yourselves. This place is not safe."

"It is too late for any of that, Sir Henry," said Holmes. "We are here now and we are going nowhere. You may as well accustom yourself to the idea. If you insist on proving recalcitrant, I shall simply ask Grier to overpower you with a chokehold again, and this time he will not relent until you are out cold. Alternatively, you can invite us to the Hall and we shall walk there together. Which is it to be? The three of us ambling up the drive side by side, companionably, or Grier carrying your insensible form? The choice is yours."

Sir Henry wisely plumped for the former, and soon he, Holmes and Grier were shaking the rain off their clothes in the Hall's main vestibule, surrounded by stained-glass windows and oak-panelled walls that were adorned with portraits, coats of arms and stags' heads. Holmes noted that Sir Henry had made sure, upon entering, to lock and bar the door behind them. He noted, too, that a revolver lay on a shelf beside the door, a bullet visible in every chamber.

"A high shelf, I hope," said I. "What about his son? To leave a loaded weapon within easy reach of a three-year-old child would be the acme of irresponsibility."

"You will be relieved to hear that it was a high shelf, yes, Watson. Sir Henry might have been at his wits' end but he was not wholly bereft of common sense."

Nevertheless it was apparent that the baronet was taking no chances. To him, Baskerville Hall was in a state of siege, and it was towards guarding his home that he was directing all his energies. No log fire crackled in the hearth, as one had, welcomingly, when I myself had first come to the Hall five years before. The air indoors was as frigid as the air without. Sir Henry was plainly too preoccupied to give thought to such comforts, and no servants remained in the house to do so on his behalf.

Holmes, recalling that the Barrymores had accused their master of defacing portraits, swiftly scanned those in the vestibule. It seemed, however, that they had exaggerated, because he found only one that had been damaged.

"It may not astonish you to learn, Watson," said he, "that the recipient of Sir Henry's violent attentions was Hugo Baskerville."

"I do not follow. Why Hugo?"

"Is it really so perplexing? Perhaps it is. You seem to forget that the author of Sir Henry's woes last time was Jack Stapleton, and out of all of their common ancestors represented at Baskerville Hall it was Hugo, more than any other, to whom Stapleton bore such a marked likeness."

The face on the portrait had been slashed with a blade, Holmes said. The image of Hugo Baskerville was now so savagely, vindictively disfigured that not a trace of it remained from the neck up, only a jagged hole in the canvas. I asked what this act of vandalism might signify, since Stapleton, being dead, could in no way be held accountable for the current state of affairs.

"It is not inconceivable that Sir Henry, having no concrete enemy to lash out against, felt the need to vent his anger upon a painting that reminded him of an erstwhile source of vexation," Holmes replied. "Or could it be that some deeper motivation compelled him?"

Whether or not this last question was rhetorical, he continued his narrative without expounding further upon it, at least not straight away.

As his gaze roved around the vestibule, it fell upon a face staring at him from the first-floor gallery above – a living one rather than a long-dead one represented in oils. A pair of solemn blue eyes looked down from between the spindles of the banister, much like a prisoner through the bars of his cell. These eyes were set amid youthful, rather winsome features, below a mop of dark hair. Their owner was dressed in a nightgown and sat cross-legged on the gallery floor, the tip of one finger in his mouth.

"Ah-ha," said Holmes genially to this watcher. "Is that young master Harry Baskerville I spy up there?"

Sir Henry directed his gaze, as did Grier, towards the object of Holmes's scrutiny.

"Harry," said the lad's father. "It's late. Why aren't you in bed?"

"I heard voices, Daddy," lisped the little thing. "I thought it might be Bammow and Mrs Bammow. I thought they had come back."

"No, it is not the Barrymores, son. These two gentlemen are friends of mine. This is Mr Holmes and this is Corporal Grier. You may have heard me mention both of them more than once in the past."

Harry looked noncommittal. "Is that man a chimney-sweep?" he said, pointing at Grier.

"Me?" said Grier. He smiled. "No, youngster, I am not, but I can understand why you might think so." He rubbed the skin of his face and showed Harry the palm of his hand. "See? If I were a chimneysweep, the dark would come off. This isn't soot. It's my own skin colour, as natural to me as the pinkish-white colour of yours is to you."

"Oh," said the boy, taking this in. "And are you a scarecrow?"

Now he was addressing Holmes, who put a hand to his chest, mock-offended. "I? A scarecrow?"

"You look like one."

"I am a trifle scrawny, I suppose. Well then, perhaps a scarecrow *is* what I am, Harry. But if so, rather than frighten off birds, I frighten off evildoers; and in that endeavour I am, even if I say so myself, quite successful."

"Is that why you have a gun? To scare bad men with?"

Holmes was holding Sir Henry's shotgun in the crook of his elbow, having carried it up from the lodge. "As a last resort, yes. More often, my greatest weapon is my brain."

"Daddy, are the Bammows coming back?" Harry, as with any child his age, moved from thought to thought like a squirrel hopping from branch to branch.

His father sighed sadly. "Not as far as I know."

"Is it like Mummy? Have they gone away to Heaven?"

Sir Henry trembled. Holmes could tell he was having great trouble keeping his emotions in check.

"No," he croaked. "Not like your mother. The Barrymores have merely... left. Now then, son, you really must go back to bed. Run along, there's a good boy. I will be up shortly to tuck you in."

Harry stood. "Goodnight, Mr Scarecrow. Goodnight, Mr Chimneysweep."

Holmes lofted a hand in farewell, while Grier saluted.

As the lad scampered off, Sir Henry shepherded his guests through to the drawing room. Here, as in the vestibule, no fire blazed. A few candles provided fitful illumination. Sir Henry busied himself pulling the curtains, which had the effect of making the room seem marginally cosier, but the atmosphere remained dull and dank. At the final window he paused to peer out into the night through the rain-speckled panes, as though searching apprehensively for something, before at last, with a show of relief, he swept the curtains shut.

"A drink, gentlemen?"

"That would be most welcome," said Holmes, and Grier similarly assented.

Their host poured out three generous measures of whisky from a decanter, and while he did so, Holmes took the opportunity to study him. The baronet was gaunt and haggard, with dark rings around his eyes and hair unkempt. Two of the buttons on his waistcoat were undone and his shirt collar was awry. His every gesture was quick and uneasy. A goodly proportion of the whisky, for instance, did not make it into the tumblers.

"A man quite so near the end of his tether, Watson," said Holmes, "I have yet to meet. His nerves were so close to the surface, you could practically see them."

Passing a tumbler each to Holmes and Grier, Sir Henry raised his own and wished them good health. He drank the contents of his glass in a single gulp and refilled it immediately. It was a rather fine single malt, and Holmes and Grier elected to sip and savour it.

"I would like to apologise," Sir Henry said. "First of all,

for nearly shooting you both. I am…" He faltered, fingering the black crêpe band that encircled his left upper arm, the traditional token of mourning. "Life is difficult. My thoughts – they keep running away from me, like wild horses. I am not the master of my own mind."

"Corporal Grier and I remain intact," Holmes said. "It is the best outcome either of us might hope for."

"Second of all, I would like to apologise for Harry's remarks just now. Holmes, there is scant similarity between you and a scarecrow. As for you, Benjamin, all I can say is that my son has led a rather sheltered life and has never before seen anyone with your complexion. Forgive him for not understanding."

"I am not offended," said Grier. "Children say whatever comes into their heads. Their judgements contain no rancour or prejudice. He did not condemn me for my race, merely made an observation about me based upon the only comparison he knew. Besides, now Holmes and I have nicknames for each other. Don't we, Mr Scarecrow?"

"I would consider it a great honour if you refrained from ever calling me that again, Grier," Holmes rebuked him, with a modicum of levity. "In return, I shall refrain from ever calling you Mr Chimneysweep."

"Oh, don't be a spoilsport, Mr Scarecrow."

"Really, it is one thing coming from a child, quite another from a grown man."

Grier was not to be deterred. "I'll have you using it before we're done," said he jauntily. "You see if I don't."

"You will be waiting a long while." Turning back to Sir Henry, Holmes said, "Since the spirit of reconciliation is moving us, I feel apologies are necessary on Grier's and my behalf, too. Our treatment of you at the lodge, manhandling you as we did, might seem unduly harsh. Please understand that I would not have resorted to such a course of action if I had thought there was any other way."

"No, no, it's quite all right," said Sir Henry. "I realise I am not at my most hospitable at present. I would not have let you into the house willingly, so you forced the issue."

"It was done with the best of intentions," said Grier.

"I know." The baronet tenderly rubbed his neck, which was doubtless sore after his partial strangulation. "I can only thank the Lord you didn't use your full strength on me, Brother Benjamin. As it was, it felt like my head was about to pop clean off like a champagne cork."

"But let us get down to business, Sir Henry, if we may," said Holmes. "Grier has apprised me of your circumstances. With regard to the loss of your wife, you have my deepest sympathies."

"Thank you, sir." Sir Henry, with unsteady hand, helped himself to a third shot of whisky.

"I know, too, about the giant moth which is alleged to have been haunting the moor of late and which may or may not have some connection with your calamity. I appreciate that the subject is not easy to discuss, but discuss it we must. I noticed how you looked out of the window just as you were closing the curtains. It was the creature you were checking for, was it not?"

"It was."

"Have you yourself seen this apparition?"

"I have not."

"Yet you do not query its existence."

"Neither would you, Holmes, had you seen how Audrey…" The sentence trailed off, Sir Henry's eyes all of a sudden brimming. A loud sob escaped him, and for a time he buried his face in his hands, his shoulders heaving. Grier moved to his side and laid a consoling arm around him. At last the baronet collected himself, straightening up and mopping his tear-soaked cheeks with his sleeve.

"It would be a tremendous help," said Holmes, "if you were able to describe in full the circumstances of your wife's death and furnish any other details you might feel relevant."

"To what end, Holmes?" came the rejoinder. "What good will it do? Will it bring Audrey back? No. Can you prevent this murderous beast from attacking again? I doubt it."

"I beg to differ. Not only may I be able to avenge your wife, I may be able to ensure that you and Harry go on to live long, prosperous lives."

Sir Henry looked up, and Holmes descried a faint glimmer of hope in his eyes. "You mean it?"

"I make it my solemn oath to you that I shall do everything in my power to resolve this matter to everyone's advantage."

"As do I," Grier chimed in.

"But in order to facilitate that, Sir Henry, you must take your courage in both hands. Tell me what happened on the night of your wife's death."

Chapter Nine

MORE OF SHERLOCK HOLMES'S "THREE-PIPE RECITATION"

Fortifying himself with yet another tot of whisky, Sir Henry Baskerville recounted his wife's final hours and tragic end.

"Audrey had had a trying day," said he. "Harry was fractious. Everything he did, from dawn to dusk, was in opposition to her wishes. Nothing was good enough for him, nothing would placate him. You know how children can be at that age. Contrary. Even with Mrs Barrymore to help her, by the time Harry went to bed Audrey was quite wrung out. The Barrymores, incidentally, are now my only household staff – or rather *were*, since I appear to have driven them away. There used to be a scullery maid, but she left to marry the postmaster's son, and old Perkins the groom was getting rather long in the tooth and retired last year. I can afford to employ as many servants as I wish, but I am not a demanding man and like to keep things simple. I have a gardener, who comes and goes pretty much as he pleases. Aside from him, it has been just Mr and Mrs Barrymore, who between them were quite capable of fulfilling all my domestic requirements, and willingly did so. And when Harry came along, they proved to be like a second set of parents to the lad. Having no offspring of their own, they treated him much like a surrogate son. They indulged him. Spoiled him rotten, in point of fact. Barrymore, in spite of chronic lumbago, would give Harry a piggyback ride whenever asked, while Mrs Barrymore invariably let him lick the spoon when she was making cakes. Harry has been fortunate in that regard. He has grown up in a household where he is universally beloved."

"The Barrymores themselves were fortunate," Holmes said. "After all that happened with Mrs Barrymore's brother, you would have been quite within your rights to sack them, and for that matter to turn them over to the police. In the event, you showed remarkable forbearance in not only absolving them but keeping them on."

"Well, their motives in aiding Selden were honourable, even if their deeds broke the law. I don't have a brother myself, but if I did, I reckon I would try to protect him, come what may. Blood is thicker than water, and all that."

"Speaking as one who does have a brother, I can echo the

sentiment. Mycroft and I may not always see eye to eye, but he has been there in my hour of need and I likewise in his, and I trust that that shall long continue. But please, go on."

"Audrey, though tired, decided to go for an evening walk," Sir Henry said. "This was a frequent habit of hers."

"How frequent?"

"Practically every day, unless the weather was unduly inclement."

"A regular occurrence, in other words."

"Yes. Is that significant?"

"It may be. It may not."

"She always maintained that a stroll upon the moor soothed her soul and restored her energies," said Sir Henry. "She grew up around here, you see, and Dartmoor was her childhood playground. Her family, the Lidstones, are landed gentry, with roots in the area going back generations, much like the Baskervilles. Audrey herself, however, was born with something of a wild streak. As a young girl she was forever straying from home. Once, she befriended a tribe of gypsies, and she told me she almost ran away with them, seeing untrammelled freedom in their nomadic lifestyle. Another time, without her family's knowledge, she camped out overnight in one of the prehistoric stone huts which dot the region."

"A form of accommodation I am only too familiar with," said Holmes.

"She was the despair of her mother and father, as you can imagine. Even Cheltenham Ladies' College and a finishing school could not tame her. Her parents truly believed she was never going to settle down and would one day bring unconscionable shame upon the Lidstone name. I think they were profoundly relieved when she and I met and formed an instant connection. I was, at the time, considered one of Devon's most eligible bachelors and was forever receiving dinner invitations from people with unmarried daughters my age. When the Lidstones asked me over, I thought it would be just another evening spent sitting next to some simpering spinster of modest attractions who would shower me with compliments and insinuate what a good match we were. Miss Audrey Lidstone was anything but that. She challenged and teased me throughout the meal, and I, gentlemen, adored every minute of it. And as if her personality alone was not enough to enrapture me, she was blessed with dazzling eyes, a sweet, heart-shaped face and an irresistibly impish smile.

"Up until then, during my first months as a resident at the Hall, I had had a couple of brief dalliances that had come to naught. One of those was with Beryl Stapleton, widow of my would-be nemesis. But alas, that did not develop as I might have hoped."

"Any particular reason why not?" Holmes asked.

"Shame," said Sir Henry. "Beryl felt a certain complicity

in all her husband had done and had tried to do. Although she had acted against him, in my favour, and indeed had been the victim of his strongarm tactics, she was nonetheless guilty by association, in her mind at least. She could not live with that, and against my protests she decided to quit the area. Where she has gone, I don't know. She left abruptly and gave me no indication whether she might return or where I might find her. I think she felt it was better for the both of us just to cut herself out of my life. It was the impulsive Latin temperament at work. But perhaps she was right. Perhaps it could never have been a successful match, the two of us, given the nature of the events that brought us together in the first place. A relationship born in blood and tragedy is surely not destined to last.

"So, in the circumstances, I had begun to doubt I would ever find a mate. For that matter, I had begun to question whether Dartmoor was really the best place for me. I was lonely. It had occurred to me that I might be better off selling Baskerville Hall and relocating somewhere a little more populous and civilised.

"All that changed in a trice, the moment I encountered Audrey Lidstone. Not to put too fine a point on it, we fell head over heels in love. Within a fortnight we were engaged. Within two months we were wed and honeymooning in Paris. We were deliriously happy, the more so when, a little under a year later, Audrey blessed me with a baby boy.

It seemed to me that after the horror and suffering that attended my inheritance, the baptism of fire that was my introduction to Baskerville Hall and the baronetcy, I could finally put all that behind me. Life from now on would be carefree and easy. Little did I know..."

Sir Henry paused, then picked up his thread again.

"At any rate, out she went that evening. All that week it had been relatively balmy for this time of year, and I offered to accompany her, but she refused. I had been up in London all day, visiting my stockbroker on Threadneedle Street, and was exhausted. Financial affairs make my head spin. I do not know one end of a ledger from another. Audrey told me to put my feet up and rest. Besides, she never minded going for walks on her own, in many ways preferring it. She knew every inch of the moor and felt as safe on it as you or I might in our back garden.

"Nonetheless I exacted a promise from her that she would return before nightfall. As a concerned, devoted husband, I could do no less. Her last words to me, as she threw on her cloak, were kindly ones. I shall never forget the gentle loving glance she cast at me over her shoulder as she set off down the drive.

"It was perhaps an hour later that I awoke from a light doze. I had nodded off in my study armchair. I glanced at the clock, then out of the window. It was full dark outside. I assumed that Audrey had come home already, and so went in search of her. I was startled to learn from Mrs Barrymore that she was not back yet. Availing myself of a lantern, I went outside to wait. I was not fearful, not then. As I said, Audrey knew every inch of the moor. I approached the gates, shining the lantern around in the hope that she would see it – a friendly beacon to guide her homeward.

"I loitered at the gates for a good twenty minutes, with still no sign of Audrey. That was when needles of apprehension first began to prick. Had she got lost? Or had she – perish the thought – met with some kind of accident? I discounted the first possibility but not the second. Dartmoor can be a treacherous place, as you well know, Holmes. I pictured the lip of some steep rocky precipice crumbling beneath Audrey's feet, sending her plummeting to the bottom. That or her stumbling and turning an ankle, even breaking a leg. There are vagabonds out there, too, human wolves who pose a threat to the unwary traveller and to whom a lone young woman would be a choice target.

"As these dire imaginings filled my head, I was seized by self-recrimination. I should have forbidden Audrey from venturing out. At the very least I should have been more insistent about going with her. What a fool I had been! Fired with sudden resolve, I thrust open the gates and headed out.

"There is, just beyond the eastern edge of the shallow bowl in which the Hall lies, a large rock. It projects up from the earth at an acute angle, rising some twenty feet into the air, and seen from a certain viewpoint it resembles an old, hunchbacked man. The locals have christened it Crookback Samuel. The name, I am told, derives from a long-ago Samuel from hereabouts, an itinerant pedlar who was indeed afflicted with severe curvature of the spine. My path took me towards this rock. I had planned on scaling its slope in order to gain height, so that my lantern's light might be more widely visible to Audrey. In the event, there was no need.

"I… I saw a pale form, prostrate on the ground at the foot of Crookback Samuel. I knew in an instant that it was Audrey. I ran to her, my heart in my mouth. I presumed she had fainted, or else, as I earlier surmised, had met with some kind of accident.

"But she lay so still. Too still. Not a breath stirred within her. And the lantern's beam showed me a face that was deprived not only of animation but of hue, whiter than white.

"My God, gentlemen! You cannot know the agony I felt then. It was as though a part of my soul had been torn from me. I collapsed to my knees and howled. My cries were guttural, primal, like those of a trapped animal. I pleaded with the heavens to return my wife to me. I would have given anything – my wealth, my health, even my life – if the other end of the bargain was Audrey brought back to this world.

"The Barrymores heard my lamentation. Mrs Barrymore remained at the house, so that the sleeping Harry would not be left unattended, while her husband rushed out to look for me. Somehow Barrymore managed to get me back to the Hall. I was in such a wretched state, I could barely walk. It was Barrymore who summoned the police. He sent a message to Dr Mortimer as well. You remember Mortimer, don't you, Holmes, from last time?"

"Very well. An excellent young man."

"Mortimer came post-haste," said Sir Henry. "He prescribed me a sedative, then took charge of the body and all the related arrangements. He really was an angel, and I am eternally grateful to him.

"Thereafter, things become hazy in my memory. I dimly recall the funeral. Audrey was interred in the Lidstones' vault, at the parish church near the family seat. Her parents and siblings were quite broken. Her mother did not even make it to the end of the ceremony; she swooned halfway through and had to be taken home. Beyond that, all I know is that I have been alternately wracked with grief and overcome by mindless rage. Then, between times, there has been terror.

"I can date the origin of the terror to the day after Audrey died, when Mortimer was kind enough to drop round and enquire after my welfare. He told me he had just conducted an examination of the body. Whether or not I asked him to – I suspect I did – he informed me of the cause of death. Audrey's blood had been drained out of her through a wound in her neck, by some means or other. He tried to assure me that, as deaths go, it would have been comparatively peaceful. After the initial pain of the incision, Audrey would have swiftly lost consciousness as the blood flowed out. It would, he said, have been much like drifting off to sleep.

"These words were clearly intended to comfort me. They did not. Rather, I was reminded immediately of the reports of sheep being killed on the moor in just the same fashion. These stories, and rumours of a gigantic moth being seen at night, were rife. Everyone knew about it.

"To think that the method which had been used to slay mere sheep was also used to end my Audrey's life. To think that she had been butchered as though she were... she were just a piece of livestock."

Sir Henry's expression was a mixture of incredulity and raw disgust.

"But for me," he said, "there was more to it than that. For I was sure then, as sure as I have ever been of anything, that this moth must be real; and not only that but Audrey hadn't been simply some random victim of its unholy appetites. The connection was quite clear in my mind. And, now that I think of it, it must be clear in yours too, Holmes. Doubtless you have divined the significance of the fact that it is a moth that murdered the wife of Sir Henry Baskerville – a moth rather than any other species."

"The line of logic is certainly one along which my thoughts have travelled," said Holmes.

"Whereas I am one upon whom the significance is lost," Grier interjected. "Would either of you care to enlighten me?"

"It all depends, Grier," said Holmes, "on you knowing the professional specialism of the man who murdered Sir Henry's uncle and almost succeeded in murdering Sir Henry."

"Stapleton, right? Jack Stapleton."

"The very same. Born Jack Baskerville, later known as Jack Vandeleur, later still as Jack Stapleton."

"He was a naturalist, yes?" said Grier.

"A naturalist with an interest in entomology, whose particular area of expertise was Lepidoptera."

"Lepidoptera. That's butterflies and moths. You're saying—"

"I'm saying," Sir Henry declared, clenching his fists and narrowing his eyes, "that Jack Stapleton has returned from the grave to plague me once more, and he has begun his campaign of vengeance by engineering the death of my wife in the most loathsome fashion imaginable."

Chapter Ten

IN THE SHADOW OF CROOKBACK SAMUEL

The following morning, at first light, Holmes sallied forth from Baskerville Hall to visit the scene of the crime, the rock formation known as Crookback Samuel.

The day had dawned blustery but bright. The weather on Dartmoor was nothing if not mutable, and all trace of the previous day's gloomy dampness was gone as if it had never been. The grass and gorse gleamed as though newly minted. The rocks and trees seemed to bask in the sunlight. A few small breeze-driven clouds scudded overhead like racehorses at the gallop.

As he walked, Holmes reflected upon the previous night's conversation with Sir Henry. It had drawn to a close not long after Jack Stapleton's name came up. Sir Henry was by then quite inebriated, and Holmes, believing he would get little further out of him of any use, proposed going to bed so that they could all reconvene in the morning, refreshed and rested. Although Sir Henry had promised Harry he would tuck him in, it was Holmes and Grier who ended up tucking Sir Henry in. The baronet fell asleep still fully clothed, but his face, in repose, was more tranquil than before, or so it seemed to Holmes at any rate. Now that allies were there in the form of Sherlock Holmes and Benjamin Grier, men whose stout hearts and steadfast support could not be in doubt, Sir Henry was able to relax for the first time in many days.

Had Jack Stapleton really come back from the dead to bedevil Sir Henry once more? Was it possible? And if so, was the lepidopterist, so well-regarded as an authority on the subject that he had even had a species of moth named after him, now in possession of an inordinately large vampiric moth that he had trained to kill, much as he had trained his hound?

Holmes turned these questions over in his mind.

"And your conclusions?" I asked.

"You know that I spurn the very idea of ghosts and revenants, Watson," replied he. "Not for one second was I prepared to entertain the notion that Stapleton had arisen from the great Grimpen Mire after five years of immersion and was now shambling around Dartmoor as some half-rotted, hate-driven ghoul, engaged in an elaborate scheme to bring about Sir Henry's downfall. And yet…"

"And yet?"

"Cast your mind back to the postscript to the climax of our adventures on Dartmoor."

"If I must."

"The morning after we slew Stapleton's hound, we went in search of Stapleton himself. His wife assisted, directing us to the safe path through the Grimpen Mire, which was marked out by wands. There were signs that someone had passed that way before us, the most obvious of these being Sir Henry's stolen boot, which Stapleton had evidently discarded during his flight. Of the villain himself, however, nothing was to be seen, and the only reasonable inference one could draw was that he had failed to reach the little island of *terra firma* in the midst of that morass where lay the old, abandoned miners' cottage in which he had kept the dog hidden; and that, instead, becoming disorientated in the fog on his way to this refuge, he had veered off the path into the mire."

"You mean, what if you were wrong?" I said. "What if Stapleton did not perish as you surmised? By leaving the boot for us to find, he was laying a false trail and wished us to conclude exactly what we did conclude. Good Lord, Holmes, can that be it?"

"In which case," Holmes said, the corners of his mouth turning down in a dour grimace, "I would be guilty of the gravest of blunders, one that led directly to Lady Audrey's death."

He sat in contemplative silence for a while, puffing at his pipe.

"I am not so arrogant as to think I am infallible, Watson," said he at last. "You have seen me, on more than one occasion, admit to an error, and there have been times when those errors have put in jeopardy the very people I am aiming to protect. If, however, Stapleton did outwit me by leading me to believe that he was dead when he was not, it could surely be considered the nadir of my career, a catastrophe beyond redemption."

There was no denying the severity with which Holmes spoke, yet he did not strike me as despondent. Hence I felt safe in saying, "Am I to take it that this has proved not to be the case?"

"All in due course, old fellow. I am mimicking the format of one of your narratives, remember. It would not do to give all the answers at once. One must consider dramatic tension. Now then, where was I?"

It amused Holmes to think that he was giving me a taste of my own medicine. I refused to be irked. "Approaching Crookback Samuel," I said evenly.

"Just so."

The rock formation was as advertised. It jutted steeply from the earth, flattening out at its apex to form an overhang. Holmes, though not of a notably fanciful bent, had little trouble seeing the profile of a man in its configuration, one who appeared to be striding doubled over, bandy-legged, with his head raised questingly forward.

The chances of uncovering clues at the site were, he freely admitted, remote. Ten days on from Lady Audrey's death, most if not all of the evidence was likely to have been erased by the weather. Holmes performed several circuits of Crookback Samuel anyway, subjecting the ground immediately around its base to intense scrutiny. What he found, imprinted in the muddy soil, were examples of the spoor unique to what he termed "a certain peculiarly destructive breed of cattle, the common or garden variety policeman". Regrettably he knew only too well the signs, from previous cases. Judging by the sizes of the various footprints, the tread on the soles of the boots, and above all the pattern of the paths they followed, which meandered and overlapped seemingly at random, a grand total of three members of Her Majesty's constabulary had explored the vicinity of the rock, and as usual the policemen had gone about their task with a zeal that was in no way tempered by methodicality or thoroughness. If anything, this particular herd had trampled more comprehensively than was their wont. Whatever useful data the ground might have yielded to the expert criminalist was lost for good.

Stepping back to get a better view of Crookback Samuel, Holmes did establish, if nothing else, that this was a prime spot for an ambush. A man crouching on the rock's uppermost face might easily leap down onto someone below, catching his victim unawares. Likewise, a man lurking in the lee of the overhang would be well hidden from sight, until he chose to make his presence known.

To prove both theories to his satisfaction, Holmes first climbed halfway up the rock's slope. Perching on the edge, some ten feet high, he jumped. He landed safely, albeit a trifle awkwardly, jarring his knees. Had there been someone below, not only would it have cushioned the impact, but this other would have been knocked flat and left stunned by the weight of an attacker descending from above with some force.

Next, Holmes took himself beneath the overhang. There was a cleft in the rock whose dimensions were more or less those of a coffin laid upright. Snug within, he was afforded a severely restricted field of vision, and by the same token it was safe to presume that only a person approaching from dead ahead would have a chance of spying him. Anyone coming by from either side would not realise he was there until the very last moment.

It was while he was ensconced inside this natural concavity that Holmes's sharp eye alighted upon a proper clue at last. Wedged into a fissure by his shoulder, only just visible, was the stub of a small cigar. He extricated it carefully using a penknife.

To one well versed in the intricacies of tobacco in all its forms – one who had authored more than a few monographs on the topic – identifying the brand of cigar was child's play. Given the narrow diameter of the stub, it must belong to that subset of the cigar, the cigarillo. Close inspection, including several deep sniffs, denoted that the tobacco itself came from Nicaragua and was grown in one of the valleys famed for the crop in that country, either the Estelí or the Condega. The cut of the leaves with which the cigarillo was wrapped, and the tight clockwise spiral of the rolling, enabled Holmes to state with complete confidence that the manufacturer was the Vargas y Araya company.

"In case you didn't know, Watson, Vargas y Araya are one of South America's premier cigar producers," he said, "and their operations are based in Costa Rica."

"Costa Rica," I echoed.

"Let it sink in. Give it a moment to percolate."

"Costa Rica!" I exclaimed. "Birthplace of Jack Stapleton."

"Precisely."

"But then, the smoker is very likely to have been Stapleton."

"Stapleton may well have a preference for tobacco from his native land."

"And therefore the cigarillo stub is proof that he faked his death."

"It is certainly suggestive of that."

At Crookback Samuel, Holmes slipped the cigarillo stub into one of the small envelopes he kept on his person for collecting evidence. Pocketing this, he checked at his feet for fallen tobacco ash, which might give him some inkling as to how long the smoker had stood there and what sort of smoker he was. He could be the type who left the coal to grow long and drop off of its own accord, or he could be the type who punctiliously tapped off the excess ash. This, in turn, would give Holmes some insight into the nature of the man.

He was not hopeful of finding any ash, however, and indeed the search was to no avail. There was precious little space around his feet to begin with, given the dimensions of the cleft, and wind and rain had long since scoured that small patch of ground clean.

Holmes then delved further into the fissure with his penknife. The smoker could have used the narrow crevice as a makeshift ashtray, in an effort to avoid leaving traces of his presence. There was no ash there either, in the event, although the fissure did offer up a small reward in the form of a spent match.

The placement of match and the cigarillo stub were, Holmes averred, illuminating. It was self-evident that someone had secreted himself in the cleft beneath the overhang and, while loitering there, indulged in a smoke. When had this happened? If not kept in a humidor, tobacco grows stale swiftly, and Holmes, who had made a detailed study of the rate at which tobacco's freshness declines, could tell from the texture and odour of this particular cigarillo that it had been smoked somewhere between eight and eleven days earlier. It was a broad margin, but nevertheless the date of Lady Audrey's death fell firmly within that period.

A cigarillo was a quick smoke compared to a cigar, although not as quick as a cigarette. On average it took fifteen to twenty minutes from start to finish. Yet this cigarillo had not burned all the way to the end. A couple of inches remained when it had been discarded. Why would the smoker not have enjoyed it to the full? One possible explanation was that he had been interrupted. He had had to dispose of the cigarillo hastily, sending it the way of the match he had used to light it.

There were two possible conclusions to be drawn from all of this. One was that the person had simply taken refuge in the cleft in order to shelter from bad weather. Running contrary to that, however, was the fact that the weather had been, according to Sir Henry, balmy all that week.

The alternative conclusion, and the likelier, was that the person had been waiting for someone. To pass the time, he had lit a cigarillo. Soon, perhaps sooner than expected, he had heard footfalls belonging to the man or woman whose arrival he anticipated. Doing away with his cigarillo, he had stepped out to accost the newcomer.

Was it beyond the bounds of probability to suggest that the one being accosted was Lady Audrey? If so, then the odds were good that the smoker of the cigarillo was her murderer.

"Not a marauding man-sized moth after all," said Holmes, "just a man."

"Or," I countered, "a man with a marauding man-sized moth that he controlled."

"Well, maybe."

"And," I added, "not just any man but Jack Stapleton."

"Again, maybe. Whoever he was, if he was lying in wait for Lady Audrey, then he was familiar with her habits. He knew of her evening walks, most likely through observation of the comings and goings at the Hall. He knew her route might well take her past Crookback Samuel, which was, anyway, an unimprovable hiding place. That he felt in need of tobacco implies that he wished to quell his nerves or, equally, that he was a fellow of considerable composure and *sangfroid*, able to smoke a casual cigarillo while contemplating murder. Whichever is the case, we may say with some assurance that the killing of Her Ladyship was not spontaneous and opportunistic but premeditated and planned. The killer, furthermore, had a predilection for cigarillos manufactured in Costa Rica."

It was at this point during Holmes's survey of the crime scene that his solitude was intruded upon. All at once, as he emerged from the cleft, he was beset by a barking, leaping hound.

Chapter Eleven

SWIFT AND NEAR-TOTAL EXSANGUINATION BY METHODS UNKNOWN

I started in my seat, feeling a sudden thrill of horror.

At this, Holmes burst out laughing.

"Oh, Watson!" he cried. "Your face is a picture! Don't think I am ignorant of your antipathy towards canines. I have noted your tendency to shy away from even the smallest and most inoffensive dogs, even the ones that are little more than balls of cotton wool with eyes. It has been thus since our time on Dartmoor in 'eighty-nine, and I suspect that therein lies the true reason behind your decision to stay in London rather than return to the West Country – not a superfluity of patients but chronic cynophobia."

"No, no, not at all."

"Come on, old fellow. Don't deny it."

Somewhat abashed, I relented and nodded.

"There," said Holmes. "It is better to admit these things than cover them up. That way, we all know where we stand."

"And to think I used to be rather fond of dogs," I said. "That bullpup I once had, back when we first met, was an adorable little scamp."

"Yes. A pity he couldn't be housebroken."

That was all too true, alas, and I had not been happy when Mrs Hudson told me either the pup must go or I did, although I fully understood why she gave the ultimatum. There is only so much floor scrubbing and carpet cleaning a woman can be expected to do. Happily, her spinster sister in Chatham had been willing to adopt him, and by all accounts the two of them, lady and dog, had become boon companions.

At any rate, it was no phosphorescent hellhound that went bounding up to Holmes on the moor that day, barking volubly. It was a brown curly-haired spaniel, and it was falling over itself in excitement, having, so it thought, flushed this man out from cover as it might a game bird.

"Hallo!" came a voice. "Is that you, Holmes?"

The owner of the voice, and of the dog, proved to be none other than Dr James Mortimer.

The young medic was little altered in appearance, Holmes told me. That same beaky nose. Those same gold-rimmed glasses perched atop it, through which a pair of keen grey eyes peered. That same rake-thin physique, which the intervening years had neither added to nor subtracted from. His posture was somewhat more stooped now, so that the forward thrust of his head was more pronounced, but his clothing still had the endearing shabbiness of old.

"And his battered, dog-chewed Penang lawyer?" I said, referring to Mortimer's walking stick, the one from which Holmes had been able to deduce a remarkable quantity of data about its owner's profession, personality and inclinations without yet having met the man. "Was he carrying it as ever?"

"Very much so," my friend said.

Holmes and Mortimer shook hands vigorously, while the spaniel gambolled around them.

"I was out taking my morning constitutional," Mortimer said, "and spied you from afar. I thought to myself, 'Dear me, if it isn't Sherlock Holmes. I must go and greet him.'"

"Rather far from your usual stamping ground, aren't we?" said Holmes. "As I recall, you live over at High Barrow."

"Oh no. Not these days. I've moved to Merripit House, just up the road from here. You know it, of course."

"Jack Stapleton's one-time residence."

"It must seem an odd choice, I realise," said Mortimer. "A cottage in the middle of nowhere, its recent past chequered, to say the least. But that is precisely why I have taken it. Given its dark associations, the owner was having trouble finding a tenant, meaning I was able to negotiate a very reasonable monthly rent. A country doctor does not make nearly as much as his city equivalent, and every penny counts. Besides, I find the place agreeable. Galen and I are very happy there. Aren't we, Galen?"

"That would be this lively fellow." Holmes indicated the dog, which was still leaping about their legs, its tongue lolling, its tail spinning like a child's paper windmill.

"Not bothering you, is he?"

"Not a bit."

"He's still only a year old and not quite out of his puppyish ways. I bought him as a replacement for Asclepius, my last spaniel. The one that had the misfortune of…"

Mortimer did not finish the sentence, and did not need to. Holmes knew as well as he did the fate that had befallen Galen's predecessor, which had been of the same breed and colouration. It had been killed and eaten by Stapleton's hound, in a ghastly act of canine cannibalism.

"It took me a goodly while to get over the loss of Asclepius," Mortimer went on. "But Galen has been proving a more than adequate substitute."

A few further pleasantries were exchanged, then Mortimer said, "Actually, it comes as no great surprise to see you here, Holmes, what with this recent terrible business at the Hall. I take it Sir Henry has engaged your services to look into Lady Audrey's death."

"Not he but a friend of his."

"And is Dr Watson with you?" said Mortimer, glancing

around as if Sherlock Holmes's constant companion must perforce be nearby. "I don't see him."

"Not this time, alas," Holmes replied. "He is too busy. You yourself know all too well how it goes in general practice. Either flood or trickle, and right now it is flood."

"Shame. I should have been happy to renew his acquaintance. He is a first-rate fellow."

"The best."

"I suppose that, in pursuit of your goal, you are inspecting the spot where Lady Audrey came to grief." Mortimer shuddered. "On such a beautiful morning, one could almost forget that something so dreadful happened here."

"Sir Henry said you were of invaluable help to him in that regard."

"I did what I could," the other man said with a modest shrug. "What any friend would. Any doctor, for that matter. I even volunteered to conduct the autopsy. It made sense, since Lady Audrey was already a patient of mine, as is Sir Henry. Being familiar with her case history, I would know if she had some pre-existing condition that might have brought about her death. I was likely to know, too, which blemishes upon her person were ante-mortem and which were fresh. It was not an easy task, I must say."

"I should imagine not."

"Lady Audrey was my patient, yes, but I considered her a friend too. You see, I'd known her longer than Sir Henry.

I became the physician for her family, the Lidstones, shortly after I moved from London to Devon. That was in 'eighty-seven, a couple of years before Sir Henry came into his legacy and arrived at the Hall. Such a charming, vivacious thing, she was. She and he made a wonderful match. I was best man at their wedding, in fact. Did you know that?"

"I did not. I was invited to attend, as was Watson, but just then – it was early 1890, was it not? – we were abroad, pursuing the notorious French swindler, le Duc d'Alençon. This was the culmination of an investigation that had encompassed three of the noble houses of Europe and occupied over a month of my life, and affairs had reached such a critical juncture that I could not possibly abandon them. Monsieur le Duc, with his network of chambermaid spies and his rather brilliant cryptographic system involving knots in items of laundry, was as slippery a felon as can be imagined. I am pleased to say that he now languishes in La Santé prison in Paris."

"Well, you missed a joyous occasion," said Mortimer. "I am also godfather to their son, young Harry, whom I helped deliver. No reason you should know that either. Harry's christening was another joyous occasion. But now we –" He broke off. "I'm sorry, Galen really is bothering you, isn't he?"

The spaniel was now on its hind legs, pawing at Holmes's thigh. Holmes was steadfastly not giving it the attention it craved.

Mortimer made a swift double cluck of the tongue, and at this command the dog returned to all fours and trotted over to its master's side. Mortimer passed it his walking stick.

"There, boy. Amuse yourself with that instead."

The spaniel took the bulbous-headed Penang lawyer in its mouth and strode off. Settling down on its haunches nearby, it held down the ferrule end of the stick with a forepaw and gaily gnawed the handle end.

"As you are here, by great good fortune," said Holmes, "perhaps you can assist me, Mortimer."

"In any way I can, Holmes."

"I know from Sir Henry that when Lady Audrey was killed, you came and took charge of the body. May I ask you a couple of questions concerning that?"

"You may."

"First of all, where did you find her lying?"

Mortimer studied the scene, clearly casting his mind back to the fateful episode. Then he indicated a patch of grass situated some three yards along the base of the rock from the overhang. "Just there."

"You are certain?"

"Quite certain. The events of that night are etched in my memory."

"And how did she look? Sir Henry has been somewhat forthcoming on that front, but he is not what one would call a dispassionate witness."

"Neither am I, to be honest." The physician took a deep breath as if to steel himself. "She was prone."

"Sprawled?"

"Yes. And her head was turned."

"Meaning the side of her neck, and the carotid artery on that side, was exposed."

"Yes."

"And in her neck, through the skin and the wall of that artery, an incision had been made," said Holmes.

"I would describe it more as a perforation."

"You examined the body in the morgue, so you will be able to furnish precise details about this perforation."

"There is no reason why I cannot, as it is a matter of public record," Mortimer said. "The wound was half an inch in diameter, but deep, created by a sharp implement of some kind."

"Was the hole perfectly round?"

"Oval, I would say. As if some metal tube or cylinder had been inserted, forcefully and at an angle."

"A metal tube such as a needle with a relatively broad diameter."

"Possibly. Not necessarily."

"And the angle, was it downward?"

"Downward, yes, towards the clavicle."

"In such a way that the tube would catch the outflux of blood being impelled up towards the brain by the heart."

"Yes. It was the carotid artery on the right side of her neck, and as you may or may not be aware, the contents of that blood vessel – rising as it does from the brachiocephalic artery, which in turn rises from the aorta – are under some considerable pressure and, if freely released, are apt to spray out in a jet to a distance of several feet."

"Yet, by all accounts, few bloodstains were in evidence on the ground," said Holmes, "or on Lady Audrey's clothing, for that matter."

"Suggesting that the implement involved – tube or cylinder or whatever it was – was hollow and that the exiting blood was channelled through it into some receptacle."

"You have heard, of course, about the sightings of a giant, vampiric moth in the region."

Mortimer nodded. "Several of my less sophisticated patients are quite agitated about it. They're a superstitious lot, country folk, and anything that carries even a whiff of the unearthly will have them muttering prayers under their breath."

"What is your opinion? Do you think the moth is pure bunkum? A hoax, perhaps?"

The other man's expression turned pensive. His head moved from side to side, pendulum-like, as he deliberated.

"I have spoken to more than one farmer who has lost livestock lately in bizarre and gruesome circumstances," he said eventually. "No question, *something* has been wounding and killing sheep on Dartmoor. Whether this bloodletting fiend is a giant moth, I can only speculate. Equally, whether Lady Audrey fell victim to such a creature is open to debate. All I know for certain is what I observed upon her body."

"But it is just conceivable that Lady Audrey was preyed upon by a large, haemophagic insect, which pierced her neck with its proboscis and imbibed her blood."

"As outlandish as it sounds, one cannot rule it out. I couched my words carefully on the death certificate. I listed cause of death as 'swift and near-total exsanguination by methods unknown', but I did add that it was not impossible that the deceased fell victim to the attentions of some predatory animal."

"Aside from the perforation," said Holmes, "were there other injuries upon the body? Any signs of a struggle?"

"None that I could discern."

"Nothing around the nose and mouth, perhaps?"

"No. Why might there have been?"

"If Lady Audrey had been subdued with chloroform, say, before her artery was pierced, there could have been bruising around the nose and mouth where a handkerchief soaked in the compound was held there."

"I see. No, there was nothing of the sort. I can state that categorically."

"It is not always the case that when chloroform is applied in that way a mark is left," Holmes said with a shrug.

"Regardless, she was overpowered somehow, and then the blood was drained out of her."

"That is so," said Mortimer.

"You told Sir Henry that her death would have been painless. You said it would have been like drifting off to sleep."

Mortimer dropped his gaze. "That, I will confess, was something of a lie. But my intentions were noble. I wished to spare a friend from suffering more anguish than he already was. I will admit, the thought that Lady Audrey might have been drugged immediately prior the attack never occurred to me, although now that you've mentioned it, Mr Holmes, it does seem a distinct possibility. At the time, I could only think that she would have been conscious for some while as she was being exsanguinated, and that, alas, she was perfectly well aware of what was happening to her. As haemorrhagic shock set in, her heart rate would have increased, pumping harder to compensate for the loss of blood pressure. This would have made her brain more active, and therefore more acutely conscious of her plight. Then, as blood flow to the organs declined, muscle asphyxia would have led to seizures, and that would not have been at all pleasant. At least a further minute would have elapsed before her brain function began to shut down and faintness overcame her, robbing her of sensation."

I myself concurred with this assessment. "I did wonder," I said, "whether Sir Henry had recalled Mortimer's words aright. Then it dawned on me that partial truth may have been involved."

Holmes said to Mortimer, "You are aware that Sir Henry believes Jack Stapleton is alive and is responsible for the killing?"

"I was not, but it is, I suppose, plausible. If I recall correctly, Stapleton's body was never found. Could it be that he has spent these past five years in hiding, plotting against Sir Henry? Could he, moreover, have spent the time breeding a variety of moth large enough to kill a person? I know nothing about the lepidopteran life cycle or about the process of rearing moths, but I fancy that in five years one might nurture numerous generations of a single species, selecting for such traits as size and rapacity, until one had created a monster of the kind that has lately made its presence felt here on the moor. I tell you what, Holmes. If Stapleton *is* the culprit, I would not be at all surprised. There, truly, was a scoundrel. An abuser of women, dogged by infamy wherever he went, and a cold-hearted murderer to boot. I wish you every luck in catching him. If you need anything further from me, if I can be of any assistance whatsoever, don't hesitate to ask. How is Sir Henry, by the way? I assume, since you seem to have spoken to him at length, that he is of a more receptive frame of mind now than he has been of late."

"He is no longer seeing off all-comers with a shotgun, if that is any measure of his mental soundness," said Holmes.

"Yes. I'd heard about his aggressive behaviour and hence have been giving Baskerville Hall a wide berth. If it is safe to approach again, then perhaps I shall pay him a call in the near future. In the meantime, I must be getting on. My surgery opens in an hour. Farewell, Holmes. Delighted to see you."

"And you too, Doctor."

Mortimer emitted another of those double clucks of the tongue. Instantly, his spaniel sprang to its feet and hurried over. It proffered its master his Penang lawyer, which Mortimer took, and raising the stick aloft in a salute to Holmes, he turned and ambled away.

Chapter Twelve

A GURT BIG GODHAN

With no Mrs Barrymore there to cook for them, the residents of Baskerville Hall were forced to prepare their own breakfast. Benjamin Grier, however, proved to be a dab hand at the stove, and soon he, Holmes, Sir Henry and little Harry were all tucking into heaped plates of bacon, sausage and scrambled egg, accompanied by grilled mushrooms and small cakes which Grier called "biscuits" but were essentially scones.

Afterwards, Holmes announced he was going out to find local farmers to interrogate about the sheep killings. Grier asked to accompany him. "The chance to witness Sherlock Holmes exercising his much-vaunted powers?" he said. "I'd be a fool not to take it."

"I fear it is going to be investigative work of the most plodding, banal sort," Holmes said, "but you are welcome to tag along nonetheless."

"Daddy," said Harry, "may *I* go with Mr Scarecrow and Mr Chimneysweep?"

"No, son," replied his father. "They are doing grown-up things."

"But it's not fair. I want to go outdoors. You don't let me go outdoors."

"Outdoors is… not safe right now, Harry. You know that."

"Even the garden?"

"Even the garden."

"I promise I won't go past the gate."

"The answer is still no, Harry," said Sir Henry firmly. "You must stay in the house. Why don't you do one of your jigsaws instead?"

"I've done them all," said the youngster, pouting.

"Including the jungle one? That's your favourite."

"Three times."

"Then what say you and I play with your soldiers? We can have a campaign on the drawing-room rug. Cushions for hills. The Battle of Waterloo, eh? How about that? I'll be Napoleon, you can be Wellington."

"I want to go outdoors," Harry muttered sullenly. "It's sunny."

"And you shall have that opportunity again. Soon. Very soon. I swear."

The lad brightened. "How soon?"

Sir Henry looked to Holmes beseechingly. "I reckon in a day or two. Don't you, Holmes?"

Holmes was loath to make promises he could not guarantee to fulfil. Still, for the boy's sake, he said, "I think your father has it about right, Harry. A day or two should do it. After that, you will be free to go outside and play whenever you feel like."

With a loud huzzah, Harry dashed out of the dining room to start setting up the Battle of Waterloo.

"Thank you, Holmes," said Sir Henry. He was bleary-looking and unshaven, not a little hungover, but the faint flicker of hope that had been kindled in his eyes the previous night was still there. "I realise nothing is certain, but even just the thought that there could be an end to this nightmare has lifted my spirits."

"You go have fun with your boy, Henry," said Grier. "He deserves it. So do you. Leave everything to Mr Scarecrow and me."

"Grier," warned Holmes, "I have told you. Harry may use those names, but we needn't. Especially when not in his presence."

"I guess scarecrows just don't have a sense of humour."

Holmes rose from the table. "Do you wish to come with me, Grier? Fetch your coat."

With a bemused shake of the head, Grier rose too. "All right, all right. Henry, are all Brits this brisk and businesslike?"

"You'll get used to it," said Sir Henry. "The British do have a lighter side. It's deeply buried, though, and you have to dig to reach it."

"So it's not just Holmes."

"Sherlock Holmes is in many ways the quintessential Englishman, but he is also, in almost every regard, exceptional. You cannot judge the rest by him, and vice versa. Good luck to the two of you. Godspeed."

Holmes chose not to respond to these comments about him, other than to give a nod that was, as he put it, "neither acknowledgement nor dismissal, but as modest and noncommittal as a nod can be".

All that day, he and Grier ranged far and wide over the moor, covering – by Holmes's estimate – some twenty miles all told. They stopped at every farm they came to, and at each they made enquiries of the farmer regarding sheep molestations and the giant moth. In several instances these rustics spoke with such an impenetrable West Country burr that Holmes could make out only one word in three and Grier none at all. The general consensus seemed to be that the moth existed and was responsible for the attacks on sheep, but nobody whom they interviewed had personally seen the creature or lost livestock to it.

That was until just past noon, when they arrived at a tiny, remote croft that perched in a narrow valley beside a brook whose crystal-clear waters seemed to slither over the stones of its bed. A couple of dozen sheep milled about in a pen, hemmed in by drystone walls, next to a one-room cottage, the roof slates of which bore a layer of dense, dark green moss.

The resident was a small, stooped ancient with a well-weathered face. There was but a single tooth in his mouth, clinging on like the last knight valiantly defending a castle. At first wary of Holmes, and warier still of Grier, the crofter started out by giving only the most evasive of answers. It rapidly became clear, however, that his flock was one of those that had suffered harassment, and some good-natured goading from Holmes, along with the offer of a florin for his troubles, soon loosened his tongue.

"Fortnight past, it were," said the crofter. "Oi'd left they sheep out for pasturin' overnight, loike. Them's not apt to stray. This valley's their 'ome, and the bellwether knows a thing or two. Good as a sheepdog, he is, for keepin' they others where them oughter be. Anyways, come the mornin', Oi were callin' they in, as is moy routine. In them trotted, all nice and orderly, and blow me if the flock weren't a head short. Missin' a hogget, Oi were."

"A hogget?" said Grier.

"I believe that is a young ewe," said Holmes.

"Roight you are, zurr," said the crofter. "A ewe between 'er first and second shearings, that be a hogget. Off went Oi, a-searchin' for she. Sheep have a reputation for bein' none too bright, don't them? Mostly that be a falsehood. There's creatures far dumber than a sheep. Certain of they be smarter than zum folk as Oi know of. But this partickler hogget 'appened to be as daft as they come, and Oi wouldner been surprised if her had got 'er 'ooves stuck in a bog or wandered into a blind gully, loike, and not been able to find the way back out. Took me an 'our or so, but Oi found 'er all roight."

"Dead, I presume."

"As a doornail, zurr. Layin' flat out on 'er flank."

"Where was this?"

"On the far slope of yonder tor, 'bout a mile from 'ere as the crow flies. To begin with, Oi thought 'er had just collapsed and expired, loike 'er 'eart had given out or zummat. Bain't be a common occurrence but it 'appens, even with an 'ealthy youngling. There weren't a mark on she, see. Least, not as Oi could tell from first lookin'. It were only when Oi inspected the carcass proper close did Oi notice the 'ole in 'er neck."

"Describe this hole."

"'Bout as big around as moy little finger, it were, and sunk deep in 'er throat. Difficult to find on account of the flass that were coverin' it."

"The fleece?" said Grier.

"That's roight, zurr. The flass. And there weren't 'ardly much blood there, neither. Wound like that, you'd think the blood woulder gone here, there and everywhere. That got Oi to thinkin', maybe 'er were dead because the blood had been removed from she. To put it to the test, Oi got out moy knife and slit open 'er belly. Won't say it were bone-dry, not zackly, but Oi will say that scarcely a dribble of blood came out."

"Had you heard, by then, about the giant bloodsucking moth?" said Holmes.

"Oi'm not one as consorts much with others," said the crofter, shaking his head. "But it were so passing strange to me, 'ow that hogget had died, that Oi went into Clyst St Margaret that evening – which be the village nearest – and Oi took moyself to the pub there, The Turk's Head, and asked around. Weren't long before Oi discovered that moine weren't the first sheep to be attacked in such a wise. Oi also learned about the gurt big godhan that were supposed to be at large and that were said to be doin' mischief to flocks all over."

"A godhan being a moth, I take it."

"That be what folk calls they round these 'ere parts. Godhans. Seems 'ard to credit that there might be one what were of a size to kill a sheep, but then Dartmoor be a place full of oddities. There's Kitty Jay's grave, just north of Ashburton. She were a suicide, died in shame, but there be always fresh flowers where 'er body lies, even a 'undred years on, and nobody knows as who puts they there. The Devil himself rode into the church at Widecombe one mornin' on a coal-black steed and made off with a young lad who'd fallen asleep during the service. Left in such a tearing 'urry, 'e did, that the church roof fell in on itself. The ghost of a fraudster called Benjie haunts Cranmere Pool, cursed with the task of emptying the water out of that place for all eternity. On some nights you can 'ear his miserable wailings over in Okehampton, close by. Giants, pixies, 'eadless 'orsemen, black dogs from Hell – there be no lack of that sorter thing on the moor, zurr. So a gurt big godhan? One that can drain a sheep of its blood, down to the last drop? Why ever not?"

Holmes and Grier made their goodbyes and left the crofter gazing sombrely at his flock as if unhappy to have been reminded that he was minus one ewe.

Holmes had secured directions to Clyst St Margaret from the fellow, and it was towards this village that the duo's footsteps now turned.

"Why are we going to Clyst St Margaret?" Grier asked.

"I don't know about you, but I am famished," said Holmes. "A hostelry such as The Turk's Head will allow us to wet our whistles and fill our stomachs. Furthermore, a village public house is the centre of rural gossip. If you want to know what is going on, a pub is invariably the best place to look."

In the event, village was too generous a term for Clyst St Margaret. Hamlet would be more accurate. Holmes counted no more than a dozen houses, clustered around a crossroads. Aside from a tiny Methodist chapel, the only building of note was the pub.

With pints of ale and great slabs of ham sandwich set before them, Holmes and Grier replenished themselves. Then Holmes went about endearing himself to the other patrons of The Turk's Head, seven in number, by buying a round of drinks. He played the part of a glad-handing tourist who was passing through the region and keen to absorb a bit of local colour. It wasn't long before he had them discussing the giant moth, and one man confessed to having seen the creature.

"It were a month ago, no more," said this eyewitness. "I were walkin' home from this very pub. The hour were just gone eleven. Up in the sky, I spied movement. There it were, 'overing afore the moon. A moth as big as I am. I'd be lying if I told you I were not affrit, gents. A proper shock it gave me, seeing it up there. Swoopin' and swirlin', it were. And them eyes... bright red and staring down at me, all baleful like."

"How many pints of scrumpy had you had aforehand, Jethro?" jeered one of the other patrons. "The usual nine or ten?"

"I knows what I saw," Jethro shot back. "I mayn't have been full sober, but these eyes of mine don't never play tricks on me."

"Where did this encounter take place?" said Holmes.

"On the lane leading up to my 'ouse, which runs north out of the village. A lonely road at the best of times."

"What lies on either side of the lane?"

"Open moor one side, grazing land the other."

"And on which side was the moth?"

"The moor side."

"It was a clear night, I presume."

"Aye," said Jethro, nodding. "Clear as anything, and bright. Moon full, stars out. A mite breezy, mind."

"How long was the moth present?"

"I stood there watchin' it for a good three to four minutes, I'd say. Then downward it flew, out of sight. I rushed 'ome to my Ethel and told her all about it. She were more alarmed than even I was. Didn't get a wink of sleep all the rest of the night, she didn't, and neither did I."

As Holmes and Grier left The Turk's Head, they were followed out by another of the patrons, a man who had maintained a steady silence throughout the conversation about the moth. He cleared his throat to get their attention, then furtively beckoned them to one side.

"I saw the moth too," said he in low tones. "Only, I daredn't mention it in the pub because, well… let's just say, at the time I saw it, I weren't where I should've been."

Holmes studied the fellow briefly. "You are a poacher."

The man patted the air with both hands in a hushing motion. "I wouldn't call myself that."

"No, that is true. Normally you would call yourself a farrier."

"You know me, sir?" the other said, startled. "Have we met? I thought you said you was a tourist."

"Two small injuries give away your profession. The first is an abrasion on your left palm, one among several cuts and scrapes I see on that hand. It shows the mark of a rasp, one of the principal tools of the farrier's trade. The other injury is on your forehead, an old scar. Its curved shape matches the arc of a horse's hoof, suggesting that one of your charges kicked you. The likeliest product of these two factors is farrier."

"I see. Well, I did not think it so obvious."

"Everything is obvious to one who knows how to look," said Holmes. "Shoeing horses brings in a variable income, greatly dependent upon season and demand. In lean times, when work is thin on the ground, one must resort to other methods of making ends meet. When you said you weren't where you should have been, poaching seemed the most logical inference. More often than not, when a countryman is in straits, he turns poacher."

The farrier sighed. "I has five children by two wives. That be mouths to feed aplenty. On Lord Torkington's estate, near Chagborough, there's rabbit warrens galore, 'undreds of plump little coneys what's just waitin' to be trapped."

"And it was there, while trespassing on this nobleman's land, that you saw the giant moth."

"This were the Wednesday afore the Wednesday afore

last. It were a night much like the one Jethro Satterley described. The air so clear, you could see for miles, and with enough of a wind blowin' for the noise of it to mask your movements."

"A perfect night for poaching, it would seem to me."

"You would not be wrong, sir. Around midnight, that moth loomed up in the distance. It didn't ride in front of the moon for me, like it did for Jethro, but there was so many stars out that its shape stood out against them, stark and black. Four wings, all flutterin'; a body thick in the middle, narrowin' to a point at the tail; a pair of stalks atop its head, curved like a demon's horns; and of course those red eyes…"

The farrier and part-time poacher gave an involuntary shiver.

"Nothing the good Lord has made has eyes like that," he said, "and I 'opes with all my heart that never again does I see the beast as them belonged to. I ain't mentioned this to a single soul, until today. That be because I don't want to answer questions about the whereabouts of the sighting, but also because even the act of rememberin' it makes me come over all queasy."

"Then why tell us now?" said Grier.

"To relieve myself of the secret, sir, which has been something of a burden to me all this time."

"You would trust a pair of complete strangers with this confession over any of your close acquaintances?"

"You are both grockles. That is, outsiders to the county. A Londoner and an American. Doesn't matter if I lose face with you nearly as much as it would with them as whom I rubs shoulders with day after day."

"That makes sense."

As a parting shot, the farrier said, "Not once since that night has I ventured abroad after dark, sirs. All across Dartmoor, people are doin' likewise. There hasn't been a mood like this round 'ere in years. Doors locked at night. Children kept inside. It takes a lot to intimidate us moor folk, but that giant moth has done it. The last time we was anything close to this fretful were some five years past, when a devil dog were on the prowl. That turned out to be a hoax. I pray this monster moth will do too, although," the fellow added darkly, "havin' seen the thing myself, I be right proper doubtful."

Chapter Thirteen

THE PLEASURES AND PITFALLS OF BEING A PROXY WATSON

As Holmes and Grier made their way back towards Baskerville Hall, they reviewed their findings.

"It is at times like this," Holmes said to his companion, "that I usually ask Watson for his opinion."

"But in his absence, I shall have to do," said Grier.

"You will more than suffice. You are easily his equal in intellect, and even when Watson is wrong, which is not unheard of, his wrongness has been known to set me on the right path."

"Then I shall endeavour to be intelligent and, if wrong, intelligently wrong."

I must admit to feeling a stab of jealousy as Holmes related this exchange. Was I so easily replaced? I did not resent Grier for it. Rather, I resented myself for having left a void that required filling.

"What we have," Grier said, "are three eyewitnesses whose accounts corroborate the circumstantial facts we have already ascertained. Sheep have been attacked. A giant moth has been observed at night."

"For me," said Holmes, "the truly intriguing element is the similarity between Mr Jethro Satterley's tale and that of our farrier-cum-poacher. Consider, in particular, the climatic conditions at the time of each sighting."

"A clear night in either instance."

"Ideal for the moth to show itself off to its best advantage."

"You mean it wished to be seen?"

"That might not be the desire of the creature itself, but of its owner, trainer, handler, whatever you wish to call him."

"Stapleton."

"If it *is* he."

"What you're saying is that Stapleton, or whoever the culprit may be, has been releasing the moth and allowing it to disport itself publicly," said Grier, "with the express intention of the creature entering into the purview of some passer-by. He is deliberately sowing alarm and consternation for his own nefarious ends."

"That is one possible interpretation of the facts, yes."

"Alternatively, might not the moth be roaming free at all times, and it is simply the case that on other nights the weather was not so conducive to a sighting? It was cloudy, or misty, or pouring with rain. The moth flew but nobody was around to see it or, owing to an overcast sky, *could* see it. Anyway, don't moths prefer dry, bright conditions for their nocturnal outings? Moonlight attracts them."

"Those are all very reasonable arguments," said Holmes.

"I am meeting the mark as your proxy Watson, then?"

"Most commendably."

Hearing this, my stab of jealousy deepened, and so did my feelings of self-reproach.

"The difficulty I am having with all this, Grier," Holmes continued, "is that I am unsure how feasible it is to train a moth. Arthropods are not higher-order vertebrates like dogs or monkeys. I wonder whether one could ever be coaxed to perform even the most basic of tasks."

"If this one is as large as it is reputed to be, then would its brain not be of a commensurate size, and its intellect therefore greatly enhanced? Perhaps even to the level of a man's?"

"Again, a good point."

"Then, of course, if it is a skinwalker…"

"Oh, Corporal Grier," Holmes said. "We're back to this Navajo 'were-moth' theory of yours, are we? And you were doing so well."

"I have gone down in your estimation," said Grier, with a note of chagrin.

"Somewhat. Watson would know better, I think, than to persist with intimations of the supernatural, especially after I have soundly rejected them."

"You think me credulous," Grier said.

"I think you all too ready to reach for the least plausible explanation when there are others that are likelier and more easily testable," said Holmes. "You know of my dictum concerning the impossible and the improbable?"

"I am familiar with it from Dr Watson's writings."

"It applies here as much as it does anywhere. Skinwalkers belong in the 'impossible' category. Let us eliminate them from our considerations and instead seek out whatever remains, no matter how improbable it is."

The asperity with which Holmes made these remarks seemed to take Grier aback. By the sound of it, the American – not as inured to my friend's sometimes waspish temperament as I – was subdued for the rest of the journey to the Hall. As for Holmes, he was blithe to having caused offence, in so far as I could judge. I doubt he will mind me saying that he has a notorious blind spot where human sensibilities are concerned.

As the two men drew near to Baskerville Hall, the sound of childish laughter reached their ears. In the front garden they came upon young Harry cavorting with a mid-sized brown dog. Holmes had no trouble identifying the animal as Galen, Dr Mortimer's spaniel. Harry was throwing a small tree branch for Galen to fetch and chortling deliriously as the spaniel came lolloping back with its prize and dropping it at his feet.

"Henry has let the kid go outside," said Grier. "That, surely, is progress."

"Yet he is keeping a very close eye on him," Holmes said, indicating the main entrance to the house.

The door was open and Sir Henry Baskerville stood on the threshold, arms folded. He exhibited little of the paternal contentment one might expect to see in a father watching his child at play. His gaze was less on Harry than on the surroundings, scanning near and far for potential threat. His shoulders were hunched, and overall his posture spoke of alertness and caution. Holmes fancied that the baronet was poised at any moment to snatch up, if necessary, the pistol that was shelved just inside the door. Woe betide any intruder, be it man or moth, who might wish to menace his son.

Holmes hailed him, and Sir Henry responded with a distracted wave.

"Mr Scarecrow! Mr Chimneysweep!" Harry cried, catching sight of the two returnees. "You are back. Daddy and Uncle James have let me play with Galen." By Uncle James, he clearly meant his godfather, Dr Mortimer. "Galen is a clever dog."

The spaniel came bounding over to greet Holmes and Grier. Holmes scratched it behind the ears.

"Galen!" said Harry, holding up the stick. "Galen. Get it, Galen." He hurled the branch, and the spaniel dutifully scurried off to retrieve it. "See? He always brings it back."

"Dr Mortimer is visiting, I presume," said Holmes to Sir Henry.

"He is within," came the reply.

"I ran into him this morning, out by Crookback Samuel. He said he might call by the Hall, and it seems he has been as good as his word."

"How have your investigations gone today?" Sir Henry enquired.

"Profitably."

"Anything to report? Has there, dare I ask, been a breakthrough?"

"It has, above all else, been a day of substantiation," said Holmes. "What I have hitherto learned at second hand, I have now learned at first hand. I have turned up some promising leads nonetheless."

"Excellent," said Sir Henry. "Would either of you care for a cup of tea? Mortimer has the kettle on even as we speak."

"I can think of nothing I would like better."

"Myself, I'd prefer coffee," said Grier, "but tea will do in a pinch."

"You go in," said Sir Henry. "I shall remain here a little longer, keeping vigil, until either Harry or Galen gets bored of their game."

"My money is on the dog," said Grier. "Harry looks like he could throw that darned piece of wood all day."

"He's certainly making the most of his freedom," said the lad's father.

"And why shouldn't he? It's his first taste of it in a while." Grier patted his friend on the shoulder. "Brave of you to give him this opportunity, Henry. I know it can't have been an easy decision."

"It is a small step." Sir Henry essayed a smile. "The first, I trust, of many."

In the kitchen, Holmes introduced Grier to Mortimer. Then, teacups in hand, the three men repaired to the drawing room. There, on the floor, lay the aftermath of Sir Henry and Harry's restaging of the Battle of Waterloo in miniature. Dozens of lead soldiers were strewn about, the red-jacketed British troops standing mostly upright while their blue-jacketed French counterparts were, almost to a man, horizontal.

Between grateful sips of tea, Holmes regaled Mortimer with a brief synopsis of his and Grier's experiences that day.

"What I require now," said he, "is a map."

"A map of what?" said Mortimer.

"Dartmoor. Would you know if Sir Henry has one?"

"As it happens, I think he does." Mortimer disappeared to the library and returned presently with an Ordnance Survey plan of the local area, which he unfolded on the drawing-room table. The map covered almost the entirety of the tabletop.

Holmes pored over it for several minutes. Then, with a peremptory snap of the fingers, he said, "Pencil."

Mortimer duly fetched the requested item. He and Grier leaned in to watch as Holmes began collating, in visual format, various of the data he had gathered that day.

"First, let us identify the spot where the sheep belonging to our friend, the venerable crofter, was killed," he said. "He told us it was a mile from his homestead which, unless I am much mistaken, is here. The scale of the map is an inch to a mile, and an inch, conveniently, is the same length as the top joint of my thumb." He swept his thumb round in a circle, his first knuckle pivoting upon the point where the croft lay. "There we are. Now, to judge by the closeness of these concentric contour lines, here lies a tor. It is the correct distance away from the croft, and in the correct direction, and is thus the likeliest candidate for the location of the ovine death."

He put an X on the map.

"Then let us plot the two confirmed sightings of the moth. One was here, to the north of Clyst St Margaret. We cannot be certain of the exact place but we know it was on the lane leading out of the village in that direction. That puts it roughly here."

He drew another X.

"The second sighting occurred on Lord Torkington's estate. That, I have it on good authority, lies near Chagborough, which is here. Mortimer, can you tell me which of the five large houses proximate to that village is his lordship's?"

Mortimer hesitated, then picked one out.

"You're sure?"

"I have been there just the once. I believe I am right, though."

"Thank you," said Holmes. "The fence lines indicate that the estate covers several hundred acres, making it hard to pinpoint with any great accuracy where our poacher was when the moth flitted into view. Still, we may make an educated guess. Rabbit warrens are usually found on hillsides. A ridge of low hill abuts the property just here. That, then, for want of an alternative, is where we shall put our cross."

He sat back.

"As you can see, gentlemen, our giant moth has a somewhat circumscribed territory. All the crosses I have made are within a few miles of one another."

"I can add a further two crosses, if you would like," said Mortimer.

"The more the merrier," said Holmes. "I was hoping your local knowledge would come in handy."

Taking the pencil from him, Mortimer added yet another X. "The moth was seen by the vicar of Thorsley parish, no less. He was heading home on his bicycle after a round of evening visits, ministering to housebound parishioners.

He was less than half a mile from the vicarage when the beast put in an appearance."

"Very good. What more trustworthy testimony could there be than a man of the cloth's?"

"Quite. He says the moth passed above him, scarcely ten feet from his head, its wingbeats loud as thunderclaps. He was so rattled, he steered his machine into a ditch."

"And the other sighting?"

"Not a sighting but a sheep killing," said Mortimer. "It took place at the farm at Foulmire. There."

"Capital!" Holmes exclaimed. "Here, now, we have five marks. And what is common to them all?"

"Nothing, as far as I can see," said Grier. "They seem to be scattered at random."

"They are. It is not the placement of the marks themselves that counts so much as their locus. Look. They encircle a town. This one, Coombe Tracey. Imagine spokes radiating out from the centre of that municipality, each extending to one of the X's which marks a sighting of the moth. In fact, there is no need to imagine them. If you will give me back the pencil, Mortimer, I shall draw them. There we go. See how the lines are more or less the same length as one another. Coombe Tracey, by that reckoning, would appear to be the hub of the moth's activity."

"What does that signify?" said Mortimer.

"Perhaps nothing. Perhaps everything. It may merely be

coincidence. We would need to record many more confirmed moth sightings and sheep killings on the map before we could state with any certainty that the giant insect calls Coombe Tracey its home. Militating against this theory is the fact that Baskerville Hall lies further from Coombe Tracey by some margin than any of the other locations. If the moth strayed from its usual stamping ground in order to kill Lady Audrey, why? Why this one exception to the rule? If it even *is* an exception. Hum!"

Bent over the Ordnance Survey map, Holmes sank into a profound meditation. The other two men left him there, Grier to go to the kitchen and prepare the evening meal, Mortimer to collect Galen and go home. Lost in his musings, Holmes did not stir from this position until Grier came in an hour and a half later to announce that supper was served.

Chapter Fourteen

A WILD MOTH CHASE

That night, during the small hours, Holmes was awoken by a scream.

It was a high-pitched, thready wail, filled with terror, and it came from Harry's bedroom.

Holmes sprang from his bed and hurried along the darkened corridor. Sir Henry was also up, and arrived at the boy's room before Holmes, for his own room lay nearer. The baronet flung open the door and rushed in, crying, "Harry! Harry! My God, Harry, what is it?"

Holmes entered the room hot on his heels. Harry was sitting bolt upright in his bed, wide-eyed, his face a mask of fright.

"Harry," said his father. "Speak to me, son. What has happened? Was it a nightmare?"

In answer, the distraught little creature pointed to the window.

"Th-there," he sobbed. "I saw it. It – it tapped on the glass, and it was looking in. It was looking at me. Its eyes were red and shiny."

Unhesitatingly, Holmes darted for the window. The curtains were not fully drawn, and through the chink between them, which spanned perhaps four inches, he spied movement. He snatched them apart and peered out.

A waxing moon shed light over the landscape. By its butter-coloured glow Holmes could see, with absolute clarity, a winged figure in silhouette. It was flying away from the Hall, out over the moor, already some fifty yards off and receding fast.

It was, indisputably, a giant moth.

Even Sherlock Holmes, hard-headed rationalist that he was, could not help but feel a twinge of atavistic fear as he beheld this unnatural entity hurtling through the air. Its jigging, uneven flight was exactly that of a moth, as was the rippling motion of its wings. A thick, tapered abdomen and a pair of curved antennae were equally moth-like attributes. What made it exceptional was, of course, its size – beyond question, it was six foot from wingtip to wingtip, and almost as long from head to tail – and its luminous red eyes, bright as any train lamps, which Holmes caught brief flashes of as the thing retreated further and further into the distance.

Grier came thundering into the room. "What's going on?" he demanded. "Is Harry all right?"

"I have him," said Sir Henry. He was on the bed, clutching Harry to his breast and shielding the child's head with one hand. "Holmes! What is out there? What do you see?"

Grier joined Holmes at the window. "By all that's holy! Is that what I think it is, Holmes?"

"It's the moth, isn't it?" said Sir Henry, his voice cracking. "I knew it. I knew it would come back sooner or later. First Audrey, and now…"

At that moment, a cloud passed in front of the moon. All at once, the scene outside was cast into darkness. Holmes squinted, desperate to keep track of the moth, but it was gone, swallowed up by the gloom. Eventually, a minute or so later, the moon reappeared. Holmes scanned in all directions from the window, but the giant insect was no longer to be seen.

"Well?" said Sir Henry. "I'm right, aren't I? The moth is here, trying to get in."

"The moth *was* here," said Holmes. "Not any more. Sir Henry, stay in this room and comfort your son. Grier? Fetch a lantern. We are going outside."

"Outside?" said Sir Henry. "Are you mad? That blood-thirsty abomination could come back."

"Is there not a pistol beside the front door still?"

"There is."

"Then we shall take that with us, as a hedge against such an eventuality."

Downstairs, Holmes and Grier emerged from the front door at a cautious pace, the former brandishing a lantern, the latter Sir Henry's pistol. The night wind buffeted their faces and made the branches of the trees thrash and seethe. Each man had donned an overcoat over his nightclothes and had put on his boots without socks.

"Stick with me, Grier," said Holmes. "Keep an eye out and, should the moth return, feel free to fire every last bullet you have into it. That should bring it down."

"With pleasure. What shall you do?"

"What I do best: look."

So saying, Holmes moved along the side of the house towards its south-facing elevation, lighting his way with the lantern. He stationed himself below Harry's bedroom window and inspected the ground there. Then he proceeded outward in a line perpendicular to the Hall, crossing the garden until he reached the fence. This course followed that which had been taken by the moth. Grier hovered at his back, watchful as an owl. Holmes straddled the fence and continued onward in a straight line, over the undulating moor. The wind hissed through the thick grass and rattled the clumps of gorse.

After the two men had gone a couple of hundred yards, Holmes halted and went down onto his hands and knees, setting the lantern on the ground beside him. He bent his head towards the grass until the tip of his nose was mere inches above it.

"Footprints?" said Grier.

"Not as such, but rather a small but well-trampled patch of earth," said Holmes. "The grass stems are freshly flattened. It is apparent as much to the nose as the eye. Grass that has just been trodden on exudes a distinctive sharp smell. Someone stood here only minutes ago, shifting around from foot to foot in such a way that I cannot make out individual prints, only their cumulative impact."

"This 'someone' being the moth's owner."

"It could certainly be the case that this is where the moth went after it flew away from the house, returning to its waiting master."

"Stapleton. He bade the moth fly to Harry's window and summoned it back when the task of frightening the boy was done."

"A plausible enough scenario."

"Or…" Grier began.

"Or the moth, which is a skinwalker, alighted here and reverted to its other form, that of a witch," said Holmes. "Is that what you were about to say?"

"No. Well, yes, I was, until I stopped myself."

"You were wise to do so." Holmes straightened up. "If luck were on our side, there would now be a trail of neat footprints, showing the direction taken by our miscreant as he arrived at and, more importantly, departed from the scene." He tutted. "However…" He aimed the lantern's beam ahead, oscillating it slowly from side to side. Even without its light it was possible to make out an expanse of flat, rocky ridges which began just a leap away and spread outward in a broad swathe to the left and right, row upon row of them. Their pale, moss-flecked surfaces glimmered like waves at sea. "There is no hope of finding spoor on such terrain. Somewhere out there, even now, our foe is watching us from a place of concealment. I am convinced of it. He has done his wicked work and is quietly gloating as he sees us flounder."

"I am willing to spend as long as it takes searching for him," Grier said, "and when we find the villain in whatever cranny he is hiding in, I shall drag him out by the scruff of the neck and give him a good thrashing."

"Your resolve is as worthy as it is misplaced," said Holmes. "See the cloud bank amassing to windward? We will soon lose the moonlight altogether, and then a darkness will descend that is nigh on impenetrable. It is clear that our enemy knows the moor well and is more at home on it than you or I. After all, he did not choose this spot by accident. He knew it afforded him the opportunity of escaping without leaving a trail. If we hunt for him using our lantern, its light will give away our position and make it even easier for him to elude us; and if we eschew the lantern, we shall stumble about like blind men, with no hope of finding him at all. No, Grier, we must accept, if only with the greatest reluctance, that we have been outfoxed. For tonight, at least."

"I have just had a terrible thought, Holmes," said the American, looking back over his shoulder at Baskerville Hall. "Suppose this has all been a ruse. Suppose you and I have been lured away from the house deliberately."

"The notion did occur to me even as we were leaving the Hall," Holmes said. "I weighed up the probabilities and decided that, on balance, it was unlikely."

"Still, Sir Henry and Harry are on their own in there, and I do not like it. We closed the front door but did not lock it, and an accomplice could be sneaking inside even as we speak. I am going back. There may not be a moment to lose."

Suiting the action to the word, Grier spun on his heel and hastened off the way they had come. Holmes followed, matching his pace to the American's. His own disquiet, he told me, was hardly as great as that expressed by Grier, but all the same he felt a certain apprehension. He wondered if he had been overconfident. Perhaps he ought to have instructed Grier to remain behind at the house to safeguard the baronet and his son. If, in a moment of inattention, he *had* allowed himself to be decoyed, and the two Baskervilles were to suffer as a result, he would never forgive himself.

No sooner were Holmes and Grier indoors than Grier sprinted up the stairs, calling out Sir Henry's name.

To Holmes's relief, and doubtless more so to Grier's, there came a soft answer from Harry's bedroom.

"Here."

Both men slowed their pace. The baronet's voice was taut but evinced no greater panic or distress than earlier. They re-entered the bedroom to find the pair on the bed, just as they had left them, Sir Henry still hugging Harry tight. The only difference now was that the boy was asleep in his father's arms.

Sir Henry put a finger to his lips, indicating that they should speak in a whisper.

"He has just this minute dropped off," he said.

"All the better for him," said Grier. "Perhaps, in the morning, he will wake up and think it all a bad dream."

"Let us hope so. I am going to stay with him the rest of the night. I am not letting him out of my sight again for a single moment, not until this whole thing is over. Am I to take it that your quest was fruitless?"

Holmes gave a rueful shrug of the shoulders. "Our quarry got away."

"You have seen the moth for yourself now. Do you doubt any longer that it is real?"

"No, it is real enough. Whether it is as real as it seems, or indeed corporeal, is another matter."

"You are being enigmatic."

"Merely circumspect. I am only just beginning to grasp what forces are at work here and do not wish to postulate anything, even tentatively, before I am in possession of the full facts."

"But you have some kind of theory?"

"A theory without empirical proof is worthless," said Holmes. "It is a roof without walls. You are simply going to have to trust me, Sir Henry. Soon enough I will have erected those walls, and then we may act decisively and put paid to this moth menace once and for all."

Chapter Fifteen

A CONSIDERABLE UNDERTAKING
IS PROPOSED

"Holmes, I have been thinking," said Sir Henry as they sat together at breakfast the next morning.

If ever a sentence is a hostage to fortune where Sherlock Holmes is concerned, it is this one. I myself am never so imprudent as to utter it, or anything like it, within earshot of him. Almost inevitably it will elicit a sardonic response along the lines of "Thinking is a practice best left to the professional" or "The brain is a delicate organ – one must take care not to overtax it."

On this occasion, however, Holmes was charitable, as well he should have been after the alarms Sir Henry had endured the previous night. All he said was, "And what, pray tell, is the outcome of your deliberations?"

The baronet cast a look over at Harry, who had finished

his meal and was now squatting in a corner of the dining room, playing intently with a spinning top and oblivious to anything being said at the table. The child seemed little the worse for his night-time encounter with the giant moth. He might even have forgotten it had happened or thought it a dream, as Grier had surmised. At any rate, he had not mentioned it once since waking, and his demeanour was that of someone quite untroubled. Holmes ascribed this to that remarkable resilience of children, which enables them to withstand shocks and upsets with far greater equanimity than any adult.

"I am," Sir Henry said, lowering his voice somewhat, "going to have the Grimpen Mire drained."

Holmes's coffee cup halted halfway to his lips. "I beg your pardon?"

"You don't see why?"

"I see exactly why. I was simply expressing surprise."

"Think about it," Sir Henry insisted. His eyes were bloodshot from lack of sleep, his gestures somewhat agitated, even aggressive. "It's the best way – the *only* way – to establish beyond all doubt whether or not Jack Stapleton is alive."

"You mean if you fail to uncover his remains by draining the Grimpen Mire, the only inference to be drawn is that he was never there in the first place."

"Just so."

Holmes mulled over the proposition. "It will be a considerable undertaking."

"Then it is fortunate that I am a man of considerable means."

"And you will oversee the work yourself?"

"No," said Sir Henry, with a nod towards Harry. "Remember what I told you last night?" He was referring to his vow about not letting the boy out of his sight. "My place is here at the Hall. However, I am going to prevail upon Brother Benjamin to supervise in my stead."

"What's that? Did I just hear my name taken in vain?" Grier walked into the dining room from the kitchen. "By the way, Henry, we are running low on essentials. Your Mrs Barrymore kept a good larder, but unless we wish to survive on tinned food for the foreseeable future, someone needs to go into town today to buy groceries."

"Are you volunteering?"

"By default. I don't fancy Holmes will do it, nor you. But what is this thing you want to 'prevail upon me to supervise'?"

"As a soldier you have been engaged upon construction projects, have you not?" said Sir Henry.

"When I was down near Mexico, our duties consisted of that and little else. My regiment built a number of roads and erected more telegraph lines than I care to count."

"Then you are just the man for the job."

"What job?"

"Draining the Grimpen Mire."

"That's the huge bog not far from here, yes?" said Grier. "Where…" Understanding dawned in his eyes. "Oh, I get it."

"Do you think your engineering skills are up to the challenge?"

"I'd have to look over the place to be sure, but I reckon they are. It'll take manpower, though, and money."

"You have a blank cheque. You'll find plenty of casual labourers in the locality with strong backs and a taste for coin. The odd employable layabout too, I should imagine. Recruit as many of them as you think you need and pay them whatever it takes. I don't care how much it costs. All I care is that it's done, and done quickly. Does that sound reasonable?"

"But it'll take me away from the Hall," said Grier. "Won't that defeat the whole object of my coming back here?"

"Holmes will remain with me."

"I'm not sure I shall, as a matter of fact," said Holmes. "I have plans that require me to be elsewhere, for periods both during the daytime and at night. All related to the case, of course."

"Then I shall be responsible for my own protection," said Sir Henry staunchly. "I have managed well enough thus far, before you two came."

His mind was made up and it seemed nothing could

deter him. He wanted the mire drained, and drained it would be.

As it happened, Holmes did not think the idea was a poor one at all. He had far from ruled out the possibility that Jack Stapleton was still alive. It was among the several strands of enquiry that he was exploring in his mind, and to confirm the death, or otherwise, of the lepidopterist would certainly help narrow things down.

He knew, too, that it would give Sir Henry something to dwell upon other than his late wife and the threat to himself and his son, made all the more imminent by the manifestation of the moth at the Hall during the night. If the baronet's energies were focused even partly elsewhere, it would be a useful distraction and could well prevent him from lapsing back into the maelstrom of madness that had hitherto engulfed him. To have a project, even if it was to be conducted at one remove by someone else, would give him purpose and a sense of accomplishment. It was Sir Henry's way of fighting back.

"Well, Grier? Holmes?" Sir Henry said. "What do you say?"

Grier looked to Holmes for guidance, as I myself would have.

"I say that you have my blessing, Sir Henry," Holmes replied, "and that Corporal Grier had better get going, because he has his work cut out for him."

Chapter Sixteen

FRANKLAND OF LAFTER HALL

Holmes escorted Grier out to the Grimpen Mire, and at his first sight of that swampy morass the American was somewhat disheartened. With a wary eye he surveyed the patches of bright green sedge – that treacherously innocuous-seeming surface layer which masked deep, sucking pools – and the small hills that formed islands of solidity in the mire's midst. It was another bright morning, but still there was an atmosphere about the place which dampened one's spirits and even somehow dimmed the sunlight. The trilling of skylarks and meadow pipits had attended the two men on their journey from Baskerville Hall all the way until they had neared the mire. Then the birdsong had dwindled to nothing, and thereafter an eerie hush prevailed, the only sound the sighing of the breeze passing through the sedge's soft fronds and spiky flowers.

"It is not small," said Grier eventually. "But," he added, demonstrating the indefatigably optimistic spirit that typifies his nation, "I will tame it."

Holmes directed him towards the village of Fernworthy, its rooftops just visible a mile distant. There Grier would find shops and also might muster up workers for his great enterprise. He himself, meanwhile, turned his footsteps towards Lafter Hall.

Holmes had not previously met Frankland, the owner of Lafter Hall. He knew the place, for I had pointed it out to him when, at the climax of the first Baskerville affair, he, I and Lestrade had driven past it in a wagonette on our way towards our confrontation with Jack Stapleton. Any knowledge he had of Frankland himself, however, was derived solely from my reports of my interactions with the man. He was aware that Frankland was gruff and liverish; that, in short, he was what one might call "a bit of a character".

How much of a "character" Holmes soon discovered in emphatic fashion. For, as he left the main road and strolled up the front path of Lafter Hall, he heard from within a bellowing cry of "Where?" Moments later, with his hand grasping the knocker of the imposing, boss-studded front door, he heard the cry repeated, even more loudly this time. "Where?" There followed, in swift succession, a litany of imprecation: "Where, where, where, where, in God's name *where*?"

At that point, Holmes knocked. The door was opened by

a butler who looked as harassed as his station allowed, which is to say that there was a slight discomfiture in his surface that betokened deep currents of perturbation running beneath.

"Yes?"

"Who is that at the door?" barked the same voice responsible for the reiterations of "Where?" This unseen questioner continued, "Not another lawyer, is it? Or some representative of my daughter, come begging?"

"I am not in a position to say, sir," said the butler.

"Is it Laura herself?" Here, the voice sounded less irate, more plaintive.

"I'm afraid not."

"Let me see."

The butler opened the door the whole way, to permit full view of Holmes to the other man. The ruddy cheeks and the receding, wayward white hair were familiar to Holmes from my descriptions: this fellow could only be Frankland.

"Mr Frankland?" Holmes said. "I apologise for arriving without announcing my visit beforehand. However…"

Frankland turned away, seemingly uninterested. To the butler he said, "My spectacles, Loach. Have you seen them? I've dozens of papers to read this morning, and I'm damned if I can find the blessed things."

"Regrettably, sir, I have no idea where they might be," the butler replied. "Do you not have a spare pair?"

"Lost those too," Frankland grumbled.

"If I might, Mr Frankland," Holmes offered. "The commonest place for a pair of missing spectacles is upon the head of the wearer."

The other laid a hand on his thinning pate and patted it. No spectacles were there.

"A joke, I see," he growled. "One I fail to see the humour in."

"But in this instance," Holmes went on suavely, "that is not the solution to the mystery. Rather, I wonder – have you thought of looking in the conservatory?"

"I beg your pardon?"

"I noticed a conservatory attached to the southern end of the house. I strongly suspect that that is where your spectacles are. I would not be at all surprised, in fact, if they were stowed on a shelf where you keep your indoor horticultural tools."

"But…! How…? What…? Can it…?"

This spluttering outburst preceded an abrupt departure as Frankland dashed from the hallway in the direction of the conservatory.

Holmes and Loach the butler waited, each not quite meeting the other's eye. A minute later, Frankland reappeared, and he was a man transformed. His previous ill temper had given way to a brighter mood, like the sun coming out after a storm. In his hand he waved a pair of gold-rimmed reading spectacles.

"Bless me! Bless me!" he declared. "It is a miracle. You are a complete stranger, and yet you knew exactly where they were. How, sir? How is it possible?" His look turned sly. "Are you some kind of spy, by any chance? Have you been watching me?"

"Watching, no," replied Holmes. "Observing, yes. The windows of your conservatory are opaque with condensation. The air within is therefore kept warm and humid, implying that you are a keeper of tropical plants."

"I am."

"Earlier today you were tending to them."

"That is also so, but how can you tell?"

"There are encrustations of dirt beneath the nails of both your hands. Your fingertips are, moreover, lightly dusted with the same dirt. You have been tamping down soil. Meanwhile, adhering to your right sleeve are a few tiny leaf clippings, further evidence of horticultural industry. Above all else, there is a small set of secateurs protruding from your breast pocket, the kind used for trimming botanical specimens. I put it to you that you had your spectacles on in order to facilitate your endeavours in the conservatory, which require close-up scrutiny. When you were done, you somewhat absent-mindedly slipped the secateurs into the pocket where you are wont to store your spectacles and conversely put your spectacles in the place where you are wont to store your secateurs. The rest was simple logic."

"My goodness," laughed Frankland. "Who are you, man? Sherlock Holmes himself?"

"As a matter of fact…" Holmes gave a bow.

"You don't say!"

"This should serve to confirm it." Holmes proffered his card to Loach, who in turn proffered it to his master.

"Well, gracious," said Frankland, putting on his spectacles to peruse the card. "An honour. Whatever can have brought the great London detective to my humble abode? You would care for coffee, perhaps? Step this way, sir. To my study. Loach will accommodate us. Loach?"

"Coffee it is, sir," the butler said, and glided off. Frankland, meanwhile, ushered Holmes into a well-appointed room that boasted walls lined with bookcases, a desk burdened with stacks of manila folders and a floor littered with legal documents.

"Take a seat," he said, gesturing towards one of a pair of plush leather wingback chairs that flanked the fireplace. He planted himself in its identical twin. "How clever of you to discern my interest in matters botanical," he added, tapping the secateurs that were still lodged in his pocket. "It is a new hobby of mine. I am slowly amassing a fine collection of exotic orchids. Remarkable things. Infinite in their variety, extraordinary in their beauty. As you may know, I am also something of an amateur of astronomy."

"I was aware."

"I still maintain a fascination with the stars, but lately I have diversified into that other branch of the sciences. *Branch*. Ha! The pun was unintended. Astronomy remains my first love, but botany is gradually supplanting it. Sup*plant*ing. I pun again."

The conversation strayed into the field of astronomy for a while. It was a topic of no particular consequence to Holmes but one in which he was capable of holding his own if need be. On this occasion, he was happy to feign an interest in it if this would ingratiate him with Frankland. Together, they discussed planetary conjunctions and occultations, meteor showers, transits of Venus and other such celestial events. At one point Frankland mentioned Professor James Moriarty.

"Died not so long ago, didn't he?" he said. "It was in the papers. Great loss to the discipline. I have a copy of his *Dynamics of an Asteroid* somewhere. Read it three times. Not sure I understand all of it, but a sterling piece of erudition nonetheless. Now that I think about it, you had some involvement in his death, did you not, Mr Holmes? It was said to have been a climbing accident in Switzerland, but there was more to it than that."

"To most, Moriarty was merely an academic and a mathematics tutor," said Holmes. "In truth, he was one of the most egregious villains ever known."

"That's right. Bit of a fuss about it last year, wasn't there? Hard to credit that someone so brilliant could also be so evil."

"Genius he may have had, but in him it had become corrupted and profane. If he had turned his talents to the pursuit of good, he might have contributed greatly to the betterment of mankind. As it was, he was a stain on the world, and deservedly was erased."

"I gather his younger brother lives hereabouts," said Frankland.

"Yes. Colonel Moriarty. A station master by profession. Curiously, his forename is also James."

"Two brothers, both called James? How queer. Their parents cannot be very imaginative people."

"Perhaps they were fond of the name."

"It is an excellent name," Frankland said. "Had I ever had a son, I might well have called him James. It derives from Jacob, I believe, and means 'a supplanter'. Ha! There's that word again."

I myself had had some dealings with this other James Moriarty, who in 1893 wrote a number of letters to *The Times*, *The Telegraph*, and a couple of other national broadsheets, in which he excoriated Holmes and mounted a vigorous defence of his brother – this being the "bit of a fuss" Frankland had referred to. In response, I had felt moved to set the record straight and publish the truth of the matter in the form of my story "The Final Problem". The tale, I believe, successfully rebutted the slander on Holmes's reputation and put paid to any attempts to rehabilitate Professor Moriarty's.

At this point in Holmes's and Frankland's conversation, Loach brought in a silver pot of piping-hot coffee. He served both men with polished efficiency before withdrawing.

"But it cannot be that you have dropped by simply to talk about stargazing, Mr Holmes," Frankland said. "Only a fool would presume this were a social call."

"It is not, I regret to say."

"I imagine it has something to do with the recent appalling business at Baskerville Hall. Poor Lady Audrey. And poor Sir Henry too, to be a widower so young and after so brief a marriage. An estimable couple, those two. Both so civilised - and there is not a great deal of civilisation in this neck of the woods, Mr Holmes, believe you me. Many's the fine dinner I enjoyed in their company. I can hardly countenance the tragedy of it all. Truly the Baskerville name is an accursed one. Not that I believe in curses, but what else can one call such a run of tribulation? Sir Charles and that hound, and now this… It was murder, of course, was it not?"

"I am minded to think so."

"Can only have been. Someone – some*thing* – emptying the blood out of her like that. Makes me shiver to think about it. I shiver all the harder when I consider that, but for the grace of God, it might have been my own daughter."

"Mrs Lyons, you mean?" said Holmes, canting his head inquisitively.

"Yes. I recall that you met her when last you were down

here. It is in no small part thanks to you that she was able to gain some sort of redress against that scoundrel Stapleton. How he abused her trust, the fiend!" Frankland's frown turned doleful. "She is not a woman who chooses men wisely, my Laura. She has many good qualities, but the ability to distinguish a worthy suitor from an unworthy one is not among them. First there was Lyons himself, that brute of a fellow. I knew from the outset that he was no good and the marriage was headed for disaster, but Laura could not see it, not until it was almost too late. She was forever excusing his wicked behaviour, even blaming herself for it. At last, thank heaven, she came around. Then there was Stapleton, and not long after that whole sorry business was done with, she and Sir Henry formed an attachment. I did harbour the hope, then, that she had at last learned discernment. I hoped, too, that their association might lead to something more, especially once the court ruled on a decree absolute and her marriage was annulled. But it was not to be."

Holmes remembered Sir Henry speaking of "a couple of brief dalliances that had come to naught" before his engagement to Audrey Lidstone. One of those dalliances had been with Beryl Stapleton, and it was clear, now, that the other had been with the newly divorced Mrs Laura Lyons.

"Do you know why it did not work out between her and Sir Henry?" he asked Frankland.

"Oh, just the way of such things," Frankland replied with

an airy wave of the hand. "I hold neither of them to blame. Certainly not Sir Henry. Laura, on the other hand... My daughter can be awkward, Mr Holmes. Very awkward. She combines vulnerability with touchiness, and that is not a stable mixture in a female."

"In anyone, for that matter," Holmes opined.

"Yes, yes, true. But it gives Laura a viperish tendency that men find highly unattractive. I suspect – I do not know, but I suspect – that Sir Henry was the unhappy victim of her venom, and it put paid to any romantic entanglement which might otherwise have developed. Nor would he be alone in feeling the sting of her spite." Frankland gazed off into the distance, his manner wistful. "All I can say is that my daughter has had a lucky escape, for if she were to have married Sir Henry and become Lady Baskerville, it might have been her lying out on the moor, stone dead, rather than Audrey. That is the one redeeming feature of it all."

"You say 'suspect', Mr Frankland. This rather suggests to me that you and your daughter are not in close contact, and have not been in some while, else you might be better informed with regard to the ins and outs of her dealings with Sir Henry."

Frankland exhaled a sorrowful breath. "It has not been good between the two of us, not for some time. Our relations were always strained, but of late Laura and I have fallen out

completely. We have become – what's the word? – estranged.
I don't really want to go into it."

"I heard you when I was at the front door, expressing the
hope that it was your daughter calling or her representative.
You believe some sort of reconciliation is still possible?"

"If you were a father, Mr Holmes, you would know that
you never give up on your children, no matter how far from
you they stray. I have made countless overtures towards
Laura, only to be rebuffed every time. I have done all I can.
The onus is now on her to reach out to me. I have faith that
one day she will."

Holmes gently probed him, trying to get him to expand
further on the matter, but Frankland would not be drawn.

"Really," said he. "I have already told you more than I
ought. It is too personal. Too painful."

Holmes gave it up, thinking that there were other methods
by which he could get at the truth. He did not know whether
the gulf that yawned between Frankland and his daughter
was in any way pertinent to his investigation. Yet he felt it
could not be ignored, just as the fact that Sir Henry and Mrs
Lyons had courted, however briefly, could not be ignored.

At this point Holmes interjected, to me, that his
impression of Frankland was very different from the one he
had gleaned from my depiction of the man. "Given everything you'd told me about him, Watson, I was expecting
someone cantankerous and spiteful," he said.

"So I adjudged him."

"Whereas I found that, although there was, admittedly, something of the pompous busybody about him, he was an agreeable and also a rather melancholy sort."

"Could it be that time and the difficulties with his daughter have changed him?" I offered.

"That may very well be so. Misfortune is the great abrasive. It smooths a person's character, rounding off any rough edges."

Returning to his encounter with Frankland, Holmes said that eventually he was able to get down to the nub of the conversation, the reason for his visit to Lafter Hall.

"I have come, sir," said he to Frankland, "seeking a favour."

"And I will be sure to grant it, Mr Holmes," Frankland replied, "if it lies in my power to do so."

"I require the use of your telescope. I know from my great friend Dr Watson that you have one on the roof of this house."

"I do indeed. Made by Dollond of London, in the Cassegrain reflector design. Two hyperbolic mirrors. Achromatic lenses. Brass casing. Two-inch aperture on a three-foot barrel. A marvellous instrument."

"It sounds it."

"Your Dr Watson availed himself of it when here, I recall," Frankland said.

"Indeed. Through it you had spied a boy making regular deliveries out on one of the most desolate parts of the moor, and your presumption, which you conveyed to Watson, was that he must be taking food to the escaped convict Selden."

"The good doctor saw for himself the lad going about his errand, through the telescope."

"And thus, by chance, did he uncover my hiding place."

"Yes, so I learned later. It was you to whom the messenger boy was ferrying supplies, not Selden at all. You had sequestered yourself secretly on the moor during your investigation into the 'hound' affair. And I can only assume you require the telescope for a similar purpose now, as part of another investigation. Am I right?"

"You are, but I'm afraid I cannot tell you any more than that at present," said Holmes. "My enquiries are at a delicate stage, and I must take care not to do anything that might tip my hand. You understand."

"I understand."

"I mean to cast no aspersions on your integrity."

"Quite, quite," said Frankland. "Better that I don't know than that I inadvertently let slip the truth and the wrong ear is listening. Then everything would be ruined."

"I am grateful for your indulgence."

"Think nothing of it. If I have learned anything from the many lawsuits I have filed over the years, it is that no matter how painstakingly you build your case for litigation, it may be undone by a single careless comment. Tact is the watchword."

"I shall need to be able to come and go at Lafter Hall more or less as I please," Holmes said. "There are certain criteria that must be fulfilled first, you see, in order for your telescope to come into play, and I have no control over the timing of them."

"I am almost always at home," said Frankland, "and should I happen to be out, I shall make sure Loach and the rest of the staff know that you have the run of the place."

"You are too kind, sir."

"Anything to help, Mr Holmes. If I play even a minor part in catching Lady Audrey's murderer, I shall be most gratified. Most gratified!"

Chapter Seventeen

THE STRAITENED CIRCUMSTANCES
OF LAURA LYONS

Frankland showed Holmes how to obtain access to his telescope. The windows of an attic room opened onto a small area of flat roof situated between pitched sections. There followed a quick lesson in collimating the mirrors and adjusting the focus, and then the two men went back downstairs and enjoyed a convivial luncheon.

Afterward, Holmes struck out for Coombe Tracey. It was a long walk but his reserves of energy were always substantial, and with the sun on his face and a gentle zephyr at his back, he was content.

His path took him within sight of the Grimpen Mire, whereupon he made a deviation, for he had spied the mighty figure of Benjamin Grier standing at the edge of the bog, deep in conversation with another. He hailed the

American, who introduced him to his companion, a fellow named Damerell.

This squat, swarthy local was a ditch digger by trade, whom Grier had had the great good fortune to encounter in Fernworthy and whom, after just a few minutes' acquaintance, he had hired to act as site foreman.

Damerell was under no illusion as to the enormity of the task facing them. The mire was on low-lying ground and, in order to drain it, it must be emptied into yet lower-lying ground. The nearest suitable example of the latter lay quarter of a mile to the west, where a gentle declivity led down to a stream.

"I were just tellin' Mr Grier that if haste be required then it's going to take men, sir," Damerell said to Holmes, scratching the back of his head beneath his cloth cap. An unlit clay pipe was clamped between his teeth. "Lots of men. We starts diggin' the main ditch there, close to the stream, where the ground begins to slope downward. Ditch don't need to be too deep but it do need to be broad. We works our way back 'ere, and meantime we also starts diggin' ditches as be comin' inward at angles from the mire to the main ditch. Four of they oughter be enough, so I thinks. Don't you reckon, Mr Grier?"

"Maybe five to be on the safe side," said Grier. "Think of them as tributaries to a river, Mr Holmes. We stop them up at the ends with boards, so as they're dammed. Then, once all of the ditches are joined up – the main one and its feeders – we pull up the boards. Gravity does the rest."

"And how long will all this take?" Holmes asked.

Grier looked to Damerell. Holmes could tell that the pair, only recently strangers, had already developed a good rapport, one founded on mutual respect. "For the answer to that, I shall defer to my colleague," Grier said. "When in the company of an expert, it's always best to draw upon his expertise. That way, you yourself look wise."

The creases that bracketed Damerell's mouth trebled in number as he smiled around his pipe. "It all depends on how many men be doin' the work. I reckons as I can get a dozen 'ere by tomorrer mornin', easy as pie. The money Mr Grier's offerin', folk'll jump at the chance. As word spreads – and it will, sir, fast – more'll come. Be swarmin' in like flies, shovels at the ready. Three days, and water'll be flowin'. Four days, five at the most, and that there mire will be a shadow of its former self."

"Capital," said Holmes. "I'm sure Sir Henry will be pleased at the news."

"What also matters is the weather," said Damerell. He cast a wrinkly-eyed glance at the sky. "If there be rain, it'll hamper us for sure." He took in a couple of deep breaths through his nose. "But I doesn't smell none. The wind's calmed, and I reckons things'll stay set fair for a while to come."

"Your country-born instincts are telling you that?"

"And the barometer at home," came the jocular reply, "the one what my missus inherited from her da and what I checked this morn afore leavin' the house."

"For what it's worth," said Grier, "I am not content just to oversee. I am going to lend my strength to the project and dig."

"Someone your size could, I'd imagine, do the work of ten men," Holmes said.

"You won't find me slacking, that's for sure," said Grier with a reverberant chuckle.

Holmes continued on his way to Coombe Tracey. Having visited the place myself, I am able to furnish a brief description of it here. It is one of those small Devon towns whose buildings huddle closely together like sheep in a storm, seeking comfort in one another's proximity. Dark houses, small windows and narrow, treeless streets give an impression of cloister-like confinement, so that even on a bright day everything is cast in gloom. The one spot where the sun may shine unhindered is a market square whose significant feature, aside from a cattle trough, is a buttressed clock tower, each dial of which, famously, tells a slightly different time from its three cohorts.

Mrs Laura Lyons – for she was the goal of Holmes's visit – was no longer living at her old apartment, and had left no forwarding address. However, locating her proved relatively straightforward. Holmes needed to ask only three shopkeepers before he found one, a butcher, who knew her whereabouts.

"I've had reason to call on the lady in person more than once," the man said. "She be the very devil for settlin' her bills. There be gentlefolk as pay up all prompt like and proper, no questions, and there be those as'll give you no end of trouble. Always it's 'I'll 'ave it for you tomorrer, I promise', ever so polite, and then when you insists on the money, them 'ands it over but it be as though them's doin' you a kindness."

She rented a room in a boarding house on one of Coombe Tracey's meaner side-streets. A mob-capped landlady with a lazy eye showed Holmes up to the third floor, saying, "Mrs Lyons already has a gentleman caller, as it happens, sir. I hopes you and he ain't love rivals or nothin', for I shan't have squallin' and fisticuffs in my 'ouse."

"You need have no concerns on that account," Holmes assured her. "I am merely a friend of the woman."

The room was a far cry from the comfortable, spacious quarters Mrs Lyons had called home five years earlier. It was cramped and dowdy, with a musty dampness to the air which the strong perfume favoured by its occupant did little to dispel. Rags of curtain swathed the windows, and a narrow cot occupied one corner. Here and there were a few items of furniture – an oak wardrobe, an occasional table, a gilt-framed etching, a chinoiserie folding screen that cordoned off the cot – whose smartness suggested they did not come with the room but were Mrs Lyons's own. Her Remington typewriter sat upon the leaf of a fold-down desk, with a small sheaf of papers perched beside it.

The gentleman caller to whom the landlady had referred turned out to be Dr Mortimer. He greeted Holmes warmly.

"Sir, this is an unexpected pleasure. You know Mrs Lyons? What am I saying? Of course you do."

"Mr Sherlock Holmes," said Laura Lyons. "Yes, I remember you. How could I not?"

Just as her accommodation was not what it once had been, so was the lady herself. The extreme beauty that had left a marked impression on both Holmes and me was still in evidence, but it was like a great ancient temple now fallen into decay. It retained a majesty of old but was still, all said and done, derelict. Gone was the bloom on her cheeks. The lustre of her brunette hair was dulled, like tarnished bronze. In place of these lost qualities, the coarseness that had previously lurked just beneath the surface and somewhat marred her attractions had come to the fore. It was as if she had been stripped of her veneer, and now the raw truth of her was laid bare.

She offered Holmes a limp hand, not rising from the threadbare armchair in which she sat. She was, he noted, thin to the point of emaciation, and her clothes were consequently ill-fitting, her blouse hanging loosely off her frame, its cuffs gaping around her scrawny wrists.

"Dr Mortimer has told me that there is trouble afoot at Baskerville Hall," said she in a wan, wavering voice, "and that you have returned to Dartmoor to resolve it. Sir Henry will doubtless be greatly obliged to you again, when all has been settled." She stumbled a little over the baronet's name. "I myself am obliged to you still for the manner in which you handled my tangential involvement in Sir Charles Baskerville's murder. Your diplomacy and delicacy were second to none. I was a fool for doing what I did. The power Jack Stapleton had over me – I cringe to think how easily I was manipulated. After him and my former husband, and Sir Henry himself, my faith in men has been eroded. About the only member of the opposite sex I can still trust is the dear doctor here."

"Your servant, madam," said the physician.

"Dr Mortimer has been my rock," Mrs Lyons said. "You see that I am in straitened circumstances, Mr Holmes. I cannot pretend otherwise."

"You are earning a living as a typist, I see."

"A meagre living. A halfpenny a page, but there is not much call for that kind of work around these parts. How did you know?"

Holmes indicated the desk. "The papers next to your typewriter are fanned out in such a way that one can see they are written in various different hands. The inference is obvious."

"Of course. Typing is my sole source of income, aside from some much-depleted savings that I draw on only reluctantly, as a last resort. I can barely afford to live. I could certainly not afford to pay for Dr Mortimer's medical services. Thank heaven he is kind enough to waive his fees. He has been so good to me, so solicitous." She patted his arm. "I have been abandoned by all others. Only he has stuck by me."

"Your father—" Holmes began, but she cut him off.

"Do not mention him in my presence," she said stiffly, with some of her old fire. "Yes, I am sure Papa would help me out financially, if I asked him to. But I would rather slit my own throat."

"He retains a great affection for you. Were you but to—"

Again, Mrs Lyons brusquely cut him off. "I said we shall not talk about it. Is it he who has sent you? You are an emissary of peace, bearing some kind of olive branch? If so, you have had a wasted journey."

"No, madam, I am here merely to renew acquaintance with your good self," said Holmes. "I could hardly come down to Dartmoor and not call on the bewitching Mrs Lyons."

Holmes had always had a winning way with women and could ladle on the flattery in just the right amount to allay any suspicions they might have.

"Bewitching," she echoed. "Once, perhaps. Yes, once."

A spasm passed through her which Holmes realised was an attempt to stifle an enormous yawn.

"Mrs Lyons is tired," said Mortimer. "Perhaps we should not tax her with our presence too long."

"No, no, quite," said Holmes, picking up on the hint. "I shall bid you good day, Mrs Lyons. Perhaps at another time, when it is more convenient, I might return?"

"Perhaps," said the lady faintly.

"And I, madam," said Mortimer, "shall see you anon."

"The day after tomorrow? The usual time?"

"The usual time."

"Thank you, Doctor. For everything."

Chapter Eighteen

HOPELESS IMPASSE

A s they walked away from the boarding house, Holmes said to Mortimer, "There is something the matter with that woman, some disease."

"I cannot betray patient confidence," came the reply.

"And I would not ask you to. But she *is* ill. Anyone with eyes can see it."

Mortimer thought hard, then seemed to come to a decision. "I believe it would be acceptable to tell you that, medically speaking, there is nothing wrong with Mrs Lyons, at least in so far as I can diagnose. If she suffers from a sickness of any sort, it is one of the spirit. She has, not to put too fine a point on it, given up on herself. She whiles away her hours, hardly ever going out. The typing work comes in piecemeal and she puts off doing it until the last minute, which does not endear her to her clients, such as they are. If ever there was a woman willing herself to die, it is Laura Lyons."

"Does her condition stem from her estrangement from her father?"

"In a roundabout way, yes. What did old Frankland tell you about how it lies between the two of them?"

"Precious little. Might you be able to fill me in?"

"I cannot see the harm," said Mortimer. "Knowing you, you would be able to find out some other way regardless."

"Then allow me to treat you to tea while you expound. If you have the time, that is."

"I can spare half an hour."

They repaired to Coombe Tracey's one and only café. Mortimer ordered scones with jam and clotted cream, putting the cream on first, then the jam, in the Devonian tradition. Holmes, by contrast, confined himself to simple buttered toast.

"It began," said Mortimer, "not long after the horrid business with the hound. Sir Henry and Mrs Lyons met. I, indeed, was the agent of their meeting. I had them both over for a little soirée, along with a few other friends. I was keen for Sir Henry to enter more fully into Dartmoor society, for at that time he was something of a fish out of water here. I had a sneaking suspicion he and Mrs Lyons might get along, but I could hardly have foreseen what the outcome would be. Mrs Lyons was the one who made the running. She has a determined streak in her, that woman. When she sees something she wants, she will move heaven and earth to get it. Not only that but she was in sore need of a mate, especially one of means. A handsome millionaire like Sir Henry was just the ticket. She latched on to him like a tigress on a deer. He, for his part, was not immune to her charms, and reciprocated the interest, at least to begin with."

"I know that it was short-lived, their affair," said Holmes.

"I would not even call it an affair. It dawned on Sir Henry soon enough that Laura Lyons was not for him. He is an honest, forthright soul, and something about her machinations, her frank acquisitiveness, repelled him. He did his best to disentangle himself from her. He tried to be subtle about spurning her advances, but when that did not work, he was forced to be somewhat blunt."

"Which she did not take well."

"To put it mildly. She treated the breaking off of relations as an affront, a betrayal of trust. To hear her talk, you might think Sir Henry had left her stranded at the altar. That is patently not how it was. There was no engagement, not even the discussion of an engagement. Sir Henry is innocent of all blame, I must assure you. He could never be accused of having led her on. Nevertheless that was how she saw it. Her vituperation was fierce. Then Sir Henry and Audrey Lidstone announced *their* engagement. As soon as she learned of that, Mrs Lyons went straight to her father and insisted that he sue Sir Henry."

"On what grounds?" said Holmes. "Breach of promise, I should suppose."

"Exactly that. Now, as you know, Frankland is a lover of lawsuits. He doles them out like confetti. Usually they concern rights of way, land use, trespass, all issues he has great knowledge of. He seems to enjoy litigation for litigation's sake, not caring which side of the argument he is on as long as he is arguing. But what do you think he said when his daughter made her request to him with regard to Sir Henry?"

"From the way you phrase the question, I would say he gave her an unequivocal no."

"He wouldn't hear of it," Mortimer confirmed. "He said he had no interest whatsoever in pursuing the matter. There was not, as far as he could see, any actionable claim to be made, and it would be a waste of everyone's time and money to try. He knew his daughter and he knew Sir Henry, and he could tell that they had not even come to an understanding, let alone agreed to wed. Mrs Lyons was motivated by vindictiveness, that was all. A sheer, deep-seated hatred of men."

"Pardonable, perhaps, given her history."

"She pressed and pressed, but Frankland was not to be moved. There were slanging matches, so I am told. She accused him of taking Sir Henry's side over that of his own offspring. She scorned him for his willingness to go to court over a tree bough falling across a path but not over the gross indignity that had been inflicted on her. A final blazing row saw her storming out of Lafter Hall, vowing never to speak to her father again. And she has been true to her word. Frankland has made several tentative approaches. All have been rejected. That is how things stand between them now, and while it has wounded Frankland, it has destroyed Mrs Lyons. The results are all too plain, as you have seen."

"At least she has you to tend to her," said Holmes. "It would appear that you visit her on a regular basis."

"Every other day, if only to provide her with company. Nobody else comes by. Any friends she once had have deserted her."

"Yet you provide her with medical treatment, too. That is implicit in her comment about you waiving your fees."

"All I can do," said Mortimer, blinking through his gold-rimmed glasses, "is give her something to ease her chronic nervous tension."

"Laudanum?"

"It is the best thing for her. It alleviates her worries and enables her to get through each day. I allow her two bottles a week and strictly monitor the dosage. Apart from that, and a few kind words, I cannot offer any more help. Unless she herself decides to pull out of the vortex of misery that is sucking her down, there is no hope for her."

"A tragedy."

"It is pride, Mr Holmes, that has been her downfall. A single kind word in her father's direction and Frankland would come running. But she has burned that bridge and cannot see a way of rebuilding it."

"There is his own pride to consider, too. I feel that Frankland needs only to force his way back into Mrs Lyons's life and she would succumb. She would accept money from him, and his largesse would heal the divide. But he wants a show of contrition from her before he will act."

"And the result is a hopeless impasse," said Mortimer with a sigh. "Well, anyway. I must be going. My gig awaits down the road. I have still three patients left to see before I can go home to Galen."

"Thank you for your time, Dr Mortimer."

"Before I leave," said the physician, standing, "might I enquire what really brought you to Mrs Lyons's door? I did not believe in the slightest your talk of 'renewing acquaintance', even if she did. Is she…?" He cast a look around at other patrons of the café, and dropped his voice. "Is she perchance a suspect in your case?"

"As of this moment, I am unsure," Holmes said. "Having seen her for myself, how enfeebled she is, and how ridden with ennui, it is hard to see how she could possibly be involved. She lacks the least spark of dynamism. All the same, she would appear to have a motive for wishing harm upon the Baskervilles. She despises Sir Henry and must have regarded Lady Audrey as a usurper, taking the vaunted position she thought was rightfully hers. It is a paradox. Here is a malcontent who quite abundantly has reason to be the murderer, but would seem physically incapable of it. How could she have subdued Lady Audrey and killed her in that extravagant style, when she scarcely has the wherewithal to leave her room? You are quite certain that she is not putting it on, I suppose."

"Mr Holmes, nobody, not even the greatest actor of our age, could feign such a depth of lassitude. Nor would one willingly allow oneself to waste away like that, to such an extent that one's health, even one's life, is threatened. Unless, that is, one's mental balance were genuinely disturbed. The poor woman, she is little more than a skeleton! She consumes perhaps a bowl of broth a day. A slice of bread as well, maybe, if she is feeling up to it. She might have an accomplice, I suppose," Mortimer added, cocking his head to one side, "some sort of co-conspirator. But given how she shuns all company, I rather doubt it."

"Perhaps, in her rage, she briefly found the strength to venture forth and commit a killing. Desperate people have been known to tap some hitherto undiscovered reservoir of vigour when necessary."

"That is true, but if Laura Lyons were one of them, I would be astonished."

"I shall defer to your medical expertise, Doctor. Goodbye."

"Goodbye, Mr Holmes."

The two men cordially parted company, and Holmes wended his way back to Baskerville Hall.

Chapter Nineteen

FOUR DAYS WITHOUT GAINFUL EMPLOYMENT, AND ONE NIGHT WITH

By this point in Holmes's narrative we had both finished the second of the prophesied three pipes. Tobacco smoke hung in a haze above our heads, like the pall sent up by factory chimneys in a northern industrial town. Holmes helped himself to a fresh wad of shag from the Persian slipper, inviting me to do the same.

"After the visit to Mrs Lyons and tea with Dr Mortimer, Watson," said he, "there followed four full days in which I was not at all gainfully employed."

"Why ever not?" I asked.

"The desired criteria were not met."

"What *were* these criteria of yours? Can you say yet?"

"Not yet."

"More suspense. I must say, Holmes, you do seem to be

relishing the role of storyteller. And, what's more, you have quite a flair for it."

"It is an easy skill to acquire," he said dismissively. "Any fool can do it – even you." Then, having gauged my reaction, he laughed. "Come now, Watson. Don't look so embittered. I spoke in jest. I rate your talents as an author highly, you know that, and it is an esteem I share with countless others. I simply wish, at times, that the literary success you enjoy with my cases did not come at the expense of the proper scientific explication of my methodology."

Pipe relit, and me somewhat mollified, Holmes resumed his account.

The sole pursuit in which he could engage himself over those four otherwise idle days, he said, was the ditch digging at the Grimpen Mire; and in this he was an onlooker only. He followed the progress of the earthworks with keen interest. Damerell had been correct in every regard when it came to the number of eager artisans who showed up. The first day, it was a dozen. The second, twice that. On the morning of the third, no fewer than fifty men assembled. From near and far they flocked, spurred by the news that riches were on offer to anyone with callused palms and a labourer's physique.

Gradually the main ditch grew, like a brown snake crawling up from the stream's edge towards the mire. At the same time, the tributary ditches wormed their way down towards it. Grier and Damerell had staked out lengths of twine to show the course and width of each channel, and within these demarcations the diggers hacked away the soft grass and exposed the soft, peaty flesh of the moor.

Hard though these men toiled, none toiled harder than Grier himself. The man was indefatigable. He was always the first to lift his shovel in the morning and the last to down tools at dusk. He scarcely stopped for lunch, and never to rest.

By noon on the third day, more or less on schedule, the groundwork was complete. The tributaries forked up from the main channel in a delta shape to their plank-stoppered heads. Each had been dug so that its bed was on a gradient, starting a few inches deep and shelving steadily until it achieved a depth of some two feet at its destination. Likewise the central ditch went from two feet to three at its terminus, the point where it adjoined the bank of the stream.

Now all that remained to be done was remove the planks that formed dams.

There was no great surge of water. Rather, a brown trickle seeped through the wall of earth separating each of the tributary ditches from the Grimpen Mire. These flows of muddy water slithered down their courses like melted chocolate, converging in the central ditch and continuing onward. A pool formed at the end of the ditch and slowly spilled its contents into the stream.

The stream's limpid tide became polluted by the influx of stagnant mire water. Its level rose and soon it was bursting its bounds and spreading to either side in a greasy flood. The current was strong enough, however, to carry along the bulk of the additional volume all the way to whatever river the stream decanted into.

A cheer went up from the assembled labourers. Holmes clapped Grier on the back. Damerell permitted himself a nod of satisfaction.

Gradually, in imperceptible increments, the great Grimpen Mire began to drain.

Whereas the progress of this enterprise had been smooth and trouble-free, by contrast life at Baskerville Hall was anything but. Sir Henry was a constant brooding presence at the house, alternately jumpy and despondent. He was drinking a lot, seldom seen without a glass in his hand. Now and then he would patrol the house's interior, looking out from each window like a prowling cat. He snapped at Harry over the smallest infraction, then would feel moved to apologise to the child in fulsome terms and beg his forgiveness. His eyebrows were perpetually knotted.

Both Holmes and Grier tried to jolly him out of his disagreeable mood, and when that failed they resorted to stern admonition, which was no more effective. Sir Henry's response was usually a sullen silence, or else just a sigh.

Harry, infected by his father's volatility, became awkward.

Holmes was witness to one or two tantrums of quite spectacular intensity. To watch the lad scream and shout, you might have thought he was invoking the wrath of God upon the world. One evening at bedtime, he could not find a beloved picture book and became so enraged that he started ripping the pages out of other volumes whose only fault was not being the one he desired. Grier was on hand to resolve the crisis. He began singing to the boy in a deep, rich baritone. A lilting lullaby tripped from his lips, and Harry became entranced, so much so that when the song was done he demanded another, and then another. "I bought me a cat, the cat pleased me," Grier crooned, and, "Swing low, sweet chariot," and "Hush, little baby, don't say a word." Soon Harry fell into a contented doze, and Grier scooped him up and carried him to his room, saying to Holmes and Sir Henry, "My mother used to sing like that to me when I couldn't sleep. Worked like a charm every time."

That was the evening of the day after the day that the mire started to drain. It was also the first time Holmes returned to Lafter Hall since his initial visit. After dinner, as he was getting ready to depart, he drew Grier aside for a word in private.

"Make sure Sir Henry gets to bed in good time," he said.

"That should not be difficult. The way he's drinking right now, he is usually close to passing out by ten."

"Encourage him to turn in earlier than that, if you can.

And, just as importantly, I want you to make sure all the curtains in the Hall are tightly drawn. Those in Harry's bedroom most of all." Sir Henry had taken to sleeping by his son's side the whole night through, on a camp bed made up next to Harry's bed.

"You suspect another manifestation of the moth is imminent?"

"Yes, but if it does appear, I must ask you to do your utmost to ignore it. Whatever happens, even if it awakens Harry or Sir Henry, let it be."

"Why?"

"Please just take my word on it."

"Very well," said Grier, "but what if the moth should attack? What if it tries to break in through the window this time?"

"If I am right about it, it shall not," said Holmes.

"And if you are wrong?"

"I seldom am, but should that unlikely event come to pass, then feel free to repel the thing with all the force you can muster."

Confident that Sir Henry and Harry were safe in Grier's care, Holmes strode out across the moonlit moor, heading into the teeth of a turbulent wind. It was around ten o'clock when he knocked up Frankland's household.

"I was wondering if you were ever going to come back, Mr Holmes," said Frankland.

"Tonight is an auspicious night for telescopy," Holmes said.

"But it isn't the stars you'll be looking at, is it?"

"No. What I am hoping to see is somewhat more terrestrial, albeit not necessarily earthbound."

"The moth, you mean? Is that what you're after?"

"Well guessed."

"I've been thinking about it, and it's the only reason I can come up with as to why you might want the use of a telescope. You are moth-spotting. I have looked for it myself on a couple of occasions, out of curiosity more than anything."

"But not seen it, presumably."

"Nor much wanted to," said Frankland. "By the sound of it, it is fearsome to behold."

The two men ascended to the roof. Frankland fussed over the telescope for a while until he had it calibrated exactly as he wanted. Then he stepped back and invited Holmes to take command of the instrument.

"Mind if I don't stay up here with you?" Frankland said. "It's a bit brisk for me tonight. These days the wind knifes into my old bones in a way it never used to."

"Not at all. This is business I am perfectly happy to conduct on my own." Holmes did not add that in fact he preferred it that way. He knew he could concentrate better on his task without Frankland hovering at his shoulder.

Frankland left, and Holmes re-familiarised himself with

the telescope's controls, then swivelled it on its mount until it was pointing towards Baskerville Hall. This done, there was nothing to do but sit and wait.

He waited an hour. He waited two hours. The wind moaned across the top of Lafter Hall, shivering loose roof tiles. The moon hung high. Three hours passed. The stars performed their slow, inexorable cartwheel across the heavens. Four hours into his vigil, midnight now just a memory, Holmes was beginning to lose heart. Had he erred? Was the theory he had formulated about the monster moth misbegotten? Surely not! He lit a cigarette to sharpen his nerves, fastened the earflaps of his cap more tightly and huddled down deeper inside his Inverness cape.

The cigarette was almost down to the stub when the moth appeared.

Holmes hastily ground out the cigarette beneath his toe and sprang to his feet. The creature had arisen from the horizon and was flitting in the direction of Baskerville Hall. He put his eye to the telescope's eyepiece. Operating the device with as much care and precision as his night-chilled fingers would allow, he tracked the moth's bouncing, erratic journey through the air. He adjusted the focus wheel, bringing the object of his scrutiny into yet sharper relief.

Then he smiled a broad smile and uttered a low chuckle.

"I have you, you rank absurdity," said he under his breath. "Oh, I have you now."

Chapter Twenty

THE BODY IN THE BOG

The next day there was a significant development.

Holmes, having risen late after his nocturnal adventures, was on his way over to the Grimpen Mire. The sun shone and there was a breath of warmth in the air that felt like the last, sweet exhalation of summer before autumn set in for good. His mood was buoyant. He even whistled a tune, a Paganini serenata.

Earlier, upon waking, he had found a note from Grier. It had been slipped under the door of his bedroom.

Mr Scarecrow
I heard the moth last night. It fluttered noisily about the house, tapping at walls and windows. Per your instructions, I ignored it. This was no mean feat but I am pleased to say it was accomplished.

Neither Sir Henry nor Harry was disturbed from his sleep by the insidious creature this time around. It persisted for perhaps twenty minutes before relenting and departing.

I am off to the Grimpen Mire now and may see you there later.

Yours,

Mr Chimneysweep

All of this was to Holmes's satisfaction, aside from Grier's insistent use of the nicknames Harry had given the two of them. As far as my friend was concerned, matters were coming nicely to a head. The pieces of the puzzle were slotting into place, and perhaps even that very day he would be able to draw his investigation to a tidy conclusion.

Halfway to the mire, he met a man hurrying towards him from the opposite direction. It was one of Grier's ditch diggers. The labourers had been sent home two days earlier, their services no longer required and their pockets lined with Sir Henry's money. A few, however, were staying on of their own volition, unpaid, curious to see how the drainage was proceeding and what it might reveal. This fellow was one of those, and he greeted Holmes with a frantic wave.

"Mr Grier sent me to catch you. Them's found something at the mire, sir."

"What kind of something?" Holmes asked.

"A body, sir. A dead body."

Holmes quickened his pace, the ditch digger falling in step beside him. Within quarter of an hour they were approaching the mire. Among the half-dozen or so men gathered beside the morass, there was a palpable sense of excitement. Voices rose in a hubbub, and fingers pointed.

"Holmes," said Grier, "I believe we have an answer to the question of whether Jack Stapleton is dead or not."

Holmes stepped up to the edge of the mire. What had formerly been a level expanse of boggy earth was now a series of irregular-shaped depressions with a couple of narrow causeways meandering in between. The causeways represented the strips of dry land that had at one time been the only safe means of crossing the mire. Near one of these, some twenty yards from where Holmes stood, a brown form lay half-exposed by the receding waters. It was unmistakably a corpse.

"I have forbidden anyone from approaching it until you got here," Grier said. "I know you would like to be the first to examine the body and would prefer the scene undisturbed."

"And here was I thinking you could go no higher in my estimation, Grier."

Holmes set off along the nearest of the causeways and in no time had arrived at a spot as close to the body as he could get without entering the mire. The thing was lying supine, and at this distance, some six or seven yards away, Holmes could discern that it had once been a male adult. The clothing was masculine, as was the physique. However, he would need to get closer still in order to determine more than that.

He called to Grier to bring a rope. He lashed one end of it around his waist and invited the American to take a firm hold of the other.

"You are my lifeline," he said. "I am trusting you to pull me out, should I get into difficulties."

"Have no fear," said Grier, planting his feet and wrapping the rope tightly around his massive fists.

Holmes slipped off his boots and socks, and rolled up his trouser legs above the knee. Then, with some trepidation, he slid down the bank of the causeway, entering what remained of the mire. The mud came up to his ankles and rose gradually further as he waded out until, by the time he reached the body, it was at the top of his shins. Each step was an elaborate pantomime, demanding that he lift his foot fully clear of the mud's sticky grasp before setting it down again. More than once he trod in a patch of greater than usual softness and depth, which threw him off-balance and nearly caused him to plunge headlong.

He made it nonetheless, and bent down to commence a careful study of the half-submerged cadaver.

The body was in a state of only partial putrefaction, the

mud having gone some way to preserving it from full decay. The stench emanating from it was unpleasant but tolerable, not much worse than the stench of the mud itself. With one hand Holmes wiped the film of slime off its head. The withered lips and sunken eyelids thus revealed put him in mind of an Egyptian mummy. For all that, the facial features were clearly distinguishable. The jaw was lean, the nose prim, but there was also a hint of Hugo Baskerville about the physiognomy, not least the beetling forehead. The hair, meanwhile, was thin and flaxen.

"Well?" said Grier from the causeway.

Holmes straightened up. "I have not a shred of doubt in my mind that these are the mortal remains of Jack Stapleton."

He returned to the causeway. Grier extended a hand and helped him up. They walked back to the mire's edge, where Holmes cleaned off his lower legs with handfuls of grass and put his boots and socks back on.

"So where does that leave us?" Grier asked. "Our principal suspect lies yonder, incapable of doing anything but decomposing."

"Stapleton was never my principal suspect," Holmes said. "I always thought the chances of him having cheated death were slim. I consented to Sir Henry's plan of draining the mire largely because I believed it would be good for Sir Henry. That it has eliminated Stapleton from our enquiries is merely a beneficial side-effect. After all, if Stapleton had still been alive, why did he wait five long years to get his revenge? Why not effect it sooner?"

"Because it took him that long to find, or breed, his giant moth?"

"Ah, with regard to the moth, Grier, I have made a—"

Holmes did not get to finish the sentence, for at that moment a young lad came running up. He was red-faced and short of breath.

"Which of you gents be Mr 'Olmes?" he panted.

"That would be I."

"I've a message from Dr Mortimer, sir. 'E begs you to come quick. 'E sent me with a wagonette to Baskerville 'All to fetch you. Sir 'Enry Baskerville told me you was 'ere."

"Where is Mortimer?"

"Coombe Tracey, sir. But we must 'urry."

Holmes and Grier exchanged glances. The lad was already making off across the moor towards Baskerville Hall. The two men went after him.

Chapter Twenty-One

THE DEVILRY OF IT ALL

The wagonette rumbled into Coombe Tracey with Holmes and the driver in the front seat and Grier and the boy sitting facing each other, knee to knee, in the back.

Holmes told me that he was feeling an odd sense of fatalism as the carriage pulled up outside the boarding house that Mrs Laura Lyons called home. This was a journey he had been expecting to make that day regardless. Dr Mortimer's summons had merely hastened the inevitable. Holmes did not know why Mortimer had called him there and why the urgency, although he had a strong and troubling suspicion.

The landlady with the lazy eye was overwrought, near hysterical. "In my 'ouse!" she moaned as Holmes and Grier entered the main hallway. "A suicide! A suicide! What will people think? I shall never get over it."

"A suicide?" Grier asked the woman. "Whose?"

Holmes answered for her. "Unless I am much mistaken," he said with a grim shake of the head, "it is that of Sir Henry's persecutor. This is something I did not anticipate, and yet, in hindsight, perhaps I should have foreseen it."

"To be wise after the event is not to be wise at all," Grier chided him amicably.

Upstairs, they came upon a horrific scene. Mrs Lyons was slumped in her armchair, in her nightgown, as pale and still as only the dead can be. Her eyes stared sightlessly, half-lidded, while her jaw hung slack. Her arm hung over the side of the chair, and from it protruded a short length of rubber pipe. One end of the terracotta-coloured pipe was capped with a needle which had been inserted into a vein in the underside of her bare forearm. The other rested in the spout of a one-gallon oil canister.

The canister was filled to the brim with blood, and a significant quantity of the blood had spilled over from the spout. Streaks of it encrusted the canister's side, while the rest had soaked into the rug beneath, drying to form a huge brown bloom around its base. The coppery tang of it filled the air, mingling with the cloying aroma of Mrs Lyons's chosen brand of perfume in a way that even Holmes, hard-headed as he was, found nauseating.

Dr Mortimer presided over the body. His face was ashen grey and fixed in a look of appalled compassion.

"Mr Holmes, Mr Grier," said he. "I would say I was glad

to see you both, but as you can tell, this is hardly a joyous occasion."

"It is not," Holmes agreed.

"Once I saw the body, I had you brought here because I knew Mrs Lyons was a suspect in the Baskerville case. I felt you should be informed of her death immediately."

"You were sensible to do so."

"She was unwell, of course. Not in her right mind. But to commit such an act of violence upon herself... I cannot imagine the inner torment that must have precipitated it."

"Were you the one to discover her like this?"

"No," said Mortimer, "that misfortune fell to the tenant in the room below. The rug here, as you can see, became saturated with her blood. Some of it dripped through the cracks between the floorboards. Dark splotches began appearing in the plaster of the ceiling beneath. The tenant went to the landlady to complain, and it was she who first entered the room and found Mrs Lyons. I happened to catch wind of the incident as I was doing my early rounds. The whole of Coombe Tracey is abuzz with it. I dropped everything and came straight here."

"I don't know about you gentlemen," said Grier with a polite cough, "but I am not comfortable standing around talking like this in front of that poor lady, not the way she is. It seems disrespectful, not to say ghoulish. With your permission, Doctor, Mr Holmes, may I cover her up?"

Both the other men nodded assent, and Grier took a sheet off the bed and draped it over the corpse.

"I have seen death before," he said. "I'm sure we all have. But we should not carry on in its presence as if it is not there. Now the late Mrs Lyons is at least out of sight, if not out of mind."

"Your sense of decorum puts us to shame, Grier," said Holmes. After an appropriately contrite pause, he turned back to Mortimer and picked up his thread of questioning again. "At what hour did the tenant first notice the stains on the ceiling?"

"Around eight o'clock, I believe."

"Then Mrs Lyons is likely to have killed herself perhaps three hours before that. I am estimating by the rate of blood flow and the time it would take for the canister to become full and the overspill to soak through the rug. Would you concur, Doctor?"

"I should think it likely, yes."

"One may also infer that Mrs Lyons used the canister to catch the blood in the hopes of preventing it seeping through the floor. Or at any rate, seeping through too soon."

"So that she would not be discovered before she was dead," said Grier.

"Precisely. A delaying measure to guarantee the success of her endeavour. Even if the canister could not contain all the blood, it would hold enough that she would be dead well before the excess made its presence known to the tenant downstairs. Without the canister, the blood would have penetrated the floor far sooner, with the result that she might have been found just in time. Then someone might have been able to staunch the wound and pull her back from the brink of death."

Mortimer gestured towards the desk where Mrs Lyons's typewriter sat. "There is also this."

Sticking up from the machine was a sheet of foolscap octavo vellum notepaper, upon which a short message had been typed.

I have had enugh. This, my campaign of terror, must end. I beg perdon for all I have done. Now I shall die as the lady Audrey died. If any of you have ocasion to think of me, remember me kindly.

    L.L.

Holmes studied it without touching it.

"Poor spelling for a woman of Mrs Lyons's background and breeding," he opined. "Don't you think, Mortimer? She struck me as an educated woman."

"I agree. But don't forget, she was *in extremis* when she wrote the note. The last thing she would have been thinking about was correct spelling. And if her fingers slipped on the keys and hit the wrong one now and then, well, that is hardly surprising. Her hands may well have been trembling."

"Now let us consider this item." Holmes turned his attention to a bottle of laudanum which stood on the floor at the foot of Mrs Lyons's armchair, not far from the canister. "One of the ones you brought her, I take it."

"It is," said Mortimer. "Collington's. My preferred brand. I can only assume she took a draught of it before inserting the needle into her arm, in order to deaden the pain."

Holmes picked up the bottle and took it to the window to examine. He held it up to the light, then uncorked it and took a sniff.

"It smells of laudanum," he said, "and just enough has been drunk to constitute a single dose – an amount sufficient to deaden pain, as you say, Mortimer, and also to calm the nerves so that she might go through with her plan."

"'It smells of laudanum'," Grier echoed. "Were you expecting it to smell of something else?"

"Merely considering the possibility that it had been tampered with."

"Poisoned, you mean? As in foul play?"

"I have to rule these things out, else I would not be doing my job."

So saying, Holmes took a minuscule sip of the preparation, just enough to moisten the tip of his tongue.

"No," he concluded. "It tastes of nothing other than laudanum."

Setting down the bottle, he turned and scanned the room. His eye alit upon the oak wardrobe.

"Now then, gentlemen," said he, grasping the handle of its door, "either I am about to deliver a tremendous *coup de théâtre*, or I am about to do something banal and ultimately rather anticlimactic."

He threw open the door, glanced within, and stepped back with a grin of profound gratification.

Grier and Mortimer crowded in on either side of him to take a look.

Both men gasped in unison.

"Dear me!" said Mortimer.

"Is that what I think it is?" said Grier.

"It is," said Holmes, "and this wardrobe is the only object in the room with the capacity to have contained it. At least, that was my supposition, and it has been borne out."

Resting inside the wardrobe was an intricate confection of canvas and wooden dowels, all painted black. Holmes reached in, took it out, and laid it out upon the floor. Unfurled, it had the shape of a moth as tall as a man. For eyes, there were a pair of small lanterns, each fitted with a lens made of red glass and a wick that drew on a tiny reservoir of paraffin. Twin reels of horsehair fishing line were attached to the contraption.

"A kite," said Grier, scratching his head in wonder. "Well, I'll be damned. The thing was nothing but a large kite."

"Not a real moth," said Holmes, "and certainly not your skinwalker were-moth."

"A hoax."

"Exactly."

"Just as the Baskerville hound was a hoax," said Mortimer. "My God. The devilry of it all. But how did you know, Holmes?"

"It was elementary, really. Let me explain. The sightings of the moth, including our own at Baskerville Hall, all took place on nights that had two things in common: they were clear and they were windy. They needed to be clear so that the moth could easily be seen, and they needed to be windy because, naturally, a kite cannot fly unless there is a strong enough wind. That the giant moth was actually a large kite with lanterns for eyes was a notion that had occurred to me early on in these proceedings, and when I saw the moth for myself from the window at the Hall, nothing about its appearance or its manner of flight suggested to me that I was wrong."

"The patch of trampled grass you discovered out on the moor," said Grier. "That wasn't left by the moth's 'master', but rather by its flyer."

"It was where the person flying the kite stood, yes, using these reels of fishing line to control it," said Holmes. "In order to ascertain the truth beyond any doubt, I decided to avail myself of Frankland's telescope. I had to wait until the next time the weather conditions were right, as they were last night. The telescope enabled me to observe the moth in sufficient detail to confirm what I suspected. The kite might look plausible enough when seen from a distance with the naked eye, but not to the eye aided by a telescope's magnifying power."

"The purpose of the bogus moth, then," said Mortimer, "was to sow fear and panic."

"Yes, in the hearts and minds of the local populace," said Holmes, "and especially in the heart and mind of one Sir Henry Baskerville. To him, it was a second sinister beast attacking and killing his near kin, which caused him to relive the horrors associated with the first. And of course, the creature being a moth this time, that would seem to implicate the lepidopterist who assailed him the last time, namely Jack Stapleton."

"Pure misdirection, in other words," said Grier. "The real culprit being Mrs Lyons here."

"The proverbial 'woman scorned'. Mrs Lyons, in case you didn't know, Grier, had a brief flirtation with Sir Henry that went nowhere. In her mind, however, it was far more than that. Sir Henry jilted her, so she believed, and she could not get over it. For years she brooded upon the perceived insult. It grew and grew in her thoughts, gaining such towering, tormenting proportions that in the end she decided she had no choice but to wreak vengeance upon him. Thus began a grim, elaborate vendetta. Mrs Lyons built the moth kite and began flying it ostentatiously at night so that it would be seen and rumours about it would start to circulate among Dartmoor's more superstitious denizens. At the same time, she set about harming and killing sheep by extracting various quantities of blood from them. This, one may infer, was designed both to foster the illusion that the moth was a vampiric entity preying on living creatures and to serve as rehearsal for the perhaps more complicated task of exsanguinating a human being."

"Lady Audrey."

"She was Mrs Lyons's ultimate target, the woman who, in her view, stole Sir Henry from her. Mrs Lyons would have conducted covert surveillance on Baskerville Hall for some time and established that Lady Audrey liked to take twilight walks alone on the moor. Then all she had to do was lie in wait for her beside the rock known as Crookback Samuel, spring out, overpower her, and carry out the act of bleeding her dry, using this very apparatus we see here. It is called a cannula, is it not, Doctor?"

Mortimer confirmed this with a nod.

"Doubtless she brought with her a receptacle into which she drained off Lady Audrey's blood for later disposal, having done the same beforehand with the sheep she had practised on," Holmes said. "Doubtless, too, the receptacle was this very canister. At two gallons it has the capacity to hold practically the entire volume of blood from an average person. Not quite all of it, as we can see, but enough to account for a fatal degree of blood loss. That way, there would be few or no bloodstains on the ground and it would look even more as though her alleged monster moth sucked its victims dry."

"Cunning," said Grier.

"Mrs Lyons was nothing if not that," Holmes said. "Consider the cigarillo stub I found at Crookback Samuel, secreted in a fissure. She chose to smoke that particular kind of cigar while she lay in wait for Lady Audrey because cigarillos have distinct connotations of South America, whence Jack Stapleton hailed originally. She expected that the police would find it, although in the event they did not and I did. Like the moth, it was yet another way of deflecting everyone's thoughts towards Stapleton."

"We were blaming Stapleton for everything, and all along it was Mrs Lyons's doing."

"Since the majority of moth sightings and attacks were centred around Coombe Tracey, it seemed to me that the person behind them might be a resident of that town. Knowing that Sir Henry and Mrs Lyons had once been if not lovers then at least romantically involved, I went to Coombe Tracey in order to ascertain whether she still lived there as she used to. She did, and she seemed rather unhappy to see me. Whether or not it worried her that Sherlock

Holmes was investigating the case, she continued flying her moth kite regardless at Baskerville Hall."

"To what end? To keep Sir Henry scared?"

"Yes. Her thirst for revenge was such that killing Lady Audrey did not sate it. She wanted the man who had supposedly abandoned her to suffer further. To her, he was just another in a series of men who had abused her trust. What she did not foresee, however, was that Sir Henry would take the drastic step of draining the Grimpen Mire. That was when her plan started to unravel. Word must have reached her concerning the great engineering project out on the moor, and she realised the game was up."

"I'm afraid the bringer of that word was me," said Mortimer. "I mentioned it to Mrs Lyons just yesterday."

"This left her with only one available course of action, as she saw it. She flew the moth kite one more time outside the Hall, as a sort of last hurrah, a final twist of the knife. Then she came back home and…" Holmes gestured towards the corpse. "Well, need I say more?"

"But, Holmes," said Mortimer, "you saw for yourself the state Mrs Lyons was in when you met her just a few days ago. You even said she seemed too enfeebled to have committed the energetic and violent acts you describe."

"It was all an imposture, nothing more," said Holmes. "You were wholly taken in by her, Doctor, and to some extent so was I. But not entirely. I have an innate scepticism about people that has stood me in good stead in the past. Everyone, in some way or other, is a dissembler. Even me, when I have to be."

"Still, I find it incredible that I could have been so easily misled."

"And indeed you might. But then, if it isn't impolite to point this out, you were rather smitten with Mrs Lyons, weren't you?"

The physician bowed his head, as if in embarrassment.

"Nothing to be ashamed of," Holmes continued. "You are a bachelor, very eligible and perhaps somewhat unsophisticated, and Mrs Lyons was a divorcee, handsome, a woman of the world. She played the part of damsel in distress, and you, the dashing, gallant GP, came riding to her rescue. In the end, she had you wrapped around her finger. You treated her *gratis*, brought her medicine, became her companion and confidant… She had you believing she was weaker and more dissipated than she really was, precisely in order to throw off suspicion. If her own doctor thought her too ill to have committed any kind of crime, then what better alibi could there be?"

"What an idiot I have been," Mortimer lamented, burying his face in his hands. "How gullible. She *used* me. To her, I was no more than a tool in her scheme, like that kite." He kicked the moth-shaped contraption in a fit of pique, snapping one of the dowels that gave it structure and rigidity.

"I am sorry that you had to learn about it this way."

"No, no, don't be. Your sympathy is appreciated but undeserved. I ought to have known better."

"At any rate," said Holmes, "my work here would appear to be done. We have a culprit. We have what is tantamount to a signed confession. Little remains beyond alerting the police with regard to Mrs Lyons's death."

"Already done," said Mortimer. "An inspector is on his way over from Exeter even as we speak."

"Excellent. Then Grier and I shall bring Sir Henry the glad tidings that the danger to him and Harry is, at long last, behind them."

Chapter Twenty-Two

A CONCLUSION?

"**A**nd that is precisely what we did, Watson," Holmes said, as he brought his narrative to a close. "The moment Sir Henry learned the sorry saga of Mrs Lyons and her kite, he broke down crying. His tears were sadness mixed with pure relief.

"'To think,' he said, 'if I had only been more sensitive towards that woman, my Audrey would still be alive.'

"'As I understand it,' said I, 'you could not have been more of a gentleman. It was Mrs Lyons's own twisted, envenomed mind that caused all this misery, Sir Henry. You are not to blame yourself for any of it.'

"At that point, Harry entered the room. 'Why are you crying, Daddy?' he asked.

"Sir Henry pulled the boy to his bosom and sobbed. Soon Harry was sobbing too, even if he did not know quite why.

"'I swear, my lad,' said father to son, 'that I will be better to you from now on. You will have your old daddy back.'

"'And the Bammows?' Harry said, sniffing hard. 'Can they come back too?'

"'Of course they can, if they are willing. I shall send word to them at once, telling them that all is well again and begging them to resume their positions. Everything is going to be as it was, Harry. We shall both of us be happy, and so will your mother, as she looks down on us from heaven.'

"I quit the room, leaving the two Baskervilles to their touching reconciliation. I felt that a visit to old Frankland was in order, so I made for Lafter Hall. News of the death had already reached the late Mrs Lyons's father, and he consented to see me but was so overcome with grief he could scarcely speak.

"'My sincerest condolences over the loss of your daughter,' I said.

"'Is what I have heard true, Mr Holmes?' said this shattered old man. 'Is my Laura the one who murdered Lady Audrey?'

"'So it appears.'

"I explained what I had gleaned about Mrs Lyons's misdeeds. There followed a bout of sobbing so piteous, it would have melted a heart of stone.

"'If only I had been a better father,' Frankland wailed. 'My Laura! She was such a sweet girl when she was little. The apple of my eye. Why do families drift apart? Why do we grow so cold to one another? Would that people were more like the stars, fixed and constant, following their set paths forever.'

"'Perhaps,' I said, 'you might in future focus more on your botanical interests than your astronomical ones. Turn your gaze from the celestial to the earthly. Plants have plenty to teach us about the evolution and interdependence of living things.'

"He gave the suggestion some thought. 'It is probably too late for me to learn that lesson,' he said, 'but that should not stop me from trying. Thank you, Mr Holmes. Those are wise words.'

"I made my excuses and left. Back at Baskerville Hall, I gathered my belongings and prepared to depart from Dartmoor for good. Before going, however, I sought out Grier and had a word with him.

"'Corporal Grier,' I said. 'You have been an invaluable adjutant throughout this entire business.'

"'I have done what I can,' said that modest fellow.

"'If I may, I would like you to continue to serve in that capacity. How long do you anticipate staying in England?'

"'Another couple of weeks, I should imagine. Three at most.'

"'That ought to be enough. I want you to remain with Sir Henry the whole time.'

"'Such is my intention.'

"'Maintain a careful watch over him.'

"Grier looked at me shrewdly. 'You do not think this is over, do you?'

"'Let us just say that it would not be prudent of me to leave Sir Henry unattended,' I told him. 'There remain one or two elements to the case that give me pause for thought.'

"'You can rely on me, Holmes,' said Grier. 'Henry is safe in my custody, as is little Harry. I will protect them with my life, if it comes to that.'

"We shook on it.

"'Until we meet again, Mr Scarecrow,' said Grier.

"'A valiant attempt, Grier, but I shall not be calling you Mr Chimneysweep. Not now, not ever.'

"'Can't blame a fellow for trying!' were his parting words to me."

Holmes stood and went to the hearth to tap out the dottle from his pipe. "And now, Watson, you are up to date with everything that has transpired in your absence. What do you make of it?"

"It is a remarkable tale," I said. "A web of murder and deceit that you have unravelled with your customary aplomb. The case would seem to be, as the lawyers say, open and shut. The murderer has been unmasked and, in a way, brought to justice. Her motivations and deceptions have been laid bare. All is settled. Yet," I added, "you remain riddled with misgiving, I can tell."

"I am," Holmes confessed. "There is something about it that I cannot put my finger on. I feel that I am missing something obvious, something so glaring that by rights I should have seen it long ago. For a start, Mrs Lyons's whole scheme seems inordinately complicated. She never struck me as a woman of great imagination. Great determination, yes, but not great imagination. Yet what are that glowing-eyed moth kite, that cigarillo and that cannula but the hallmarks of a formidable imagination? Then there is her suicide note with its misspellings. Was that the handiwork of a woman who felt the net closing in around her, so drug-disorientated and panicked that her fingers were clumsy on the typewriter keys? And the bottle of laudanum…"

His voice drifted off, and I saw a peculiar fixity come over his face and a faraway look enter his eyes. Both were traits that I knew of old. Holmes had withdrawn into himself, entering that fantastic, labyrinthine mind of his to explore its many chambers and consult its vast repositories of knowledge and logic. It was clear that I would not get any further conversation from him for the time being and that my presence was superfluous. Discreetly I tiptoed out of the room and returned home to await the call to arms which, if I knew Sherlock Holmes, would surely not be long in coming.

PART THREE

Chapter Twenty-Three

BASKERVILLE HALL REVISITED

The call to arms was sounded not three days later.

It took the form of one of Holmes's typically terse telegrams.

> Watson
> Come at once. Bound for Devon again. This time no
> excuses brooked. Pack a bag. Bring revolver.
> SH

Nor were any excuses forthcoming from me. I was resolved to make up for my previous timidity. I appreciated that I had developed cynophobia, but a phobia of Devon? Was it possible to be scared of a *county*?

Then there was Benjamin Grier. I had found it galling to listen to Holmes recount their exploits together on Dartmoor and give example after example of the consummate teamwork that had so swiftly instituted itself between them. Everything Grier had done was something *I* should have done. He had stepped into the shoes I had vacated. It had been an act of necessity, prompted by neither malice nor ambition. Yet they were still *my* shoes, and no one should wear them but me.

One of my locums was back in town and agreed to take on my caseload. I packed a bag, and presently Holmes and I were at Paddington, boarding a Devon train.

Throughout the journey Holmes was in subdued mood, barely exchanging a word with me. He did not vouchsafe the reason why we were travelling to the West Country with such haste, but I could tell from his silence, which was interspersed with occasional sighs and irritable flourishes of the hand, that he was deeply disconsolate; that, indeed, he was angry with someone. My intuition was that this someone was most likely himself.

As we passed from the rolling green hills of south Somerset into the rougher, russet-tinged terrain of Devon, I felt my heartbeat quicken and my mouth go dry. Again and again I told myself that my fears were baseless. I reminded myself that during my time with Holmes I had faced murderers, convicts, blackmailers, vengeful mariners, a deadly Indian swamp adder, an Andaman Islander armed with poisoned blowdarts, a rogue shikari who was a crack shot with an air-gun, and

God knows how many pistol-wielding maniacs; and before any of that, hordes of Afghan ghazis who had made it their business to take potshots at me with their jezail rifles. I had also dealt with countless medical emergencies that called for a steady nerve and an equally steady hand. It was ludicrous that a man of my age and standing should be so timorous.

This inner talking-to brought some relief to my anxiety, and by the time we pulled into Bartonhighstock station I was almost calm, almost my usual self.

Grier himself was there to meet us with a wagonette. One look at the fellow, and I knew that some terrible catastrophe had struck. He was as solemn-faced as a mourner at a funeral. More than that, he appeared hollowed, as though half the stuffing had been knocked out of his huge frame. His eyes, which I remembered as being lively and bright, were dull and haunted.

"Let's go," he said tersely, whipping the horse into motion.

Rain spat down on us from a sky the colour of glazier's putty. For several minutes I expected that one or other of my companions would apprise me of the situation, but perhaps Grier assumed that Holmes had already done so, and Holmes himself remained disinclined.

At last I could bear it no longer. "I have been as patient as a man can be," I snapped. "In heaven's name, what has happened? One of you fill me in, I don't much mind which it is."

Holmes looked at Grier, Grier at Holmes, each's grave expression mirroring the other's. Eventually Holmes said, "To start with, Mrs Barrymore lies at death's door."

At that, I groaned in dismay. "What ailment has befallen the woman?"

"According to the wire I received this morning from Grier here, she appears to have been the victim of the bite of some highly venomous creature. Dr Mortimer has been looking after her, and is concerned she will not survive. But," he added, "there is worse."

"What could be worse than that?"

"A kidnapping."

"Oh Lord," I breathed. "Who?"

"Young Harry."

I gasped. "I can hardly believe my ears! When? What were the circumstances? Spare no detail."

Holmes turned to Grier. "You know more than I. You should be the one to speak."

"I am not sure that I can bring myself to," said the American. "But if I must, I must. The facts of the matter, Doctor, are these. Yesterday morning, Dr Mortimer called round with his spaniel, suggesting he might leave it at the Hall for a few hours. He knew how much Harry loved playing with the dog, and he told Henry and me that it would be a good therapeutic tool for the boy.

"'My godson has been through a great deal these past few

weeks,' he said. 'Having Galen to look after and play with will prove a useful distraction. It will take his mind off things and perhaps help him rediscover a sense of normality.'

"Henry could see the logic in that, as could I. And Harry, well, when he got wind of Mortimer's offer, he clung to his father's legs and implored him to say yes. Henry could hardly refuse.

"By then, Mr and Mrs Barrymore were back in residence. Henry had sent them a letter pleading with them to return. He had sworn that his black moods were a thing of the past. No longer was his life overshadowed by the threat of a vampiric moth, the letter said. Sherlock Holmes had seen to that. His grief for his wife was in no way lessened, but at least now he could get on with mourning her as a widower ought.

"This importuning had the desired effect, and once more the Barrymores were tending to the Baskervilles' domestic needs.

"All that day, Harry was in a transport of delight. He fed Galen scraps from the lunch table. He tried to teach him tricks – roll over, play dead, hold out a paw to shake – which he hoped would impress his 'Uncle James' when he returned to collect the spaniel. Galen patiently endured the lessons but seemed in no hurry to learn. Seeing the two of them together was an enchanting sight, and I truly began to believe that the whole sorry affair of Mrs Lyons and her vendetta was behind us. Henry and Harry could move on with their lives, and all would be well. Ha!"

Grier snorted this expostulation.

"I should have known better," he went on, his voice curdling. "In the afternoon, Henry proposed that he and I go out onto the moor to shoot grouse. I recalled that Holmes had advised me to keep a close watch on Henry, and by implication Harry too. Obviously, if Henry and I left the Hall to go grouse-shooting, I could not also mind Harry. However, my reckoning was that the pair of us would only be gone a couple of hours. In the meantime, the Barrymores were there to look after the boy. I deemed the risk acceptable.

"We left Harry in the garden, romping with Galen, under Mrs Barrymore's supervision. Before going, I had a quiet word in her ear.

"'Never let the lad out of your sight,' I told her. 'Not for one moment.'

"'You have my promise, Mr Grier, as a Christian woman,' replied that lady. 'I would sooner die than let harm come to a single hair on Harry's head.'

"When Henry and I returned from our outing – we had bagged a brace of birds each – it was to a Baskerville Hall in the grip of a deathly hush. Sometimes one can tell when things are awry, even before the truth of it becomes known. One senses it instinctively.

"In the main hallway we found Galen hunkered at the

foot of the stairs. The spaniel looked – 'appalled' is the only word I can think of for it. You know how it is with some dogs. They are sensitive to drama and calamity. Galen's muzzle was on his paws and he barely raised his head when Henry and I entered, whereas under normal circumstances he would have hurried over to us and demanded to be petted.

"Now my hackles were up, and so were Henry's. It was then that a distant sound of sobbing reached our ears. It was coming from upstairs, from the wing that one might call the servants' quarters but for the fact that that description seems an exaggeration somehow, since the sole residents are the Barrymores. Abandoning our shotguns and our birds, Henry and I hastened towards it. The source was the Barrymores' bedroom, and therein we found Barrymore kneeling beside the bed, upon which lay his wife.

"I have never seen a man more devastated, more desolate, than Barrymore was then. There was not a trace of colour left in his already pallid face, save for the redness of his tear-filled eyes. He was wracked with anguish.

"'She is dead, sirs!' he cried upon seeing us. 'My dear wife! Dead!'

"Mrs Barrymore certainly looked dead, laid out atop the counterpane. I went over and examined her. I immediately detected the rise and fall of her chest, barely perceptible but present nonetheless. Barrymore, in his paroxysm of despair, must not have noticed it. I also found the merest trace of a pulse in her left wrist. I could not take the pulse in her right wrist for the whole of that arm, from hand to elbow, was horrendously inflamed, swollen to twice its usual size and a deep crimson in hue.

"I told Barrymore that his wife was still alive, and at this he sagged to his haunches in relief.

"'Oh, thank merciful heaven!' he declared.

"'She is terribly unwell nonetheless,' I said. 'We need Mortimer.'

"'Of course,' said Barrymore. 'I shall saddle a horse at once and ride to his house.'

"'No, Barrymore,' said Henry. 'Your place is by your wife's side. I shall go. Besides, I am a better horseman than you.'

"'Bless you, sir. Bless you. Might I ask, before you go – you have seen young Master Harry, have you not?'

"Something about this query made my blood run cold.

"Henry himself did not share my dread, at least not yet. 'I presume he is somewhere in the house,' said he.

"'Only,' said Barrymore, 'I heard my wife cry out in distress, and found her lying in the garden, in the state that you see her now. Dr Mortimer's dog was by her side, looking solicitous of her. There was no sign of Harry, and I assumed he had gone indoors, having tired of their game. I picked my wife up and carried her into the house, with the dog following me. It looked to me as though she had swooned. It was only after I laid her out on the bed that I realised how lifeless she seemed. And then I saw *that*.' He pointed to her arm. 'It was bad then, and it has since got worse. I still do not know what it signifies. But Harry is surely somewhere around here. Is he not?' he added in a plaintive tone.

"Now it dawned on Henry, as it already had on me, that some vile mishap might have befallen his son as well as Mrs Barrymore. Were Harry in the house, would he not have come to greet us when we returned? The fact that Galen was lying on his own in the hallway, when Harry and he had seemed so inseparable earlier, was another ill omen.

"Henry dashed out of the room, crying, 'Harry! Harry!' I followed, and together we combed the house, from attic to cellar, and then the garden. We yelled the boy's name continually, at the top of our lungs. Were he within range of our voices, and conscious, he could not have failed to hear us, and would surely have responded if he had been able. We even ventured onto the moor, moving outward from the Hall in a widening spiral, still shouting, 'Harry! Harry!' as we went. We were in a state of panic that mounted with every minute, until we could scarcely think straight. We had all but forgotten about poor Mrs Barrymore. Harry alone occupied our minds.

"'Gone!' Henry wailed after an hour of futile searching. 'My son is gone!'

"'We do not know that, Henry,' I said. 'Not for sure.' These words rang hollow even to my own ears. I persisted nonetheless. 'Perhaps Harry ran away when Mrs Barrymore fell ill. Perhaps he took fright and, not knowing what else to do, headed out onto the moor. Or perhaps,' I went on, warming to my theme, 'he ran for help. Yes, that could be it. The lad has a sensible head on his shoulders, even aged just three. He could have gone to Lafter Hall, say, or to that farmer who put me up for the night – what is his name? Wonnacott. Even now, Harry sits indoors, in the warm, enjoying a well-deserved treat, while a doctor makes his way here, most likely Mortimer. Mrs Barrymore will be saved, and it will be all thanks to Harry and his resourcefulness. Your son will be the hero of the hour.'

"'No,' said a forlorn Henry. 'Why would Harry go all the way to Lafter Hall, or anywhere else, when he knew Barrymore was right here? He would have sought out Barrymore before he did anything else.'

"This, gentlemen, I could not gainsay. My speculation crumbled like the fantasy it was.

"And there you have it," Grier said by way of conclusion. "We have had search parties out on the moor all through the night, equipped with lanterns and torches, and all of today as well. Dozens of local folk have volunteered their services. I myself have coordinated these efforts and led more than one of them. We have looked in the prehistoric huts. We have looked in crofts, both abandoned and tenanted. We have looked in barns, spinneys, gorse patches…"

"The Grimpen Mire?" I hazarded hesitantly.

"Even there. What is left of it. I have had the remaining areas of shallow bog dragged with hooks on ropes. Nothing of note has turned up, aside from the mouldering skeletons of ponies and sheep. I have not slept. I am running on my last dregs of energy, yet I will not abandon this endeavour until Harry is found."

"Is there any proof that Harry was kidnapped? There hasn't been a ransom demand, has there?"

"None. But given that Henry has been the object of a recent campaign of terror and murder, the kidnapping of his son is hardly an unlikely extrapolation of that. Don't you think, Holmes?"

Holmes maintained his morose silence, so I felt obliged to answer on his behalf.

"If Harry has been abducted, then a ransom demand must surely come soon," I said. "And what of Mrs Barrymore, Grier? Can you tell us anything further? I presume Mortimer has been to see her by now."

"In the event, Barrymore himself went to fetch him," came the reply. "He had no choice, given that the rest of us had all at once become embroiled in looking for Harry, a matter that seemed the more urgent of the two. Mortimer has been at her bedside ever since."

"And her condition?"

"No better, no worse."

"What do you think may have caused it?"

"There are two tiny, closely adjacent wounds on her hand which, to me, look like puncture marks caused by fangs," said Grier. "Mortimer agrees. Then there is the inflammation and discolouration arising from them. I have seen rattlesnake bites, and the symptoms they present are not at all dissimilar."

"A rattlesnake? In Devon?"

"Or some other kind of snake. Do you not have venomous snakes in this country?"

"Just one that is native."

"One!" Grier declared. "Is that all?"

"The adder," I said, "and its bite is seldom fatal. The pain and swelling are usually negligible, not much worse than a bee sting. Very occasionally a person might have an extreme allergic reaction and die, but instances of this are vanishingly rare."

Grier shook his head in mild disbelief. Hailing from a land of copperheads, coral snakes and cottonmouths, not to mention rattlesnakes, he seemed surprised that the British Isles were so free of serpentine danger.

"Well," he said, "it could be that Mrs Barrymore is one of the few who react badly to an adder bite."

"If that were so, chances are she would be dead by now from anaphylaxis. Since she is still alive, we must consider that the venom came from some animal other than an adder and that its effects are slower-acting, if far more insidious.

I will be able to tell you more once I have examined her for myself. And Sir Henry. I must ask about him. How is he faring in all this?"

"Broken, Doctor. Quite broken. As you and Mr Holmes will shortly see for yourselves, for we are here. Journey's end."

Baskerville Hall rose before us, bleak and black. The sight of it ought to have filled me with disquiet, given its connotations for me, yet at that precise moment I felt nothing but a smouldering fury. My thoughts were as sharp and clear as a diamond. I was almost pleased to be back in this gloomy, disaster-ridden place, for I was now instilled with a sense of purpose that left little room for any other considerations. Holmes and I had a mission, and I would not rest until it was successfully discharged. Neither, if I knew my friend, would he. Whoever had harmed Mrs Barrymore and snatched young Harry Baskerville would have not only the remarkable intellect of Sherlock Holmes to contend with but the dogged determination of Dr John Watson as well. And woe betide the villain!

Chapter Twenty-Four

THE HIDER IN THE HEDGE

Sir Henry Baskerville was not simply "quite broken", to use Grier's phrase. He was all but catatonic.

He sat in the drawing room with a vacant stare, rocking to and fro slightly. His hair was unkempt, as if he had torn at it, and he wrung his hands constantly. I could get little more sense from him than I might from a stone. All he did in answer to my entreaties was to intone, "My boy is gone. My boy is gone," over and over, a threnody of misery. He was lost in some private hell, beyond the reach of others.

Sir Henry was Holmes's and my first port of call. Our next was Mrs Barrymore. Grier had left us to it, having gone back out onto the moor to continue organising the parties looking for Harry. Evening was coming on, the start of a second night of searching, but the American, indefatigable as ever, was refusing to give it up.

Dr Mortimer, who was watching over Mrs Barrymore along with her husband, looked as exhausted as anyone. He sprang up from his seat when Holmes and I entered, then sat straight back down.

"A touch of lightheadedness there," said he, hand flying to forehead. "I got up too quickly, and no wonder. I haven't eaten a thing all day."

"Stay where you are, then, Mortimer," I said. "Better still, go downstairs and find yourself some food. I will take over Mrs Barrymore's care for now."

"I couldn't possibly."

"No, it is quite all right."

"Well, if you are sure," said Mortimer. "It is such a relief to see you and Mr Holmes, Doctor. For the first time since this latest dreadful business began, I am feeling that all may not be lost."

Galen the spaniel was in the room too, curled up on the rug by the fireplace. As Mortimer exited, the dog traipsed after him with an expectant eye. Evidently Galen had not been fed lately either, and was hopeful of a meal. What is telling is that I had scarcely registered the dog's presence when I came in, and as it left with Mortimer, all I thought was that it was a pretty, affectionate-looking little thing. Not once did snarls and the flashing of canine fangs cross my mind.

I glanced over at Holmes. His persistent taciturnity was

beginning to trouble me. I had never known him to be this uncommunicative or seemingly passive when presented with a vexing problem. Normally in such circumstances he was a whirlwind of activity, barking out questions and statements, his keen eyes flashing as he hunted high and low for clues. Now, his eyes were hooded and his lips tightly pressed together. To a certain degree he reminded me of Sir Henry. Both men seemed to have withdrawn into themselves. My hope was that in Holmes's case it meant he was deep in rumination, already homing in on the solution to the case. But I could not be sure.

He seemed content for me to continue to make the running, at any rate, and so I did.

"Barrymore," I said, "perhaps you should take a break too, and have something to eat. Go and join Mortimer downstairs."

"Forgive me, sir, but no," said the butler stolidly. "I am not moving from this room until I am assured that my wife will be well."

"Then let me see if I can give you that assurance," said I, moving to the bedside.

Mrs Barrymore lay tucked in under the covers, limp and still. Her breathing was shallow and slightly irregular. A sheen of sweat glistened on her forehead, and her cheek was hot to the touch. I took her pulse and found it rapid. All her symptoms betokened feverishness.

On a table nearby I spied a bottle of tincture of opium, alongside a china basin full of water and a cloth. Mortimer, clearly, had been using the medicine and cold compresses to reduce her temperature and alleviate the pain and inflammation. It was what I would have done.

Gently I drew back the covers to expose her right arm. There was puffiness and redness all the way from hand to elbow, as Grier had said, and this condition had begun to spread into her upper arm.

I took the hand and examined it. On the back I spied the two puncture marks mentioned by Grier. They were set close together, a quarter of an inch apart. Around them the swelling was at its worst, a mound of inflammation stretching the skin so tight it practically shone.

Like Grier, I too had seen snakebites. In Afghanistan once, at camp in Kandahar, I had treated a lieutenant in the North Lancashires who had put his boots on one morning without checking them first as he ought to. Overnight, a krait had crawled inside and gone to sleep. The vicious brown-and-white-striped vermin did not like its rude awakening and bit the fellow's foot. I got there in time to be able to squeeze out most of the venom from his toe, and I am pleased to say the lieutenant made a swift recovery.

The puncture marks on Mrs Barrymore's hand were too small, and not deep enough, to be those of a snake.

Their origin, however, did not concern me then so much

as their consequences. My nostrils were registering a distinct, sour odour, and I could see purple-black lines within the skin, emanating from the site of the injury and threading their way, tendril-like, up into Mrs Barrymore's forearm. The smell was that of flesh starting to turn rotten.

I turned to Holmes and Barrymore. Since my friend was being so unresponsive, it was to the butler that I addressed my remarks, but they were intended for both men.

"Your wife's body is resisting the toxicity of whatever poison is within her," I said.

"That is good news," said Barrymore.

"It is indeed. But there is bad news to go with the good, I'm afraid."

"What? Tell me, Doctor."

"Necrosis is setting in."

"My God."

"If I am to halt the spread of it, and save her life, I am going to have to operate."

"Operate? You mean…?"

It is always better when dealing with patients or their relatives to speak plainly rather than honey one's words.

"Amputate the arm from the elbow down," I said.

At that, Barrymore let out an unmanly shriek. He clamped a hand to his mouth. His eyes were round and horrified.

"It is the only way," I went on, "and it must be done forthwith. The longer we leave it, the further the destruction of the bodily tissues will progress, until it will inevitably prove fatal. Do I have your consent, sir?"

Before Barrymore could answer, there came a soft stirring from the bed. This was followed by a gasp of pain, and then a reedy, halting voice spoke.

"Husband? Is that you?"

Barrymore rushed over to his wife. "Yes, my dear. It is I."

Mrs Barrymore's eyelids fluttered. She turned her head towards him. "I heard you cry out. Whatever is the matter?"

"Nothing, now that you are awake again."

"My arm. It throbs so."

"It must do, I know."

"And I feel so weak."

"Please, don't exert yourself," said the concerned husband, smoothing her hair. "Just rest."

Suddenly Sherlock Holmes stepped forward, showing animation at last. "Mrs Barrymore," said he. "Do you know who I am?"

The housekeeper blinked up at him, attempting to bring her gaze into focus. "It is… Mr Sherlock Holmes, is it not? I remember you."

"Madam, I regret imposing upon you at a time like this, when you are indisposed so. I would not if the need were not great. Can you tell me what occurred yesterday afternoon?"

"I… I recall very little."

"You were in the garden, with Harry. He was playing with Dr Mortimer's dog. Something happened. What?"

"I cannot… I cannot remember."

"You must try," Holmes insisted. "It is important."

"Holmes," I cautioned. "Mrs Barrymore is not at all well. Do not press her." Barrymore, to judge by his scowl, agreed with me.

"Regrettably I must, Watson," said my friend. "I do not know when I might next get the opportunity."

"It… It is a blur, in large part," said Mrs Barrymore. "But… Yes. It is coming back to me. Harry was playing. He had a rubber ball and he – he was throwing it for Galen to fetch. Such merry laughter. I had not heard the child laugh like that for some time, not since… since Lady Audrey. It was a good sound. And then…"

"Then?" Holmes prompted, bending forward eagerly.

"Then there was another sound. A twig."

"A twig?"

"Snapping. *Crick-crack*, it went. Like that. In the hedge."

"The hedge. Which one?"

"The stand of wild privet that borders the old lodge. There was…" Mrs Barrymore rubbed her brow with her good hand. "There must have been someone within the hedge, or on the other side. That is what I thought. Someone who was trying to be stealthy. Galen must have thought so too, because he became excited. He ran to the hedge, yapping, and vanished through. Harry followed before I could stop him. To him it seemed… seemed a new game that Galen had started. A game of chase. He too ducked into the hedge. I was on my feet in a trice. I called out to Harry. 'Come back, lad,' I said. And he…"

She was becoming agitated, and I placed a hand on Holmes's elbow and cast him a look that begged him to relent. Harassing the woman when she was in such a delicate condition was potentially injurious to her health, not to mention unkind.

Aside from shrugging off my hand, Holmes studiously ignored me. "Please, Mrs Barrymore. I know it is difficult, but whatever you can remember, anything at all, will help."

"Harry did not come back. There was the sound of conversation on the other side of the hedge. Soft. One of the voices was Harry's. The other was too quiet for me to distinguish clearly."

"A male voice or female?"

"I cannot say. By then, I was up and striding to the hedge myself. I was keen to know who was there and what business they had with Harry. I knew, too, that I must retrieve the boy. I had promised Sir Henry not to let him out of my sight, and now I had allowed that very thing to happen. I put out a hand to part the leaves and peer in. It was then that I felt it. The pain. Oh! The pain! It was so sudden, so awful. My hand seemed all at once on fire. I snatched it back. I have this recollection of… of *something*. Something crawling over my hand. It… *writhed*. I shook it off. It fell to the ground and scuttled away. I… Did I fall too? I think I must have. I was on my back, looking up at the sky. Things went dim."

"Can you describe further the thing that was on your hand?" said Holmes.

"It was… It was black. And red. And yellow. Long. Thin." Mrs Barrymore's voice was fading. She was sinking back into unconsciousness.

Holmes leaned further over her, and it looked as though he was going to shake her in order to keep her awake.

I took hold of him again, firmly this time, and pulled him back.

"Desist at once, Holmes," I hissed. "I will not have you beleaguering her any more. She needs rest." I lowered my voice further still, in case Mrs Barrymore remained alert enough to overhear. "Not least in light of the ordeal which lies ahead for her."

Holmes gave a sign of assent. "Quite right, Watson. I apologise to you – and, Barrymore, to you. In my fit of passion, I forgot myself. Mrs Barrymore has not told us much but she has told us as much as she can, and that will have to do."

"What does it all mean?" Barrymore wondered. "What hurt her?"

"Your wife was ambushed, Barrymore," said Holmes. "What was done to her was done in order to prevent her hindering the kidnapping of Harry – and, for that matter, seeing the kidnapper. The ruthlessness of the person responsible would seem to know no bounds. Mrs Barrymore was an innocent bystander, and she has been used cruelly."

"Do you know who did it? I would dearly love to get my hands on the fiend."

"Not yet, but there will come a reckoning, you mark my words," said Holmes. "Not only will Harry be brought home safely, but his abductor, your wife's attacker, will pay the penalty for these crimes. This I vow."

Chapter Twenty-Five

THE LESS SAVOURY PRACTICES OF HOLMES'S AND MY RESPECTIVE PROFESSIONS

Within the hour, I commenced the operation on Mrs Barrymore. I availed myself of the sharpest knives I could find in the kitchen and a small handsaw from the tool shed, since none of the implements Dr Mortimer carried with him in his medical bag was sufficient to the task. Mortimer doused the blades in alcohol to disinfect them while I set up oil lamps in a circle around the bed, so that their light bathed what was to be my makeshift theatre.

A tourniquet was tied about Mrs Barrymore's upper arm. Towels were wadded beneath her elbow. Then, using sulphuric ether furnished by Mortimer, I sedated the patient and set to work.

The amputation itself went well, by which I mean it was quickly and cleanly done. Once the affected portion of limb had been detached, I tied off the blood vessels. Earlier, when making my initial incisions, I had left long flaps of skin which I had peeled back above the elbow. Now I took these, folded them down over the stump and sewed the ends together. The result looked as neat as such things ever can. To finish, I slathered the join with antiseptic unguent and applied bandages.

Throughout, Barrymore stayed in the room. I had suggested he step outside, but his refusal was total and unbending. Once or twice I heard him stifle a groan while I was working, but he held his nerve. I don't know that I could have been as brave in his position, were it my own wife I was watching be surgically mutilated. As for Mortimer, he assisted by passing various implements to me upon request and taking the ones I handed back to him. He maintained an air of professional detachment throughout, although his cheeks were notably whiter than usual.

As I cleaned up afterwards, I told Barrymore that I had done the best I could and his wife's fate now lay with a greater power than mine. The butler thanked me profusely, with much shaking of the hand and the shedding of more than a few tears.

My only recourse with the severed forearm was to take it to a far corner of the garden and bury it. I dug a hole deeper than any fox or other scavenging mammal could, dropped the limb in, covered it up, and patted the soil down hard on top.

Then I took myself off for a well-deserved stiff drink.

As I was helping myself to a snifter of brandy in the drawing room, Holmes came in. There was mud smeared liberally on his trousers and jacket sleeves, and scraps of foliage adhered to his clothing all over.

"Good grief!" I said. "Look at the state of you. If young Harry could see you now, he would think his nickname for you all the more appropriate. What on earth have you been up to?"

"While you were engaging in one of the less savoury practices of your profession, Watson," Holmes said, "I was engaging in one of the less savoury practices of mine. To wit, I have spent the past hour down on my hands and knees in the hedge near the old ruined lodge, conducting a painstaking search by the light of a dark-lantern."

"A sense of proportion, Holmes," I chided him. "One can hardly equate ferreting around in a hedge with removing a person's limb."

"No, you are right, old friend," came the contrite reply. "I spoke glibly. There is no comparison. Still, like you I find myself in need of a restorative. Any chance there's a glass of that brandy going spare?"

I poured him one.

"Thank you." Holmes cast a look around the room. "No Sir Henry?"

"Abed, on Dr Mortimer's recommendation. Mortimer

prescribed potassium bromide, and it seems to have done the trick. He told me this shortly before leaving."

"Yes, I saw him go, along with faithful Galen. He looked quite enervated."

"It was his first amputation on a woman. Apparently he found it harder to bear than if it had been a man. 'I don't know why, Watson,' he said, 'but with a female it seems more like a desecration.'"

"And how is Mrs Barrymore?"

"I am going to check on her shortly. She has a strong constitution, and barring unforeseen setbacks, I anticipate she will pull through."

"Grier, meanwhile, remains out on the moor." Holmes plucked a sprig of privet from his hair and peered at it with curiosity before flinging it into the fire. "And will continue with the hunt for Harry until exhaustion overcomes him, assuming it ever does. The word for such behaviour is self-flagellation."

"Grier feels he has much to atone for," I said.

"Pshaw!" said Holmes. "He did nothing wrong. It was Sir Henry's decision to go grouse-shooting, and Grier could not be in two places at once. He chose to stick with the person who seemed at greater risk. I would have done the same."

"You know, it is good to find you in a talkative mood once more, Holmes. All afternoon you were aloof to the point of rudeness."

"Was I? Yes, I suppose I was in a bit of a brown study, Watson. You must appreciate how galling it is to have a clear intimation of danger but misread evidence which, interpreted correctly, might have enabled one to forestall said danger. I should have known!" He smote his forehead with the heel of one hand. "I should have been able to predict this! Really, I am an idiot. Those serge-clad clowns at Scotland Yard could have done better."

"I am not sure that's true."

"No, you are right. A *circus* clown could have done better."

"Now who is flagellating himself? We are none of us perfect. Why, back when I was at Netley, I had a patient who presented with double vision and a severe headache. He was young, so I dismissed it as a migraine and gave him salicylic acid powder to take away the pain. It turned out he had had a stroke, rare in someone his age but not unheard of. I still feel a chill to the vitals when I remember how badly I erred."

"You are kind to try to console me," said Holmes, "but it won't do. I am Sherlock Holmes and I hold myself to a higher standard than others. I saw this coming. I simply did not see it distinctly enough. Now I at least know where I went wrong – now, when some of the damage done is irreversible."

"Some. That means not all."

"No, not all. And come the morning, I can begin rectifying what is in my power to rectify."

"Tell me what you found." I waved a hand in the direction of the garden. "Out there. You have fresh data, it is apparent."

"Another brandy first, if you'd be so kind."

When his glass had been refilled, Holmes said, "Harry was abducted by not one person but two. The footprints out by the hedge do not lie. There are two sets of them – and one of them, moreover, belongs to a woman."

My eyebrows rose. "Good Lord."

"A woman of medium height and build. The man is somewhat taller and, like her, of average weight for his size. I base these judgements, of course, on the depth of the footprints and their median distance apart. It would seem that the pair had been lying in wait behind the hedge, biding their time, until they could grab Harry. The moment arrived perhaps earlier than they wished, when they drew Galen's attention. They had made provision against any impediment Mrs Barrymore had to offer, however, in the form of a venomous animal which they launched at her like some sort of living missile. The intention could merely have been to frighten her off with this creature. It could, by the same token, have been to injure her in the exact way they did, rendering her powerless. In either case, the animal chosen was well suited to the task."

"What sort of thing was it? Do you know?"

"I do. Recall, if you will, Mrs Barrymore's rather vague

description. She said it was black, red and yellow, and long and thin. It writhed on her hand."

"That could be some kind of snake, I suppose. Many venomous snakes sport those three colours. It is one of nature's warning signals."

"But then consider, too, the kind of locomotion the creature exhibited after it fell to the ground. Mrs Barrymore said that it 'scuttled'. It did not scurry, as a small mammal does. It did not slither, as a snake does. *Scuttled.* What scuttles that is not insectile? That does not have a multiplicity of legs?"

"Then it was a spider, perhaps."

"No, Watson. 'Long and thin', remember."

"A caterpillar?" I ventured this half-heartedly, but thought there was an outside chance it might be correct. There had been a lepidopteran theme to Mrs Lyons's revenge upon Sir Henry, after all. This fresh offensive might be an extension of that, conducted by two collaborators of hers who were continuing her work.

"I see the reasoning behind your suggestion and applaud it," said Holmes. "However, I have never heard of a caterpillar that scuttles, nor that has a venomous bite, although there are certain of the species whose urticating bristles and spines cause a toxic reaction. No, I can think of only one creature that fits the bill. *Scolopendra gigantea.*"

"Assume that I do not know what that is."

"The giant centipede, Watson. Found in the jungles of

northern South America and capable of growing up to twelve inches long. Legs yellow, carapace red shading to black on each segment. A predator that feeds on anything from tarantulas to frogs to bats, with a bite known to kill its prey within seconds and on occasion prove lethal to humans. My knowledge of entomology is not comprehensive, and I am prepared to stand corrected, but I would wager good money on *Scolopendra gigantea* being the 'weapon' that was used to attack Mrs Barrymore."

"How is it that you know so much about this particular centipede?"

"It is a necessity for anyone in my occupation – some might call it a curse – that his brain become a storehouse for all manner of unpleasantness," said Holmes. "This includes a passing familiarity with those fauna which unscrupulous types might use to harm others. I bought that copy of Messrs Kirby and Spence's great work of entomological reference, the one I keep at Baker Street, just so that I could acquaint myself with the more sinister and potentially deadly forms of arthropod. The book, in relation to insects and arachnids, is a treasure trove of esoterica and grotesquerie. That is why I had little trouble remembering *Calyptra*, the vampire moth, when Grier was first telling us about the bloodsucking lepidoptera purportedly roaming Dartmoor. While not hazardous to humans, *Calyptra* had still lodged in my memory by dint of its common name if nothing else."

"Whereas this giant centipede is a genuine danger to people."

"And worthy of a permanent place in my mental inventory for just that reason."

"But what is one doing here in the West Country? Who would possess such a beast? Unless..."

"Unless?"

I gave an incredulous shake of the head. "It can't be Stapleton, can it?"

"I told you, Stapleton is dead."

"Perhaps you misidentified the corpse."

"No, it was his."

"Then perhaps it was a substitute corpse placed there by Stapleton," I said, "the body of someone who resembled him closely. He dressed it in his own clothing and had it ready as a decoy, so that he might effect a miraculous escape."

"Again, no. I never forget a face. The one I saw on the body in the mire was unquestionably Stapleton's. The only way this doppelgänger theory of yours would work is if it had been his identical twin."

"It could have been."

"He killed his own twin brother and threw him in the mire, simply to elude capture?" said Holmes, one eyebrow aloft.

"It is not inconceivable."

"It is not terribly likely either."

"Well then, does Stapleton have a brother, not a twin but

the ordinary kind? One that we have not heard of before? Or another relative – a cousin, say – who followed in his footsteps as a naturalist?"

"Some next of kin, you mean, who would be keen to visit retribution upon Sir Henry on Stapleton's behalf," Holmes said. "Now, Watson, you are getting a great deal warmer."

"Or it could be an assistant," I said, "a work colleague as versed in entomology as he himself was."

"Again, you stray near the bullseye."

"I am not, though, hitting the mark."

"Not quite. In fact, your last arrow landed somewhat further into the target's outer rings than the previous."

"This is damnably frustrating," I said. "You obviously have a notion who the culprit might be. Why not just say?"

"But the solution is well within your grasp. You have simply to make that last crucial step. Let me help. I told you there were two sets of footprints at the hedge, a man's and a woman's."

"Yes."

"I can also tell you that I detected the faintest traces of a feminine perfume still lingering at the scene. It adhered to several of the privet leaves and must have been transferred there through contact with the skin of the wearer."

"So? You have already established that one of the kidnappers was female."

"But the scent was familiar to me, Watson. It was the

perfume known as white jessamine. Now then, let us review the data one more time. A close relative of Stapleton's who might wish to avenge his death, who is female and who fragrances herself with white jessamine…"

Holmes made a circling motion with his hand, as if to incite the cogs in my brain to turn. They did with their usual creaking rustiness.

"My God!" I said, when at last my mental machinery churned out an answer. "Can it be…?"

"I can only think," said Holmes, "that our kidnapper, who is also the killer of Lady Audrey and Laura Lyons, is Stapleton's widow, she who was born Beryl Garcia."

"And the man with her, the other kidnapper…"

"Must be Antonio, the Stapletons' manservant and Mrs Stapleton's fellow Costa Rican."

I was thunderstruck by the revelation. "But what has turned the woman against Sir Henry and his family? When last we knew of her, she and he had developed a strong mutual attraction. I foresaw it growing into something even more, as did you, and it surely would have if she had not fled Dartmoor for parts unknown."

"I agree. I fully expected Mrs Stapleton to become the next Lady Baskerville. Sir Henry has explained why this did not happen."

"She left Dartmoor, overcome with feelings of shame. But still the two parted on good terms. It was her decision to go. She did not have grounds to think that Sir Henry had spurned her, as Mrs Lyons, in her maddened way, did."

"Something must have happened in the intervening five years that soured Mrs Stapleton's feelings towards him."

"Soured them to the point where she has become homicidal," I said.

"And to the point where she will stoop to abducting his son in order to wound him," said my friend.

"But why did she kill Laura Lyons? And why place the moth kite in her closet?"

"I should have thought the answer to those questions was obvious."

"To you, maybe. Not to me."

"Well, I shall resolve them to your satisfaction soon enough. In the meantime, let us call it a night. I am weary, and you, after your exertions, must be even more so. There is much to be done tomorrow."

"Indeed," I said, stifling a yawn. "All in all, these are very positive developments, Holmes. We now know whom we are looking for. We can furnish police forces across the land with descriptions of Mrs Stapleton and Antonio. It can only be a matter of time before they are discovered and apprehended. There is hope!"

"Is there, Watson?" said Holmes musingly. "Let us allow ourselves to think so. The alternative is too grim to consider."

Chapter Twenty-Six

THE TRAIL OF BERYL STAPLETON

All was haste and activity the next day. First thing, Holmes drove to the telegraph office at Coombe Tracey with Grier. There he sent a wire to Scotland Yard, for the attention of Inspector G. Lestrade. He asked the official to institute a country-wide alert. Police officers were to look out for a woman in her early thirties and an elderly man, both of Hispanic appearance and speaking accented English. It was likely that they would be in the company of a three-year-old boy, the Honourable Harry Baskerville, whom they had abducted. He wrote that the matter was of the utmost importance. The child's life might even depend on it.

He asked for a reply by return, and an hour later one was waiting for him. Lestrade told him that a bulletin had been sent out and that all metropolitan and rural forces were mobilising. Every available resource would be pressed into service. The kidnapping of the son of an aristocrat was a serious business, the Scotland Yarder said, and there would be no rest for anyone until the boy was safely reunited with his father.

Back at Baskerville Hall, Holmes carefully outlined the situation to a late-rising Sir Henry. The baronet was aghast.

"Beryl!" cried he. "But how could she? Why? I have done nothing to offend her. If anyone has cause to feel offence, it should be me. She went so suddenly, with scarcely a backward glance. A man could easily take that amiss. Five years without a word, and now she returns, nursing so much hatred towards me that she would kill my wife, nearly kill my housekeeper, and steal my son?" His hands made clutching actions, as though he was trying to squeeze sense out of thin air. "It beggars belief."

"I cannot explain the whys and wherefores of it, Sir Henry," said Holmes. "That will come in due course, I am sure. For now, what we must concentrate on is the fact that Jack Stapleton's widow is a known quantity, as is her accomplice Antonio. The police have their descriptions, and Harry's. We must trust the sturdy constables of this land to strain every sinew and do their best. They have the manpower and the reach. They may not be the brightest sparks but their illumination can still penetrate into the dimmer corners where villainy may hide."

The hours passed slowly as we waited for news. Sir Henry drank, copiously, to quell his inner torment. Holmes paced. Grier was in his room, catching up on the many hours of sleep he had forgone. The search of the moor had been called off. The area had been scoured thoroughly, and now that the police were involved, it seemed sensible to leave the task to the professionals.

As for me, I occupied myself primarily with Mrs Barrymore's welfare. The housekeeper had come round and was sitting up in bed. Her stump had to be causing her some significant pain but, aside from the occasional wince, she was refusing to let it show. I suggested an analgesic but she refused, saying she did not like "fuddlesome" medicines. She would much rather keep a clear head, even if it meant putting up with "some soreness".

"Your resilience does you credit, madam."

"They breed us hardy in the West Country, Dr Watson," replied she, and given the evidence before me, I was not going to gainsay the remark.

During the afternoon, a messenger arrived from Coombe Tracey with a telegram for Holmes from Lestrade. My friend unfolded the slip of paper with a slight tremor in his hand, although whether this was born of dread or eagerness I could not tell.

"Well?" I said. "What has Lestrade to say?"

Holmes drew a deep breath. "It is as I feared."

"What?" asked Sir Henry, sitting bolt upright. "Harry. Is he…?"

"No, Sir Henry," said Holmes. "Forgive my poor choice of words. Harry is well – as well as can be expected. What I feared is that Beryl Stapleton might have plans to leave the country, and so it has transpired. A woman answering her description was spotted at Portsmouth this morning, boarding a transatlantic passenger steamer."

At this, Sir Henry looked grim, with a hint of despair in his eyes. "And Harry was with her, I suppose."

"He was," said Holmes. "Lestrade reports that she was accompanied by a small boy, who it was assumed was her son. The eyewitness, a customs officer, says that the child looked dazed and sleepy."

"Drugged, no doubt," I said.

"Very possibly, to keep him docile."

"And it was just a lone woman with Harry? No Antonio?"

"Not according to this report."

"What do you think has become of the manservant?"

"They must have known there was a possibility that police would be looking for a man and a woman together. Thus they have split up temporarily, in the hope of throwing the authorities off the scent, and will rendezvous later at their destination."

"Which is where?" asked Grier, who had emerged from

his room shortly before the messenger came. "Where is the steamer bound?"

"She is the SS *Görlitz*, of the Ostdeutscher Steam Navigation Company," said Holmes. "More than that, Lestrade's wire does not reveal, but German shipping lines that cover transatlantic routes tend to follow the eastern seaboard of the Americas, down from Nova Scotia through the islands of the Caribbean, all the way south to Tierra del Fuego."

"That itinerary could well take in Costa Rica," I said.

"Indeed, Mrs Stapleton's native land is one possible port of call along the way. We can know for certain that that is where she is going if we inspect the passenger manifests at Portsmouth."

"Assuming she bought the tickets under her own name, that is," said Grier.

"Oh, if she used a pseudonym I am sure it is one that I shall be able to penetrate," said Holmes. "Besides, she and Harry will be listed as mother and son, and there cannot be many pairs of passengers on that ship fulfilling that remit."

Now Sir Henry was on his feet. He was swaying somewhat after all the alcohol, but there was no denying the fire that burned within him.

"We must go as soon as possible," he said. "To Portsmouth. And when there, we will book berths on the first ship headed for Costa Rica."

"Can we not just wire the port authorities in Costa Rica," said Grier, "and see to it that the Stapleton woman is arrested the moment she steps off the gangplank?"

"But what if they miss her? Or what if, anticipating just such a move, she disembarks early, in Honduras perhaps, or Nicaragua?"

"In that event, Henry, we ourselves would fetch up in South America with no greater likelihood of finding her than anyone else has. She could lose herself in that vast continent, never to be seen again."

"But we would be there, rather than thousands of miles away in England. It would signally increase the chances of locating her and Harry."

"I am not normally one to counsel inaction," Grier said, "but I still feel that pursuing her across the ocean seems inordinately futile."

"And I am not going to sit idle when there is something that can be done," Sir Henry countered. "I would rather waste time on a bootless chase than stay here hoping that the bodies of international justice act in successful concert. I cannot leave my son's fate to others. Benjamin, I beg you, come with me. I ask this in the name of our friendship and also in the name of our commonality as men 'on the square', for we are brothers in spirit just as Jabal and Jubal were brothers in flesh."

This was clearly some sort of Masonic invocation which

precluded any refusal from him to whom it was addressed. Grier bowed his head, then nodded.

"Very well, Brother Henry," he said. "If that is your wish, I must accede to it."

"And you, Mr Holmes," Sir Henry said, turning to my friend. "I insist that you accompany us. I shall pay you, of course. I don't care how much. Name your price."

"The going rate will be fine, Sir Henry. I cannot abandon you, not after my failure to pre-empt the drastic measures that Mrs Stapleton has taken. This thing must be seen through to the end."

"And you, Doctor?" Now it was my turn to feel the glassy-eyed vehemence of the baronet's gaze. "Can I count on your support too?"

"If Holmes is going," I said, "then so am I, willingly."

"Then it is settled. I shall make the arrangements."

"My only proviso," I added, "is that Dr Mortimer is charged with looking after Mrs Barrymore in my absence."

"Naturally. I shall have Barrymore go over to Merripit House straight away to convey that instruction."

Barrymore returned, not simply with an assurance from Mortimer that Mrs Barrymore would be his patient, but with the man himself.

"What's this I hear about an expedition to Costa Rica?" Mortimer said to Sir Henry. "You are chasing after Harry's kidnapper? Then I must come too."

"There is no need. I have marshalled an impressive force already." Sir Henry waved a hand at the three of us.

"It is not open to negotiation. Harry is my godson. I swore an oath that, while I live, I would care for him. Would you have me go back on a promise? One made in church, moreover?"

"Well, when you put it like that… Objections, anyone?"

"Is there another doctor who can minister to Mrs Barrymore?" I asked Mortimer.

"I know of at least two whom I can call on, both excellent fellows," said he. "And Galen can be kennelled with a friend of mine. That may not seem important to you but it is to me."

"Then I am satisfied," I said.

"Anyone else?" said Sir Henry, looking to Holmes and Grier. From each he got a nod of assent. "Welcome aboard, Mortimer. Now go back home and pack your things. We leave for Portsmouth in the morning."

Chapter Twenty-Seven

TRANSATLANTIC MANHUNTERS

The docks at Portsmouth were all bustle and clamour. Cranes swung, crowds milled, stevedores yelled, and every now and then there would come the deep moan of a ship's horn, loud enough to make the eardrums ache. The air was filled with the brackish smell of seawater and hosts of gulls skirling and mewing.

Disembarking from the train at the dockside terminus, our five-strong band of transatlantic manhunters divided forces. Sir Henry, Grier and Mortimer went to collect the tickets for our voyage. Holmes and I went to the customs house.

There, Holmes asked to see the passenger manifest for the SS *Görlitz*. The clerk on duty, a puffed-up little man with a tight gutta-percha collar and steel-rimmed spectacles, balked at first. Ships' records were not for public scrutiny, he said. Holmes then produced a warrant he had had sent to him from London by Lestrade, granting the bearer the rights of a police official and permitting him to view any and all documents he requested. This rather took the wind out of the clerk's sails.

The manifest revealed that a Mrs Pearl Merripit and son Harry were aboard the *Görlitz*, and that they were scheduled to disembark at Puerto Limón in Costa Rica in eleven days' time.

"Mrs Stapleton did not wrack her brains too hard when coming up with false identities," I remarked dryly.

"In Harry's case, it was sensible to keep his first name the same," said Holmes. "A child his age would be confused if asked to change it and would not readily answer to anything else. In her own case, she merely exchanged one kind of precious gem for another, and borrowed the name of her former Dartmoor home. Not what one would call cryptic, but enough to throw off most pursuers. Anyway, as I said yesterday, a woman and small boy travelling together are a comparatively rare sight, even if they are passing as mother and son. Mrs Stapleton must know this and realise that it marks them out, meaning there was no requirement for her alias to be anything but serviceable."

"She may realise that, but does she realise Sherlock Holmes is on her trail?"

"It would not surprise me in the least. Beryl Stapleton has shown herself to be a wily and resourceful adversary.

She was aware that I was investigating Lady Audrey's murder, and hence she must have foreseen it was likely that my services would be called upon when Harry subsequently went missing. She is counting on the fact that she has a significant head start on us and that once she gets to Costa Rica she will be on home territory. She knows the lie of the land there, she can blend in among the indigenes, and that will be to her advantage."

"But Harry cannot blend in so easily. He has dark features but not dark enough to pass for a Latin. Nor does he speak Spanish."

"And that will be to *our* advantage," said Holmes. "A pale-complexioned, Anglophone child will stand out from the crowd."

Joining our colleagues again, we climbed aboard the RMS *Aegean*. Sir Henry had booked us First Class cabins, and the comfort and opulence of the accommodation was in stark contrast to the conditions I had endured when last I undertook a lengthy ocean journey, travelling back from Afghanistan to this very port. My cabin aboard the troopship *Orontes* had been little better than a monk's cell. At the time, however, I had been so debilitated by my war wound and subsequent bout of enteric fever that I had hardly cared how salubrious my surroundings were. All I had wanted was to get home.

After settling in, I went out on deck. The *Aegean*'s cargo of mail, chinaware, silverware and dry goods had been loaded, her hatches were battened down, and now her mighty coal-fired engines were rumbling, sending deep, church-organ vibrations through the ship from stem to stern. Exhaust fumes began purling from her three smokestacks in huge columns, and in short order the hawsers were cast off from their mooring bollards and withdrawn. A tugboat towed the steamer away from dock and out into the harbour waters, then detached itself, gave a merry toot on its whistle, and left the larger vessel to make her own way. Back on the dock, handkerchiefs fluttered and hats waved as people saw off friends and relatives.

The *Aegean* sailed with stately slowness out through the pinch-point entrance to the port, passing between the Round Tower on the left and the fort blockhouse on the right, and onward into the Solent. Gathering speed as she circumvented the Isle of Wight, she was soon riding the swells of the English Channel westward at a good fifteen knots, forging into a hefty headwind that drove the outpourings from her smokestacks backwards in a single, swirling, grey-black plume.

All this I observed from a vantage point at the bow rail, feeling the sense of exhilaration that often attends a departure to sea. For all that we were on a mission of the utmost gravity, there is still nothing quite like the sense of limitless possibility one has when venturing out onto the open main. The horizon stretches before one – the rim of the planet! –

and the vastness of the Earth is laid bare. One may go anywhere. Anything might happen. Even the thought of our destination, South America, a continent as yet unvisited by me and forbiddingly unknown, was not as daunting as it might otherwise have been.

I was watching the Dorset coast slide by to starboard, a narrow strip of rust-brown cliff and shingle beach, when Holmes appeared beside me.

"Bidding fond adieu to the old country, eh, Watson?"

"Who knows how long it will be until we see England again. A month?"

"I hope we shall return with Beryl Stapleton in custody, and Harry and his father reunited, well within that span of time."

"So do I. I am looking forward to us achieving the desired outcome of our journey, of course. But, churlish as it may sound, I am also concerned about the effect the frequent and sometimes lengthy leaves of absence I take are having on my career. I think some of my regular patients are beginning to despair. One even called me his 'semi-physician' the other day. It was meant as a joke, but not entirely."

"There is always Verner and his proposal," Holmes reminded me. "He is offering an excellent price for your practice."

"And I am giving it serious thought."

"It would leave you with a tidy sum which, husbanded

wisely, would yield enough money to live on. Although," he added, "the reduction in income might also oblige you to find more modest lodgings than that rather palatial Kensington townhouse you currently rattle around in."

"Lodgings such as, perhaps, the upper floors at 221B Baker Street?"

"Why, the idea never occurred to me, Watson," said Holmes with a sly grin. "But now that you mention it, would it be so bad? You and I together again in the old digs? If you gave up general practice, you would have more time to write, too. You are forever complaining that I am solving cases faster than you can chronicle them, and Newnes at *The Strand* is badgering you for more tales."

This vision of the future was, like the view from the ship's prow, bright, broad and breezily pleasing.

"No need to make a decision just yet," Holmes went on. "But perhaps by the time we get back home...?"

I nodded. "Somewhat changing the subject," I said, "there's something I've been meaning to ask. You have been castigating yourself over your supposed failure to prevent Beryl Stapleton kidnapping Harry. What was it that should have tipped you off to her next move?"

"You must understand, Watson, I did not know *what* she would do. Nobody could have predicted it. Nor did I even know with absolute certainty that Laura Lyons was not the true culprit behind Lady Audrey's murder. There were a couple of anomalies at the scene of her supposed suicide, however, that nagged at me. The suicide note, for one."

"With all the spelling mistakes."

"Exactly. It would seem as though Mrs Lyons had typed it herself. Yet who *types* a suicide note? Something as personal as that – one's last, melancholy proclamation to an uncaring world – surely cries out to be handwritten. However, if we set that objection aside for the moment and assume Mrs Lyons chose neatness over passion, what about the misspellings? 'Enough' was spelled E-N-U-G-H."

"A missing 'O' could easily be excused as a typing error," I said.

"Yet the letters, as they are, give a close approximation of the word, the kind that a person whose mother tongue was not English might think is correct. Now consider the other two misspellings."

"One was 'perdon', was it not?"

"And the other 'ocasion'. These, respectively, were meant to be 'pardon' and 'occasion'. But they are also the equivalents of those words in Spanish."

"Gracious! Is that so?"

"Now, perhaps you will cast your mind back to 'eighty-nine, and the anonymous message of warning that Beryl Stapleton sent to Sir Henry in London. What form did it take?"

"It consisted of words clipped from *The Times*, all save the last, 'moor'. That was the only word which had not appeared in the previous day's edition of the paper and thus had to be appended by hand."

"Obviously the use of typeset words was intended to disguise the identity of the note's sender. But perhaps Mrs Stapleton also employed that method because she was unsure of her written English. Any misspellings might have given the game away."

"And she typed Mrs Lyons's suicide note for much the same reason, so as to avoid writing in her own hand."

"Which we might have recognised as not being Mrs Lyons's," said Holmes. "Even if you or I were not familiar with that lady's handwriting, someone like Dr Mortimer would be. However, Mrs Stapleton's uncertain grasp of our language on paper was in evidence in the misspellings."

"So that was one of the two anomalies at the scene," I said. "What was the other?"

"The bottle of laudanum. When I held it up to the light, its colour looked a little fainter than such preparations usually are, and when I tasted it, it seemed somewhat weak."

"Laudanum comes in all shades, from beer brown to pale amber, and no brand tastes quite like another. Some are sickeningly strong. Others are more palatable. In a few instances, the maker cuts cost by diluting the mixture."

"And for that reason, I could not be sure that the laudanum had been watered down by someone other than the maker, Collington's."

"Yet you suspected it might have been."

"Mrs Stapleton could have forced Laura Lyons to consume a large quantity of it, in order to subdue her. Mrs Lyons, in her fragile state, would not have put up much resistance. This happened during the small hours of the morning, so she would have been in bed and perhaps still drowsy from an earlier, self-administered dose. Mrs Stapleton surprised her and tipped the liquid down her throat, perhaps stopping up her nose so that she had no choice but to swallow. With the additional laudanum in her body, Mrs Lyons would swiftly have fallen into insensibility. Mrs Stapleton then topped up the bottle with water to make it look as though only a small amount, a reasonable single dose, had been drunk. That way one might well infer that Mrs Lyons had had a palliative nip of laudanum before typing her note and opening a vein in her arm."

"After drugging Mrs Lyons," I said, "Mrs Stapleton set her up in her armchair and bled her dry, then prepared the suicide note."

"She also planted the moth kite in the wardrobe. All this was done to frame Laura Lyons for crimes she herself had committed. I wonder whether I might have detected the telltale odour of white jessamine in the room, as I did in the hedge at the Hall, had there not been other smells masking it."

"You mean the reek of blood and death?"

"And of Mrs Lyons's own perfume. If I had caught that scent, perhaps I would have divined Mrs Stapleton's involvement in the case earlier and thus saved us a great deal of trouble and heartache. But," he added with a philosophical grimace, "there is nothing to be gained by such speculation. We are where we are."

"What I am curious to know is how Mrs Stapleton got into Mrs Lyons's lodgings in the first place."

"That is a very good question, Watson, and one I am not fully able to answer, although not for want of trying. While I was waiting for Lestrade's reply to my telegram yesterday morning, I didn't waste the time. Instead, I used it profitably by taking myself to the boarding house. There I conducted a brief interview with the landlady. I asked her if anyone had entered the property during the small hours on the night Mrs Lyons committed suicide. The landlady lives on the ground floor and would surely know if there had been any such visitor."

"And was there?"

"She told me she had heard nothing untoward that night, but then admitted that she is both a heavy sleeper and somewhat deaf. She maintained that the front door is always locked at eleven sharp, but every resident has a key for it. Her lodgers are permitted to come and go at all times, even late, provided they tread lightly and close the door softly so as not to disturb their fellows and her."

"I see. So it is conceivable that Mrs Stapleton could have forced the lock on the front door, or picked it."

"And then, having sneaked upstairs, she entered Mrs Lyons's rooms by the same means," said Holmes. "We must assume, from the timing of events, that she went to the boarding house straight after terrorising Baskerville Hall for a second time with her moth – the same occasion on which I was able to identify the moth as a kite from atop Lafter Hall. She realised she had taken her 'giant vampiric insect' charade as far as it could go, and now she must cut her losses and pin the blame for everything on a hapless, unwitting innocent, someone who was a likely candidate because she had a connection to Sir Henry that was both direct and inimical."

"I can see how it all fits," I said, "but that is only because we know now that Mrs Stapleton was the agency behind it. Those two anomalies you refer to are both tenuous, too slight to base any kind of useful conclusion on. The misspellings in the suicide note could have been just that, misspellings. It was impossible to tell with absolute certainty that the laudanum had been watered down. In and of themselves, they gave you nothing to go on. They were incidental, perhaps *co*incidental."

"I have built successful cases upon far smaller minutiae," Holmes said. "Thoughts of Beryl Stapleton did enter my head at the time. The stumbling block, for me, was simply that I could not fathom why she might harbour any ill will towards Sir Henry Baskerville, let alone a detestation so intense it might provoke her to murder. I still cannot. If one has a suspect but no motive, then one may as well not have a suspect at all."

"Perhaps her Latin blood is what has driven her into such a mania," I suggested. "The Spanish are nothing if not hot-headed, their women most of all."

"Is that enough, though? I am not sure. Even among the more emotional races, there has to be something to give impetus to their passions. A vindictive rage like Mrs Stapleton's does not arise from nowhere. Well, at any rate," Holmes concluded, resting his elbows on the rail and setting his face to the marine vista before us, like some living figurehead, "we have a week and a half at sea to ponder the matter. Let us hope it is plain sailing all the way."

Chapter Twenty-Eight

NOT PLAIN SAILING

Would that I could report that our voyage was uneventful. For the first three or four days, shipboard life was agreeable enough. Our cabins were staterooms, with facilities that would put many of London's grander hotels to shame. There was a smoking room shared among the First-Class passengers which, with its leather-upholstered chairs, ornate electric candelabras and book-filled shelves, had something of the atmosphere of a Pall Mall club. A promenade deck for the exclusive use of us elite travellers offered deckchairs to lounge in and games of quoits and shuffleboard. The restaurant was run by a Parisian chef who had studied under Escoffier. The sea was smooth. Things really could not have been nicer.

When it became widely known that Sherlock Holmes, no less, was aboard the *Aegean*, his celebrity drew attention.

Fellow passengers came up, introduced themselves, and asked him about his past cases. Mostly he dealt with these unsolicited intrusions with courtesy, although on one or two occasions, if somebody started to bore him, he or she was steered towards me. "As my chronicler," Holmes would say to this person, "my very own Boswell, Dr Watson, is far better suited to answer your queries than I." Invariably the disappointed suitor would engage me in desultory conversation for a minute or so, find that I was far less interesting than my friend, and drift off.

A few people had mysteries they wished Holmes to clear up. They would regale him with a lengthy account of some baffling crime which they or someone they knew had been the victim of, and expect him to supply a solution magically like a conjuror producing a rabbit from a hat. They did this in a purely social manner, without mention of recompense, and the irritation it caused Holmes was palpable. In every instance, even if he was perfectly able to unravel the problem based on the information given, he professed himself at a loss. "It could be," he said, with a show of pained apology, "that my reputation is overrated." Privately to me he said, "The nerve of these folk! Because I am not at my place of business, but rather seemingly at leisure, they treat me as though I am some kind of public pump from which they can draw advice, like water, at will. Would I ask a paperer to paper my wall for free? A cobbler to repair my shoes out of the goodness of his heart? No! So why do they believe a consulting detective should be any different?"

These were relatively petty annoyances, however, and could easily be dismissed. More worrisome was Sir Henry's behaviour. With time on his hands and little to do but agonise and fret, he drank. He drank at breakfast, he drank at lunch, and by the day's end he was thoroughly soused and yet still would drink more. The sideboard in the smoking room was well stocked with wines and spirits, to which passengers were free to help themselves, and the baronet made the most of it. One evening, as he staggered up to the sideboard yet again to refill his glass, a steward politely suggested that rather than enjoy his umpteenth cognac, he should instead go to bed. At this, Sir Henry bristled and growled some shocking oaths at the man. The steward stood his ground, and an altercation seemed in the offing, until Benjamin Grier intervened. He put an arm around his friend's shoulders in a way that was as much a means of restraint as a gesture of comradeship, and, speaking to him softly as one might to a skittish horse, guided him out of the room to his cabin.

As if this were not bad enough, Grier himself was subjected to more than a few barbed comments based upon the colour of his skin. It seemed that among the other First-Class passengers, for one of his race to share the same amenities and privileges as them was not simply an abnormality but an abomination. I distinctly recall a very rotund northern industrialist – a man so fat, he was practically spherical – speaking loudly from an adjacent table at dinner, saying that he had not paid all that money for his ticket only to have to consort with "members of an inferior species". Another time, a woman who was some kind of Italian aristocrat, a marchesa or contessa, made pointed comments about those who belonged on the upper decks and those who belonged in the bowels of the ship, a system of ranking she appeared to think should be based not only upon means but upon complexion.

Worst of all was a coffee magnate, on his way with his wife and eldest son to visit his plantations in Jamaica and Trinidad. Here was a man for whom his Caribbean-native employees, to judge by how he spoke of them, were little better than machines for watering and gathering his crops, and who openly expressed a yearning for the bygone era when they could have been put to work from dawn to dusk for no pay. He was rude about Grier behind his back and just as rude to his face, addressing him as "monkey" and using other racial slurs that I shall not repeat. I asked him to desist from such talk, but all I got in return was a sneer, as if to say, "I refuse, and what are you going to do about it?"

One afternoon, Grier and I were playing chess when this impudent fellow came swaggering over. He made a pretence of studying the state of the game, whereas in fact he was obviously working himself up to deliver another verbal broadside.

"Ah, the eternal conflict of white against black," said he eventually, motioning at the board. "But white has the advantage. White always goes first. For that reason, white should always win."

It so happened that I was playing white, and I was losing badly. I made this point to the coffee magnate. "It isn't the colour of the pieces that matters, it is the mind of the man who's moving them," I said, "and right now, Corporal Grier's mind is running rings around mine." I thought it worthwhile referring to Grier by his military rank, to show the coffee magnate that he was not just a man but a soldier who had served his country, and was thus all the more deserving of respect. "Indeed," I added, "he is trouncing me."

"So I see," said the other. "Does that not fill you with shame, sir?"

"Shame that I do not play better chess? Yes. Shame that I am on the verge of being checkmated by a worthy opponent? Again, yes, not least because I have made several unforced errors during this game. But do I feel shame of any other description? None whatsoever."

I thought I had spiked his guns, but I thought wrong.

"Were I to lose at chess to an *ape*," the coffee magnate said, "I would hang my head. Indeed, I would hang *myself*."

At that, I sprang to my feet. "That is enough!" I declared

hotly. My fists were clenched. "You will apologise to Corporal Grier this instant."

"It is fine, Watson," said Grier. "Let's not make a fuss."

"You may not wish to, Grier, but I do. I have listened to this insolent jackanapes long enough. Even if you can put up with it, I cannot. Sir," I said to the coffee magnate, "I give you one last chance to make amends. You will say sorry, and you will shake my friend's hand, and you will walk away and never speak to him in that atrocious manner again. I'll have you know that Grier is as courageous and noble a human being as I have met. He is worth a dozen of you."

The coffee magnate looked aghast. It wasn't my impassioned tirade that shocked him so much as the very notion that he should ever apologise to anyone for anything, least of all to someone he considered subhuman.

"You're not serious, are you?" said he. "You are? Then it is clear that proximity to this jungle creature has infected you. His stink has got all over you. Next thing you know, you'll be—"

I never found out how that sentence would have finished, for at that moment the red mist descended and I could hold myself back no longer. I lunged for the coffee magnate, fully intent on knocking him to the floor.

Grier must have known what was going to happen, for he was out of his chair and had his arms about me before I got in a single blow. He hoisted me bodily off the floor, swung me about and deposited me back down so that he now stood between me and the coffee magnate. I attempted repeatedly to get past him, in order to reach the object of my ire, but it was useless. Grier blocked me every time. I might as well have been trying to get past the Colossus of Rhodes.

The coffee magnate jeered at me from behind Grier. "A proper Englishman would not stoop to fisticuffs so readily. Some of this savage's coarser habits must have rubbed off on you."

Grier rounded on him. Coolly, almost amiably, but with teeth nonetheless gritted, he said, "I would advise you, sir, to leave us. Now. If you do not, I shall let my friend have his violent way with you. In fact, there is a very good chance that I shall join in myself."

The coffee magnate spluttered, but he was markedly more intimidated by Grier than he was by me. He backed away, murmuring about people who did not know their place and threatening some kind of legal redress. He was cowed but not, I thought, repentant.

Incidentally, some of my readers may be wondering why I am leaving this fine personage anonymous in these pages. They may feel, as I do, that someone who holds a certain stratum of his fellow men in such contempt, for no other reason than a misplaced sense of his own superiority, deserves to be exposed for the model of arrogant, smirking bigotry that he is; and naming him would undoubtedly do that.

However, I have before me on my writing desk a letter from Messrs Chalfont, Pettit and Quirke, the prestigious firm of Chancery Lane lawyers. Dated a month after the events I am chronicling, this sternly worded missive compels me to desist from ever mentioning the coffee magnate by his proper name, on pain of a libel suit that could prove quite ruinous. It seems that the fellow concerned had realised he might crop up in one of my narratives, feared the condemnation that might result, and took preventative measures. Hence I am under constraint to refer to him only by a generic descriptor. The more astute among you, though, may infer his identity from the few hints given.

"You shouldn't have interfered, Grier," I said, adjusting my jacket and straightening my tie. "The man deserves a good pasting."

"And where would that get us, Doctor? I have learned that, with people like him, you can achieve more through civility than you can through being provoked. If you show anger, it only affirms what he already thinks. If you are calm, it removes a central plank of his prejudice. You take away fuel from his fire rather than giving it. Now, shall we resume our game?"

"No," I said. I had bumped the table when standing up and the chessboard had been disturbed, with several of the pieces having fallen over or been dislodged from their squares. Even if we could have restored them all to where they belonged, there seemed no point. I was no longer in the mood. "No, I am going outside to take the air. I concede. Victory is yours."

In truth, I was jealous of how much of his dignity Grier had managed to retain during the confrontation, and how much of mine I had thrown away. That was his real victory and my real defeat.

The last straw came when, on the fourth day, our group received an invitation from the captain of the *Aegean* to dine with him in his quarters that evening. It turned out that the invitation, delivered in person to each of us by the first mate, was for Sir Henry, Holmes, Dr Mortimer and me only.

I summoned those other three to my cabin.

"I shan't be going unless Grier is going too," I said.

"I agree," said Holmes. "It would be unconscionable."

"Whether or not the snub was deliberate," said Mortimer, "we must take it as such."

"It must have been deliberate," I said. "The captain clearly knows that we are all travelling together. Why else ask the four of us jointly?"

"Perhaps he is under the impression that Grier is a servant," Mortimer said.

"Then we should disabuse him of the notion," I said. "Don't you agree, Sir Henry?"

Sir Henry merely nodded. He was in the middle stages of his daily round of drunkenness, whereby he was cogent, just about, but loath to communicate beyond the bare minimum required. The rest of us had decided collectively to allow him his inebriation for the duration of the voyage. It kept him pacified, for the most part, and should he breach the bounds of good conduct – as with the steward, for example – we could always intercede. It seemed fairer to take this approach than forbid him the bottle. Once we got to Costa Rica, we would oblige him to sober up. He would have renewed purpose – the search for Mrs Stapleton and Harry – and would want, and need, a clear head. While we were on the rolling emptiness of the Atlantic, however, there was nothing to occupy him save thoughts of his son and his own impotence. If drink afforded him release from that, so be it.

I sought out the first mate and advised him that unless the fifth member of our party could dine with the captain as well, then none of us would.

The fellow went off to discuss the matter with his superior officer, and returned to inform me that the invitation had been rescinded. Captain McCandless, he said, had been looking forward to our company at his table, especially that of the noted Mr Sherlock Holmes; but if we wished to decline, that was our prerogative.

Later, the coffee magnate sidled up to me while I was out on the promenade deck.

"Captain McCandless is a friend of mine," said he. "I travel aboard the *Aegean* on this route regularly, and over the years he and I have become close. He told me that he wished to extend a dinner invitation to you and all your colleagues. I put him straight on a thing or two."

There was no Grier around this time to hinder me; nor, it so happened, were there any witnesses. I left the coffee magnate sprawled on his back, clutching a bloodied nose.

"There's plenty more where that came from," I told him, and departed to the sound of oaths and curses, feeling both pleased with myself and a little ashamed.

That night, the RMS *Aegean* sailed into a mid-Atlantic squall.

That night, too, Benjamin Grier narrowly escaped death.

Chapter Twenty-Nine

A TRAGIC CONCATENATION OF DISASTERS

It began around teatime with a slow, steady deepening of the *Aegean*'s sway through the water. The skies darkened prematurely. The wind rose.

By evening the ship was seesawing up and down, such that the simple act of walking became a trial. It was hard putting one foot in front of the other when the floor would not stay flat.

The crew retained a blithe attitude, but among the passengers, less accustomed to the moods of the ocean, tension prevailed. Outside it was blowing a gale, and the crash of the waves over the bow boomed through the hull like beats on some enormous gong. Dinner was served as usual, with the waiters compensating for the movement of the ship by leaning deftly from side to side as they threaded their way between tables with dishes and trays held aloft. Soup slopped in bowls, and wine swirled about in glasses.

Afterwards, going to bed was the sensible option. I wasn't feeling as seasick as some, if their stifled groans and green faces were anything to go by. However, lying down seemed definitely preferable to being upright.

Grier alone found the whole situation terrifically entertaining. "Nature in the raw," he said. "The elements at their tumultuous best. I'm going outside to enjoy it. Coming with me, Watson?"

"Are you mad?" I said.

"That will be a no, then." He looked around our table. "Henry? How about you? Mortimer? Holmes? Anyone?"

Heads were shaken.

"I am an arch urbanite," said Holmes. Even he, with his iron constitution, was looking somewhat queasy. "I like the city because everything is contained and orderly there and, more than that, *stays put*. If you want to go out into the teeth of a storm, Grier, then I wish you well. Try not to get swept overboard."

"I shall do my best."

An hour later, I was supine in my cabin, wide awake. Sleep had no intention of coming, it seemed. The squall was worsening, I was sure of it. Now the *Aegean* was rolling from side to side as well as tilting fore and aft. All about me, things rattled and shuddered. The wind hissed like a demon about the ship's superstructure, and rain hammered on the portholes as though seeking entry.

Then came a violent knocking at the door.

I crawled out of bed and staggered over to answer it.

Before me stood Grier. He was clutching his head. Blood flowed out freely between his fingers.

"Good heavens, man!" I exclaimed. "What on earth has happened?"

Without answering, he stumbled in. I shut the door behind him. He fell into the chair by the dressing table with a heavy moan. His clothes were wringing wet.

I drew his hand away from his head. A very nasty gash ran down his temple from the hairline almost to the ear. It was deep and would require stitching.

"Did someone hit you?" I said.

Grier mumbled what I thought was "No".

"Then what did this?"

But the American appeared half-concussed, and at that moment was barely capable of coherent speech.

I set about cleaning the affected area with a wet washcloth, then swabbed the wound with cotton wool soaked in surgical spirit. Grier hissed with pain.

"I will need to suture the laceration shut," I said. "I have a needle and thread to hand. I warn you, it is going to smart."

Grier made a grunt of resignation. I took this as consent.

He kept his cool throughout the procedure. It must have hurt like blazes, but aside from the occasional contortion of the lips, he gave no outward indication of distress.

In spite of the ship's lurching, my hand was steady, and the suturing was, even if I say so myself, exemplary.

By the end of it, Grier had fully regained his senses. "It seems, Doctor, that you and I have very different definitions of the verb 'to smart'. But thank you all the same."

"I have done the best I can," I said, "but you are going to have an impressive scar."

"I shall tell people I got it in a sabre duel with a Prussian nobleman over some matter of personal honour."

"Fine, but perhaps you can tell *me* honestly how you came by the injury."

"My impression is," said Grier, narrowing his eyes in thought, "that it was all just an awful accident. I was out on deck, near the front of the ship. I was clinging to the rail, feeling the sheer might of the storm pounding through me, and I as small as small can be, a speck of dust in the face of God's might. It was exhilarating. Then all of a sudden I glimpsed something out of the corner of my eye. An object hurtling towards me. On instinct, I ducked to one side. This enormous weight crashed into my head. I fell to the deck, stunned. After that, I don't remember anything until I came to. I have no idea how long I was lying there. I only knew that I must get up and go inside, else the cold and the wet would be the death of me. As I got to my feet, I saw something lying nearby. It was a heap of cable, with a wooden hook block in the middle of it. Big, heavy thing, that hook block.

Must have weighed thirty pounds or more, including the cast-iron hook itself. The cable was dangling down from one of the ship's cranes that stood right above."

"One of the guy derricks."

"If that's what they're called. The jib of the guy derrick was swinging to and fro with the motion of the ship. I think the hook block must have come at me at head height and struck me a glancing blow, after which it fell to the deck."

"Thank God it *was* only a glancing blow. If you hadn't ducked and it had hit you full on, it would have stoved in your skull."

"Then it's a good thing I was born with a very hard head." Grier sheathed the sentence in a small smile.

"I suppose it was the tip of the hook that gave you that gash," I said. "Are you quite sure, though, that the whole thing was an accident?"

"Why ever not? One of the sailors didn't tie down the derrick as tightly as he ought to. The storm worked its tether loose. The reeling of the ship and sheer bad timing did the rest."

"I'm simply wondering if it might not have been foul play."

"You have spent too much time in the company of Sherlock Holmes, Watson. You see intrigue and malfeasance everywhere."

"But think about it, Grier," I said. "You do, after all, have an enemy aboard the *Aegean*."

He used the coffee magnate's name. "Him, you mean? He is a blowhard, yes. He certainly takes a dim view of my kind. But is he the sort to attempt murder? I doubt he would have the guts or the gumption. It would mean dirtying his hands, and a fellow like that hasn't got his hands dirty a single day in his life."

"Still, I cannot let it lie. Stay here. You are in no fit state to do anything but rest."

"If my head were not sizzling like a skillet, I might argue. As it is, I shall do as I'm told."

I roused Holmes in his cabin. I told him about Grier's mishap and voiced my concern that it had been not accident but assault. Holmes did not disagree – at least, he reckoned it a possibility – and presently he and I were out on the port deck, making our way for'ard. Black waves roiled and seethed around the *Aegean*. Rain pelted, seeming to come from all directions at once. The deck planks were slick underfoot, and what with that and the slamming gusts of wind and the ship's pitch and yaw, every step one took was treacherous. It felt as though one's legs might be whisked out from under one at any moment.

Eventually, after much slithering and striving, we reached the foredeck. There was the hook block, just as Grier had said, nestled amid a spill of cable like the head of a curled-up snake amid the coils of its own body. The guy derrick from which the cable hung slackly was rotating with the ship's motion on its pivoted base. Its angled jib described a ponderous to-and-fro arc several feet above our heads.

Holmes commenced one of his examinations. He looked over the scene, moving cautiously because of the conditions, with none of his usual darting, terrier-like zeal. He studied the hook block, the cable, the base of the guy derrick, and the derrick's winch with its double-handed crank. Here, his eye alighted on something lodged amid the winch's cogs. He extricated the item in gingerly fashion, held it close to his face, then slipped it into a pocket. It was a tiny, glittering object the nature of which I could not make out just then.

There was no point in talking. The howling of the squall made communicating, even at a shout, a futile exercise. Holmes signalled with a wave of the hand that we should go back inside, and this met with no protest from me.

Returning to our quarters was like going from the thick of war to a ceasefire. Although the storm raged on, we were out of it, our ears delivered from the wind's roaring barrage, our bodies no longer assaulted by salvoes of rain.

As we dried ourselves off in Holmes's cabin, my companion fixed me with a portentous stare.

"There is malice afoot here, Watson," said he.

"I feared as much. Grier was not merely in the wrong place at the wrong time."

"No. Someone swung the hook block at him, having lowered it beforehand to the level of his head. The aim was clearly to cause harm, and most probably to kill. The culprit, however, has done his best to make it appear as though it was all just misadventure."

"How?"

"In the normal course of events, when the guy derrick is not in use the cable is reeled in so that the hook block sits at the tip of the jib, some twenty feet above the deck. A ratchet is then applied to the winch to lock the mechanism. If, as we are meant to believe, the derrick broke loose from its tether of its own accord and started to swing, then in order for the hook block to be level with Grier's head, the winch ratchet would have to have come undone too, and the cable would have to have begun unspooling."

"So that as the jib came towards Grier, the hook block would have been descending and, when it reached him, it was at exactly the height it needed to be to brain him."

"One might well assume, if one were the assuming type," said Holmes, "that somehow the ratchet was jarred, perhaps by the juddering action of the jib as it butted up against its stops, and this was how the cable was released. The hook block landed on the deck after it had struck Grier, and the cable continued to pay out until there was enough of it lying on the deck to achieve equilibrium with the amount remaining on the reel. Sufficient slack still remained in the cable for the jib to continue its swinging. This is how we found things, is it not?"

"It is."

"However…" My friend wagged an admonitory finger. "It is altogether too much to accept that the hook block just so happened to be at the right height when it reached Grier, and that the jib just so happened to be swinging over him at that same moment, and above all else that Grier just so happened to be standing in precisely the right spot for this collision to take place, especially given the way the ship is moving around so unpredictably. The layers upon layers of chance stretch credulity. It is much easier to infer, if less palatable, that the derrick had been untethered beforehand and the hook block lowered, ready to be launched at Grier manually, with considerable force, by an unseen assailant. Said assailant then undid the ratchet and allowed the cable to run free. This, he hoped, would lead everyone to think, as Grier himself did, that the whole thing was a tragic concatenation of disasters."

"But if the intent was murder, would the culprit not have checked to see that he had done the job properly?" I said. "It would not take much to establish that Grier was not dead but had only been stunned."

"Having contrived this elaborate method of despatch," said Holmes, "the felon had painted himself into a corner. If the hook block did not kill Grier outright, he could not strike him a second time. That would negate the entire 'accident' aspect of the plan. Even if he knew Grier was still alive, he had no alternative but to leave him as he was and trust that his injuries were so severe that he would die of them, or else that exposure to the elements would finish him off. For what were the odds of someone coming across Grier until after the squall had blown itself out? Even the ship's crew won't go out on deck in this weather."

"It was our millionaire friend with the coffee plantations who did it, isn't it? I know it was. Grier embarrassed him in full view of several other First-Class passengers, including his wife and son, after he interrupted our chess game. He was there in the dining room earlier tonight when Grier announced he was heading outside, and he saw a chance to get his own back. Perhaps simply injuring Grier was all he was after. A man like him might not countenance murder, but badly hurting someone – especially someone he considers no better than an animal – would trouble him little."

"Granted, he seems a plausible suspect," said Holmes. "There is another, however, who is as likely to have done the deed."

"And who is that?"

Holmes produced from his pocket the tiny object he had retrieved from the winch.

It was a gold cufflink, the type that uses a hinge pin to hold it in place.

"This could well have fallen from the culprit's shirt cuff into the winch mechanism as he was releasing the ratchet," he said. "Hinge-pin cufflinks are notorious for coming loose and slipping off."

"I would not be surprised if" – the coffee magnate – "has a cufflink like that. It looks to be pure gold and rather expensive, just the sort he would wear."

"But are these his initials?"

Holmes held the cufflink out to me so that I could see its face.

A pair of letters were engraved into it in a stylish serif font:

HB

"They are not," I admitted.

"They are, however, the initials of someone else known to us," Holmes said. "In point of fact, I spied this cufflink and its mate adorning that person's sleeves a little over an hour ago. I saw them at very close hand, what's more."

"Whose sleeves?"

"Watson, must I spell out everything for you?"

"My God." A chill ran through me. "'HB'. You mean to say…?"

"Sir Henry Baskerville," said Holmes.

Chapter Thirty

A VIVID PICTURE OF FRIENDSHIP GONE AWRY

"I cannot believe it," I said. "Sir Henry? But he and Grier are bosom friends. He would no more attack him than you would me."

"Yet the evidence would seem compelling, would it not?" said Holmes, twirling the cufflink between thumb and forefinger.

"Suppose it fell from his sleeve. Hinge-and-pin cufflinks often come loose. You said so yourself. Somebody picked it up and seized an opportunity."

"An opportunity to…?"

"To kill Grier, or maim him," I said, "and make it look as though another was to blame – in this instance by planting the cufflink in the winch, so that when it was found, the obvious inference would be that Sir Henry Baskerville was behind the attempt."

"I presume that the person responsible for this cunning deception is the coffee magnate. You persist with your belief that he is the guilty party."

"He despises Grier. He might also want to pay me back for hitting him by striking at a friend of mine."

"Ah yes, your second confrontation with him. It was most intemperate of you, Watson, lashing out at the fellow like that."

"I don't regret it."

"Nor should you," said Holmes. "But it is not wise to make enemies of the wealthy. What if he takes you to court for common assault?"

"Let him," I replied. "I will deny it. It will be his word against mine." Then, my defiance wilting somewhat, I said, "You don't think he *will* sue me, do you?"

"It might prove very costly for you if he did, whether or not he can prove the offence. He is able to afford far better legal representation than you and could have you tied up in litigation for months, if not years. I feel that that is a likely response to being punched, for someone such as him, who is hardly a man of action. Far likelier than devising this rather intricate scheme of hurting Grier and trying to pin the blame on another. One must also bear in mind the fact that when Sir Henry went to bed this evening, both of his cufflinks were present and correct in the appropriate place. I recall it distinctly."

"The cufflink could have fallen off in the corridor, somewhere between the dining room and his cabin. The coffee magnate stumbled across it when going to bed himself a short while later."

"But surely if one wished to frame somebody else for a crime, one would not choose a person who is obviously a close friend of one's intended victim. One would look for an *enemy* of his instead. Moreover, the whole artifice of the hook block was designed to look like an accident. Why, then, go to the trouble of placing evidence that would confirm it was a deliberate act?"

"In case someone such as Sherlock Holmes saw through the trick. The coffee magnate had an inkling you might investigate, and so made provision against that possibility."

"You so desperately want the man to be guilty, Watson, that you are espousing a theory which pays no heed to the facts."

"It was not him, then?"

"I can say so with almost complete definitiveness."

I was deflated. I had been looking forward to watching Holmes convincingly and publicly accuse the coffee magnate of attempting murder and causing actual bodily harm. To see him get his just deserts would have been delicious.

"But it cannot have been Sir Henry either," I said.

"And why not?" said Holmes. "Has his behaviour not been erratic lately? Has he not been drinking heavily?"

"To the point where he might wish ill upon a longstanding friend, though?"

"A man may get so drunk that he is not responsible for his actions. He and Grier are longstanding friends, indeed, but might there not have arisen some animosity during that time? A rift which, although amends have been made, has not fully healed? Sir Henry's new-found wealth, for instance, could have upset the balance of their relationship. Grier might have asked him for a loan and it was refused, or, conversely, Sir Henry offered to bale Grier out of a financial tight spot and Grier was too proud to accept the help. Sir Henry has been dwelling upon it, this past insult, and now tonight, when he is in his cups, the old resentment comes welling up. Grier heads outside. Sir Henry pretends to go to bed, but actually follows Grier onto the deck to have it out with him. There is Grier, standing at the bow. Sir Henry's drink-addled brain is overcome by rage. But Grier is a big man, far outclassing Sir Henry in terms of sheer physical strength. It would be hopeless to try to beat him in a fair fight. Nor, for the same reason, would it be an easy thing to wrestle him over the rail into the sea. Then Sir Henry's eye falls upon the guy derrick. Eureka. Stealthily, his movements disguised by the din of the storm, he untethers the derrick and lowers the hook block. He swings it at Grier with all his might, then undoes the ratchet and quits the scene. He has been quite cunning, he feels. Little does he realise he has left behind a telltale cufflink."

"You paint a vivid picture," I said.

"And an all too plausible one," said Holmes.

"Then what must we do? Do we tell Grier who his attacker was?"

"No. He might wish to retaliate against Sir Henry, and if he did, who of us could stop him? You? Me? Against that giant of a man?"

"True. But we cannot leave Sir Henry unchaperoned. He might try again with Grier, or even, if he is becoming so deranged, visit similar violence on one of us."

"You are absolutely right, Watson. We must also consider the possibility that tomorrow Sir Henry may have no memory of tonight's events. It could be that he was so drunk everything will be a blank. So we must be careful not to alert him to the fact that we know what he has done."

"For fear that his remorse would be so great, his madness might turn inward," I said, nodding. "He might do himself harm."

"Exactly."

"All the same, he cannot be allowed to get away with it."

"We will deal with that after the business with Beryl Stapleton and Harry is resolved. Once Sir Henry has his son back, safe and sound, he will be a much more malleable proposition. We can then reveal what we know and find some way of achieving reconciliation between him and Grier. I'm sure it is possible. In the meantime, however, we must contain him and curb his excesses. Any thoughts as to how we might accomplish that?"

I deliberated. "What if I were to monitor him? As a doctor, I mean. I could claim to have observed symptoms in him of a condition that requires round-the-clock medical supervision. Jaundice, for instance. Then I could confine him to his cabin and keep an eye on him at all times."

"What an excellent idea," said Holmes. "I was thinking along those lines myself, but you have crystallised what was nebulous. Jaundice. A drinker's ailment. Perfect."

"The symptoms are not always easy to spot. Sir Henry's eyes are permanently bloodshot at present. I can tell him I have noticed a slight yellowing of the whites, and he might well confuse the one thing – their bloodshot state – with the other. Additional symptoms include fatigue and weight loss. He, in his current state of heightened tension, is exhibiting both."

"The power of suggestion will do the rest. When a qualified physician tells you he thinks you are ill, you are apt to believe him."

"It is unethical," I said, "but, in the name of the greater good, it is acceptable."

"However, you cannot be expected to stay at his bedside twenty-four hours a day. I propose bringing Mortimer in on the plan. That will halve the burden. Do you think he will go along with it?"

"I should imagine so. He is an amenable sort, and Sir Henry is his friend. Should I tell him why we are practising the fraud?"

"Best not," said Holmes. "It will complicate matters unduly. Just say that you are doing it in order to ensure Sir Henry's mental health. Mortimer will see the sense in that."

"What about Grier? He is waiting back at my cabin. He will want to know the outcome of your investigations. What shall I tell him?"

"Tell him that despite every effort I have been unable to draw any meaningful conclusion. Let him think that it was just an accident after all, as he already supposes."

I did as bidden, and Grier seemed content. "That's what I get for braving a storm," he said. "Next time, I shall stay indoors, like any sane person."

I saw him to his cabin and returned to mine, where I spent the night tossing and turning, much like the *Aegean* herself.

Chapter Thirty-One

PUERTO LIMÓN

By the morning, the squall had died out and the sea was serene again, with just a slight rolling swell. I got up feeling bruised and pummelled, as if I had just gone the full twelve rounds with the prize fighter Jem Mace, even though all I had done was lie in bed. I ate a hearty breakfast, then went to talk to Dr Mortimer.

At first he cavilled at my proposal, but I talked him round.

"Sir Henry could very well do himself a mischief if he keeps up this level of alcohol intake," I said. "We have another six days at sea, if the rest of the crossing is smooth. It is surely possible that we can maintain the ruse for that long. We will be saving him from his own worst impulses."

"But jaundice, Watson? Will he fall for it?"

"If we both insist on the diagnosis, there is no reason to think he won't. Once we arrive at Puerto Limón, we can pronounce him cured. Whatever you may think of the rightness or wrongness of lying to him, a few days sequestered in his cabin, drying out, is just what the man needs. That way he will be clear-headed and fighting fit when we begin looking for Harry in Costa Rica."

Mortimer and I met with Sir Henry in private and set about convincing him he was ill. It was easier than I had thought. He was suffering the obnoxious effects of a hangover, which helped. When he checked in the mirror, his skin was sallow, his eyes bleary. Outwardly he looked awful, and I had no doubt he felt just as awful inwardly.

"Jaundice," he said. "My God. What must I do?"

"We have caught it in good time," I said, "so it is eminently treatable. The simplest remedy is rest and plenty of fluids, by which, of course, I do not mean alcohol."

"No. Quite right."

"Water. Clear soups. Coffee. Tea. We must flush the excess bilirubin out of your bloodstream, in order to keep the icterus under control." I was bandying about these medical terms both to impress and intimidate him. "Mortimer and I have agreed to keep you under close observation. We shall take it in turns."

"It will be a terrible imposition upon both of you."

"Think nothing of it. Your care is our concern."

So it was that over the ensuing days I would sit with Sir Henry for six hours in the daytime and six at night, alternating with Mortimer. In between shifts I would eat, stretch my legs, and catch up on sleep.

The "patient" behaved impeccably. He consumed whatever foodstuff was put in front of him and did not touch a drop of alcohol. It was clearly a shock to him that he had contracted such a serious illness, and this had a sobering effect, in every sense.

The *Aegean* put in at New York, where as many passengers came on board as departed. Thereafter, her coal bunkers restocked, she began coasting southward. Soon the autumnal chill of the northern latitudes lay behind us and we were in tropical climes. The skies were immaculately blue, the sea dazzled, and warm breezes wafted.

In Jamaica we had to say a fond farewell to the coffee magnate and family. By then the swelling of his nose had gone down. It is worth noting that his wife walked past me as they were leaving and gave me a surreptitious nod, as if to say she condoned my conduct towards her husband. Discreetly I tipped my hat in return.

West across the Caribbean we steamed, towards the isthmus that connects the north and south portions of the American continent. We called in at Belize City, Puerto Castilla in Honduras, and Puerto Cabezas in Nicaragua. At each, Holmes went ashore to consult the port authorities, enquiring whether a Mrs Pearl Merripit and son had disembarked there. The answer was always in the negative.

At last we arrived at Puerto Limón, on a morning so sparklingly bright and pristine, it could have been the first morning of Creation.

By then I was feeling cloistered and more than a little claustrophobic. You can spend only so long aboard a ship before you begin to yearn for the liberty to go just anywhere, to have an existence not restricted to a few hundred square feet of deck space and an even lesser area of interior accommodation. Spending long spells cooped up in Sir Henry's cabin did not help matters. Nor, even, did travelling First Class, ungrateful as that may sound. A gilded cage is still a cage.

Puerto Limón sprawled inland, covering the flank of a shallow ridge of hills. The city consisted largely of low white buildings with curved red roof tiles. Here and there a church or a grand municipal-looking edifice rose above the rest. Palm trees lined the streets in between, their foliage like brilliant green bomb bursts.

The heat, even at nine in the morning, was tremendous. The five of us stood on the docks, fanning our faces and taking stock. Sir Henry looked a good deal better for the period of abstinence that had been imposed on him. The colour was back in his cheeks and his eyes had regained something of their old lustre. Of all of us transatlantic manhunters, he was understandably the keenest to get going.

"Harry is out there," he said, scanning the landscape. "Every moment we linger is a moment he gets further away."

"But we cannot go off half-cocked," said Holmes. "We must first establish whether Mrs Stapleton left the SS *Görlitz* here."

Sure enough, she had. That was the good news. The bad news was that this had been four days ago. The larger, more powerful *Görlitz* had made better time on the crossing than the smaller, if nimbler, *Aegean*.

"Don't worry," Holmes said to a frustrated Sir Henry. "Her lead has lengthened, but we may still catch up. Let me ask around among the locals. Someone is bound to have seen her and Harry. Someone may even know her current whereabouts."

Holmes had a good working knowledge of the major European languages, and although his Spanish was not the equal of his French or German, he was able to converse well enough in it. His first thought was that our quarry would have taken the train to San José, for one could more easily hide amid the teeming multitudes in the Costa Rican capital than anywhere else in the country. This, however, proved to be a false hope. None of the officials at Puerto Limón's railway station could recall seeing a woman and a boy matching the description Holmes gave them.

Next, he scoured Puerto Limón itself, with the aim of establishing whether the pair had stayed there before moving on, and whether indeed they were still in the city. Here, again, he met with disappointment. There were only a handful of hotels and boarding houses to choose from, and none of them had lately played host to a beautiful Latin woman and a three-year-old boy who spoke only English.

Undeterred, Holmes cast his net wider. As evening set in, he trawled the city's bars, buying drinks, making free with his money, trusting that his generosity would loosen tongues. Eventually a provincial by the name of Juan said that a friend of his, who ran a business transporting goods up and down the Rio Banano, had been hired by a woman sounding very much like the one Holmes was looking for.

"There was a boy with her, *si*," said this fellow. "My friend, Ramón, he takes passengers sometimes into the interior. He took her and the *niño* on his boat, I am certain of it."

Holmes rewarded Juan with a five-colón note for the information. "*Gracias, señor.* There is a second five-colón note for you if you can direct me towards another boat owner who would be able to take my friends and me upriver."

Juan eyed the money avidly, licking his lips. "I may know of such a person. In fact, it is my cousin. Gilberto is his name. Gilberto Suarez. He has a motor launch. It is not big but it is reliable. It is yours for the asking – at the right price, of course."

Gilberto Suarez drove a hard bargain. A daily rate was negotiated by Holmes and Sir Henry for the hire of his motor launch and his services as pilot. The fee was doubtless extortionate by local standards, but reasonable by ours. Sir Henry could well afford it, and said to me later that if Suarez had asked a hundred times as much, he would still have paid up.

We purchased provisions for the journey, including tents, bedrolls and mosquito nets. In short order, we were boarding Suarez's motor launch from a jetty at the mouth of the Rio Banano, where the river debouched into the sea a few miles south of Puerto Limón. With a white-hot sun riding high overhead, Suarez cast off and we headed upstream.

Chapter Thirty-Two

UP THE RIO BANANO

The motor launch was fifteen feet long, with a clinker-built hull and a shallow draught. Its engine was positioned centrally and was capped with a six-foot-tall chimney which sent out gobbets of noxious dark smoke. Gilberto Suarez sat just for'ard of this, manning the helm, while astern there was a covered area with bench seats. If we slotted our legs around one another's carefully, the five of us were just about able to squeeze into this. However, it was preferable if one of us squatted at the bow instead. We organised a rota so that each man spent an hour up front, in the open, while the rest stayed in the shade. Any longer than that would have been to risk sunstroke.

The boat chugged bronchitically along, managing a speed slightly quicker than walking pace. This did not seem fast, least of all to Sir Henry, but Suarez insisted we were making good headway, especially given that the current was against us. He was a plump, jolly-looking man in late middle age who wore a broad-brimmed straw hat perched askew on his head and a red bandanna knotted around his neck and who was forever mopping his rugged brow with a handkerchief. Even though he had some idea about the nature of our mission and must have understood that sightseeing was the furthest thing from our minds, he insisted on referring to us as "*turistas*" and pointing out various items he thought would be of interest. Over there was a macaw, over there a capuchin monkey, and over there a caiman, the reptile lurking so low in the water that only its eyes and snout showed above the surface. His English was more than serviceable. Apparently he had ferried a number of British *chargés d'affaires* and ministers up and down the river in his time, as well as explorers and gold prospectors from our country and the United States, and this was how he had picked up the language. He claimed he knew the Banano and its tributaries intimately. There was not an inch of its waters that was unfamiliar to him. His wife – God rest her soul – always used to say that he loved the river more than her, and there was, he allowed, some truth in that.

Nightfall came with startling suddenness. We pulled in at a narrow, muddy beach and made camp. Grier built a fire and cooked sausages and beans over it while the rest of us pitched our tents. Dr Mortimer seemed in a rather disgruntled mood all evening, but when I asked what the matter was, he said simply that he was not the outdoors sort. He enjoyed his creature comforts, and here we were, on the banks of a wild river, at the edge of a forest filled with screaming animals and who knew what else – pygmy tribesmen with a taste for human flesh, quite possibly. He longed for a roof over his head and carpet beneath his feet.

I could sympathise up to a point. The forest was mysterious-looking and certainly not quiet. Within its dark, lush immensity, creatures ululated and gibbered, croaked and coughed. It was noisier than Piccadilly Circus on a busy weekday, and every time there was a lull and one thought that the raucous cacophony might have abated, it would resume with a vengeance, seemingly louder than before.

There were flying insects, too. The air was thick with them – ones that stung, ones that blundered into your face, ones that whirred past your ear on wings that sounded like someone riffling through the pages of an encyclopaedia. Their presence brought out swarms of bats, which swooped around us, emitting little piping chirrups that were just audible as they feasted upon the airborne banquet.

Never, not even in the mountainous desolation of the Hindu Kush, had I had such a sense of being in a realm not made for men. We were intruders in a savage Eden where we did not and never would belong. Nature fought and bickered around us, and the best we could do was stay out of its way.

Yet, at the same time, there was a majesty about it. A moon shone down on us that was bigger and brighter than the moon above Britain. The stars glittered in their myriads, so many of them that it was hard to pick out the major constellations amid the throng. A humid breeze blew along the river that made me think of some divine primordial breath, full of fecund inspiration. Much like Grier and his appreciation of the squall, I felt awed and humbled by our surroundings.

So great was this emotion that, after most of the others turned in, I stayed up smoking a pipe and soaking in the sights and sounds. I was not alone. Grier was in a similarly contemplative mood. We sat side by side and shared a companionable silence, while the night forest continued to put up its chorus of catcalls and the river rustled past.

"Your head injury seems to be healing nicely," I said at last.

"All thanks to you, Doctor."

"No dizziness? No heightened sensitivity to noise or bright lights?"

"You asked me that when we were on the *Aegean*, several times, and the answer is still no."

"I felt I should check again nonetheless. The after-effects of a concussion can be pernicious. Those stitches should be ready to come out in a day or two."

"Will it 'smart' again?"

"Hardly at all."

"Oh dear." Grier chuckled. "You know, seeing all those stars up there, I'm reminded of a joke I once heard. Two gold miners are out in the wilderness, camping. One is significantly cleverer than the other. Let's call them Jeremiah and Cletus. No, actually they're not gold miners, they're Englishmen. Let's call them Holmes and Watson. Holmes is the cleverer one, naturally."

"Bah! It's bad enough that Holmes flaunts his intellect and compares it favourably with mine all the time. Now you're doing it too?"

"Do you want to hear the joke or not?"

"Very well. If I must."

"Sometime in the middle of the night, Holmes says to Watson, 'Look up at the sky, Watson, and tell me what you see.' Watson replies, 'I see thousands and thousands of stars.' Holmes says, 'What do you deduce from that?'"

"'Deduce'," I said. "You really are tailoring this joke to suit our characters, aren't you?"

"It does seem to fit quite nicely," said Grier. "Watson replies to Holmes, 'Well, if there are so many stars, if even a few of them have planets, it's quite likely that there are some planets like our Earth out there. And if there are planets like our Earth out there, there might also be life. It does make you wonder about mankind's place in the universe.' And

Holmes says, 'How fascinating, Watson. What I deduce from it is that somebody has stolen our tent.'"

I laughed, in spite of myself, and Grier laughed too.

"I shall have to tell Holmes that one," I said.

"Will he find it funny?"

"He doesn't have much of a sense of humour. The things that amuse him are often obscure and occasionally quite baffling to the rest of us. I suspect, however, that the absurdity of the joke – and the literalness of the punchline – will appeal to him."

"Perhaps one day the joke will actually be about you and him," said Grier. "As his stature continues to grow, and yours with it, people will tell the Holmes and Watson version. It will become the standard."

"Who knows?" I said with a shrug. "Perhaps. But I would hope posterity remembers us, if it ever does, for something more than that."

The next day we were up early and on our way again. The launch seemed more sluggish than previously, but Suarez tinkered with the engine and soon had us back up to full speed, such as it was.

Not only forest lined the river. There were villages, some little more than a few houses clustered beside a landing, others so large they could almost be called towns. There were coffee plantations, rubber plantations, coca plantations, banana plantations, and small farmsteads. These occupied plots of land were hewn out from the forest, with the river close by to draw on for irrigation. People waved at us as we went by, and sometimes Suarez hailed them and the two parties would converse in Spanish while the boat chuntered past. The first time this happened I thought that they were merely exchanging snippets of news or gossip, but it transpired that Suarez was asking for information about Ramón and his steamboat. By this method he was able to chart the progress of our quarry.

"Ramón passed this way three days ago, *señores*," he would report, or, "Ramón halted here and made a delivery but no passengers got off."

After two full days of travel, I was beginning to think that we would never overtake Ramón's steamboat. It and our launch would continue upriver in procession, separated by dozens of miles, an uncloseable gap. We were not gaining on Beryl Stapleton and Harry. They would remain forever ahead, unseen, tantalisingly unattainable.

And what if the information Holmes had gleaned from Suarez's cousin Juan was incorrect? What if Mrs Stapleton and Harry weren't on Ramón's boat at all? Then this whole enterprise would have been a waste of time and we would be no nearer finding them.

On the third day, we had not gone more than a few hundred yards before we noticed that the bottom of the motor launch was awash with river water. The level was rising rapidly, and it was apparent that the hull planks had sprung a leak. While we passengers bailed out frantically, using whatever receptacles were to hand, Suarez steered towards a nearby sandbar. When we reached the shallows, he damped down the engine and we climbed out and dragged the launch up onto the sandbar. Suarez then set to recaulking the affected seam. Holmes looked on at close hand while he worked. The rest of us found a patch of shade to shelter in. When the job was done and the caulk had dried, we hauled the boat back into the river. The setback cost us a couple of hours all told.

The setback we experienced the following morning cost us a great deal more time than that, for we woke up to discover that the launch was gone.

Chapter Thirty-Three

A SNAKE IN OUR MIDST

"I tied up properly, I swear," said Suarez, scratching his head in perplexity and dismay. "You must believe me, *señores*. Never would I be so careless that I would fail to secure the rope. I am skilled in knots. This is terrible. Where is it? Where is my boat?"

"Some way downstream, I should imagine," said Holmes. "How far it has gone depends on when it broke loose from its mooring and floated off, and also on the strength of the current, which in this stretch of the river is considerable."

"We're stranded," said a despondent Mortimer. "Stuck in the middle of nowhere, with no means of transport. What a deuced disaster."

"Not nowhere, *señor*," said Suarez. "There is a village some three miles along the river from here."

"Three miles?" said Sir Henry. "That's hardly any distance at all. Let's get going, shall we?"

Suarez shook his head. "Three miles through the forest is not the same as three miles in civilisation, across fields or along roads. It will take us most of the day. And it does not bring my boat back."

"Your boat will fetch up at the bank somewhere, Suarez," said Holmes reassuringly. "It will snag on a tree or beach itself in the lee of a meander."

"And if for some reason you never recover it, I will buy you a new one," said Sir Henry. "All I ask is that we carry on our journey. I have been as patient as I can, but every minute we delay is a minute that my son gets further away."

"*Si, señor.* I understand. You are speaking the truth that you will buy me a new boat?"

"You have my word on it."

"Then what are we waiting for?"

As we folded the tents and gathered up our belongings, Holmes wandered over to the tree trunk around which Suarez had lashed the launch's painter the previous evening. He spent a while examining it, before returning to join us again.

"Take only what you can carry," Suarez advised. "We will leave everything else and come back for it later. Of course, *los indios* might steal it in the meantime. The Tayní and Cabécar tribes both call this territory their own, and they consider that whatever they find in the forest belongs to them. But there is nothing we can do about that."

"It is just possessions," said Sir Henry. "Nothing of real importance."

Weighed down by makeshift backpacks, we began our trek. We followed alongside the Banano, with Suarez leading the way and the rest of us straggling behind. Suarez hacked through the undergrowth with a machete, but it was a laborious process. The forest was dense, and vines and bromeliads flourished in profusion, forming great thicketed tangles, while huge tree roots interwove across the ground. A troop of howler monkeys accompanied us some of the way, shrieking uproariously from the branches overhead and pelting us with fruit. Evidently we were trespassing in their domain.

After a while Suarez became exhausted. We stopped to rest, then Grier commandeered the machete and took the lead, with the Costa Rican following behind, guiding him. Dr Mortimer and Sir Henry were next in line, while Holmes and I had the rear. With a gentle tap on my shoulder, Holmes invited me to slow down and fall back. Soon he and I were separated from the others by some twenty yards.

"You have your revolver, of course, Watson," Holmes whispered.

I nodded. I had brought the pistol from London to Devon,

on his instruction, and thence all the way from England to here, secreted among my belongings.

"That is good. I fear now is the time when we finally may need it."

"In case we meet these tribesmen Suarez mentioned," I said. "Is that what you mean? So that I may deter them with a few well-placed gunshots."

"No, it is not them I am worried about."

"Wild animals, then."

"Not them either," said Holmes. "Not exactly. Although there *is* a snake in our midst."

I glanced around, suddenly alarmed. I thought he was referring to an actual serpent which he expected me to shoot dead.

There was no snake to be seen, and it was only then that I realised he was speaking metaphorically.

"You're saying that one of us…"

He put a finger to his lips, enjoining me to silence.

We picked up our pace, closing the distance between us and our colleagues.

Holmes's revelation, while disturbing, made a dreadful kind of sense. I recalled how the motor launch's engine had been faulty, and how the boat had leaked, and now – the latest and worst in this litany of hindrances – how we were in the position of no longer having a boat at all. Someone had tampered with the engine workings. Someone had put a hole in the hull. Someone had untied the painter. Each of these events had occurred overnight. The person responsible could easily have stolen out of his tent and done the sabotaging by moonlight while the rest of us slumbered.

But who was it? Which of us was the saboteur? And what was his motive?

Could it be Sir Henry? I thought not. He was desperate to find Harry. It was his overriding imperative and his sole one. That said, I could not ignore the fact that he had attacked Grier viciously aboard the *Aegean*. Even if now sober, could he have some twisted, unknowable motivation for wishing to impede us? There was hereditary madness in the Baskerville bloodline. It had manifested in Jack Stapleton. Was it now manifesting in Sir Henry as well?

What about Dr Mortimer? The young physician was hating every moment of the journey. He had been out of sorts since we left Limón and had been getting ever more sulky and refractory the further upriver we went. He surely wished for Harry's safe return as much as anyone, but the process by which we were achieving that goal was not sitting well with him. Did he so resent the arduousness of the journey and the deprivations we were experiencing that he would arrange things so that we had no choice but to turn back?

Then there was Grier. I had come to like the man a lot, but now that I thought about it, how well did I know him? The answer was: not that well. It was Grier, moreover, to whom Holmes had entrusted the responsibility for keeping Sir Henry and Harry safe, in which endeavour he had been only half successful. Could he secretly be in league with Beryl Stapleton? Was his visit to Baskerville Hall all part of some piece of sophisticated chicanery cooked up between the two of them? I hated to think this, but now that Holmes had planted the worm of doubt in my mind, I was very concerned that Grier had been misleading us all along. How had he described himself when he first came to us at Baker Street? He had likened himself favourably to a buffalo, "docile unless provoked, dangerous when it is". The "dangerous" part of that phrase might be the pertinent one now. It was not beyond the realms of possibility that he had set up the whole business with the hook block on the *Aegean*, injuring himself with it and planting the cufflink in the winch in order to redirect elsewhere any suspicions one might have about him.

Gilberto Suarez likewise was an unknown quantity. Could he and his cousin Juan have colluded together? What if Beryl Stapleton and Harry were not even aboard this Ramón person's steamboat? We only had Juan's word for it. Suarez might knowingly be leading us on a wild goose chase, not caring that he was deceiving us, caring only that he got paid at his daily rate. Hence he had been sabotaging his motor launch to waylay us and make it even less likely we would ever find the steamboat. He might even have gone to the lengths of unloosing the launch and letting it float away so as to eke out a few more days of business from his rich customers. If he knew the Banano as well as he claimed then he could have picked a spot where he was confident the river would carry the launch and deposit it safely somewhere downstream.

My thoughts were in turmoil, and they remained in turmoil even as, after several hours of hard going, we stepped out into a clearing. Here a score of mean, shabby houses huddled, inhabited by people of Spanish descent and *indios* who had adopted European ways. Chickens roamed the packed-dirt spaces between the hovels, and a couple of rag-clad *mestizo* children peeped shyly out at us from a doorway as we trudged towards the centre of the village.

We must have looked a sight – filthy, bedraggled, footsore, sodden with sweat – but the village headman, who was known to Suarez, welcomed us as though we were royalty. We were fed stew and yams. I was reluctant to ask which animal had provided the flesh for the stew, afraid it might be some form of bush meat, monkey perhaps, or caiman. It tasted gamey and had a stringy texture that meant I was picking bits of it out from between my teeth for some while afterwards. Yet it filled my rumbling belly, which, as far as I was concerned, counted for more than its provenance. We were also served a strong, very sweet cane liquor known as *guaro*, and this helped soothe our various aches and pains.

It looked likely that we would have to spend the night at the village. However, just as the sun was beginning to set, there came the blare of a steam horn from the river.

Not long after that, a mid-sized steamboat hoved into view, butting its way downstream. As we converged on the rickety wooden pier that served as a landing, Suarez let out a surprised, triumphant cry.

"*Señores!*" said he. "There it is. What you are looking for. That is Ramón's boat!"

Chapter Thirty-Four

MORAL ELASTICITY

S uarez flagged down the steamboat.

"Ramón! Ramón! It is I, Gilberto Suarez," he called out in Spanish.

A man leaned out from the wheelhouse. He was youngish, with a trim build and thick black eyebrows. He waved to his fellow river pilot with apparent pleasure.

Suarez beckoned to him. "Come. Put in. We must talk."

"Suarez," said Holmes in a low voice, "take care. Do not tell him who we are. Continue to smile and wave, as though nothing is amiss."

Suarez, however, did not hear. He was in a transport of delight, evidently glad that in spite of all the reversals and complications he had delivered to us the thing we sought.

"Ramón, these gentlemen have been looking for you," he

said. "They wish to know about your passengers, the woman and the boy."

Ramón had already turned his attention from Suarez to us, and I could see his brow furrow and his expression darken. He spun the helm, and the steamboat began to veer away from the landing. Doubtless Mrs Stapleton had instructed him to steer clear of *gringos* and perhaps had taken the precaution of furnishing him with descriptions of Holmes, Sir Henry and myself, the three of us who she knew were likely to be chasing her.

"Ramón?" said a puzzled Suarez. "You are avoiding us?"

"Watson," said Holmes. "Your revolver. A warning shot or two, if you please."

I drew the gun and took aim. The first bullet missed the boat's prow by inches, literally a shot across the bow. The second shattered one of the wheelhouse's side windows. I had meant to hit the woodwork, but at a range of ten yards and in dwindling daylight, accuracy was at a premium.

"There are more where those came from," Holmes shouted to Ramón in Spanish. "Unless you pull in, my friend will ensure that the next bullet goes into you."

Ramón cowered behind the helm binnacle. The wheelhouse, with its large windows, one of them now lacking glass, afforded scant protection. I imagined he was weighing his alternatives.

"I shall give you to the count of three," said Holmes. "One. Two."

The steamboat decelerated and began gliding towards the landing again. Ramón had made up his mind.

Sir Henry was aboard the vessel even before it had come to a full stop. "Where is he?" the baronet demanded of its pilot. "My son. Where is Harry?" He dived into the wheelhouse and dragged Ramón out by the scruff of his neck. "You dog. Show me to him now, or it'll be your hide."

"*Por favor! Por favor!*" Ramón cried out, his hands held out in self-defence.

"They are below decks, aren't they?" Sir Henry persisted, shaking the fellow roughly. "Down that companionway. Yes? No?"

Ramón continued to protest in a babble of Spanish. Sir Henry either did not understand what he was saying or did not care. He raised a fist, with every intent of belabouring the Costa Rican.

Suarez clutched the brim of his hat against the sides of his face with both hands. "*Dios mío!*" he wailed in horror. "He will kill Ramón."

"At the very least beat him black and blue," Mortimer said.

"Holmes," I said, "we must do something."

My friend, however, was already moving. He sprang agilely over the gunwale of the steamboat as its hull scraped alongside the pier. With a couple of dextrous, balletic *baritsu* manoeuvres, he was able to wrest Ramón from Sir Henry's clutches and at the same time deposit the baronet harmlessly on his backside.

Meanwhile Grier seized the steamboat's transom and arrested its progress by main force before inertia could send it drifting past the pier. He clambered aboard and tossed the mooring rope out to Mortimer, who looped it around one of the pier's uprights to secure the vessel.

"Let me have the blackguard, Holmes," Sir Henry growled, picking himself up. "I promise to show him mercy, although I cannot guarantee how much."

"Far be it from me to come between a man and his satisfaction, Sir Henry," Holmes said, "but let us think about things logically. This fellow here – Ramón – is travelling downriver. If he has been transporting Mrs Stapleton and your son upriver from Puerto Limón, then it stands to reason that he has deposited them somewhere further up the Banano from here and is making the return journey. In other words, they are no longer aboard."

"You don't know that."

"No, but it is a reasonable enough inference. Besides, Ramón does not deserve our censure. As far as he is aware, all he has done is convey a woman and her child to their destination. He is not wittingly complicit in any crime. He has been carrying out the work from which he makes an honest living, that is all."

"He must have realised something was up. He would have seen that Harry was unhappy – maybe even terrified – and had some notion that the woman claiming to be Harry's mother was an impostor. He would have been able to put two and two together."

"If so, then he is guilty of moral elasticity, but you could say the same of any man with a business to run. You wish to take out on him an anger that rightfully should be directed elsewhere."

"At the very least he can tell us where he dropped Harry and that woman off," Sir Henry grumbled. "And if I have to pound the information out of him, I will."

"I am sure Ramón will be helpful," Holmes said. He turned to the steamboat pilot, who was sitting slumped against the wheelhouse, looking ruffled and mulish. Addressing him in Spanish, he said, "You may not realise it, *señor*, but you have lately assisted in a criminal enterprise, a kidnapping. You have one chance, and one chance only, to atone. The woman and child – where did you leave them?"

Ramón shook his head. "I cannot say."

"I expect you have been rewarded handsomely for your services, and the fee, in part, was meant to buy your silence. Your discretion is laudable. It is also misplaced. This gentleman here who has just ill-treated you would be quite happy to continue doing so, with even greater roughness, in order to extract the truth from you. By the same token, he would be willing to pay you for what you know, and pay you well. How much do you make in a year on average? A hundred colóns? A hundred and twenty? He will give you double that figure."

The baronet looked on, his brows knitted. He was unaware that Holmes was being so free with his money. Had he been thinking clearly, however, and not allowed his rage to consume him, he might have seen that bribery was a more effective tool than fists.

"Give him what he is asking for, Ramón," Suarez said from the pier. "These are good people. They are also," he added with emphasis, "wealthy people."

Ramón seemed to make a mental calculation. "One hundred and fifty colóns, *señor*," he said to Holmes, "and I will tell you where I left them."

"Two hundred, and you will take us there in your boat."

"Two hundred and fifty."

Holmes gave Sir Henry a brief précis of the negotiations. "Two hundred and fifty colóns," he said. "Is that an acceptable sum?"

"I begrudge paying the rascal a single copper penny," said Sir Henry. He sighed. "But yes. If we must, we must."

Holmes nodded to Ramón, who nodded back.

"Very well," Ramón said. "There is an old estate, about a day's journey from here. It has been long abandoned."

"I know the one," said Suarez. "A mansion. It was once

owned by a tobacco baron. A very bad man. Cruel. Garcia was his name. He died, and the place fell into rack and ruin."

"Garcia," I said. "As in Beryl Garcia?"

"I have heard you *señores* speak of a Beryl Stapleton. Is she also Beryl Garcia?"

"That was her maiden name. She must be a relative of this tobacco baron."

Suarez shrugged his shoulders. "Garcia is a very common name in Costa Rica."

"Nonetheless, it is possible that this mansion is her ancestral home."

"And that is why she has gone to ground there," said Grier, "like a fox returning to its lair."

"Can you navigate at night?" Holmes asked Ramón.

"It is not recommended. The river has its ways, and they are not always kind."

"I can do it," said Suarez. "If the skies stay clear, the moon and stars will be bright enough to see by."

"There we have it," Holmes announced in English, rubbing his hands together. "The last leg of our journey. Let us set sail immediately."

"Immediately?" Mortimer echoed, sounding wretchedly weary. It seemed he really had had enough of this expedition.

"Of course, Doctor. There's no time like the present."

Chapter Thirty-Five

THE GARCIA MANSION

In the moonlit dark, the steamboat forged along the winding, silvery contours of the Banano. Suarez and Ramón, whose surname was Pérez, took turns at the helm. When not piloting, each would stand lookout at the bow. A log bobbing along in the water might hole the hull, or there might be ripples indicating the presence of rocks just below the surface. By day, such hazards were readily detectable to an experienced pilot; at night, less so.

The stars faded and dawn broke. A thin mist hovered above the river. This was the only hour at which the forest was anything like quiet. There was a pause in the ruckus, like an in-drawing of breath before the exhalation of a new day.

Shortly before noon we encountered a band of *indios*, standing at the river's edge. At first there were only two of them, then half a dozen, then a dozen. They manifested from the forest shadows like wraiths. They were small and wiry, and were clad in grass skirts, feathered headdresses and extraordinarily large, saucer-shaped nose rings. Paint adorned their coppery skin in ceremonial patterns – stripes on their faces, dots and whorls on their chests – and their jet-black hair was uniformly worn in a pageboy cut. Each carried a wooden hunting spear with a tip of sharpened bone.

They eyed us as we went by. There was something inordinately solemn in their gaze and I wondered how we must seem to them, we emissaries from another world, a world of steam power and elaborate, all-covering clothing. People like us had entered their land unbidden and taken it over, bringing guns and diseases and a lust for material acquisition. Did they hate us? Were we enigmas to them? Did they feel anything about us at all?

As the steamboat passed by, one by one, imperturbably, the *indios* turned and melted back into the forest. I expected at least one of them might turn round and look at us again, but none did. We, it seemed, did not merit a backward glance.

With the sun past its zenith, Suarez announced that we would be reaching the Garcia mansion in less than an hour. He drew our attention, too, to the clouds that were gathering to the north. They were iron grey, forbidding and mountainously tall.

"A bad storm, *señores*," said he. "There will be rain – rain like you have never known."

"Rain can be useful," said Holmes. "It can cover our approach to the house, for one thing."

"We're going to sneak up on it?" said Grier. "Is that the plan?"

"Why not just walk up to the front door and demand that Beryl give us Harry?" said Sir Henry. "We are five, and she is just one. She will have no alternative but to do as we say."

"This is a woman who will stop at nothing," said Holmes. "She has twice committed premeditated murder. She unleashed a potentially deadly insect on a hapless victim. She stole a child. She is not to be underestimated. If she feels cornered, she might resort to some desperate act whose consequences would be most regrettable."

"She might hurt Harry, is that what you're saying?"

"That is what I am trying *not* to say. We also have no idea if she is alone in the mansion. She may have servants there, such as Antonio, who could have journeyed from England ahead of her to prepare the house for her arrival. She may also have a band of local thugs hired to protect her. She may have a rifle and no qualms about shooting at us from a window. Given all these considerations, to 'just walk up to the front door' is the least wise tactic open to us. Stealth, on the other hand, is our friend."

Thunder rumbled ominously in the distance. At the sound, the noise of the forest creatures became muted. They knew what was coming. Now was the time to huddle down and take shelter.

A cool wind swept in from the north, shivering through the forest canopy. The drop in temperature would have been welcome, had one not known what it presaged. The thunderclouds continued to grow, swelling like some titanic fungus. Lightning chased back and forth within their depths.

The sunlight dimmed. Then the rain started.

It was, as Suarez had said, rain like one had never known. It was rain of Biblical proportions. It was rain to make the fiercest downpour of an English autumn seem like a mere spring shower. It hammered onto the trees, making boughs droop and leaves drop. It pounded onto the river, turning its surface to a seething shimmer. It fell in vertical streams, as though from some mighty cataract.

Suarez and Ramón remained topside, sheltering together in the wheelhouse. Ramón had boarded up the shattered side window, so that they were able to keep dry, more or less. The rest of us went below decks, hurrying down the narrow companionway and filing through a hatch into the steamboat's single cramped cabin. The rain drummed on the caulked planks above us like a thousand stamping feet.

"This is preposterous," said Mortimer. "We will catch our death if we go out in such weather."

"When we get to the house, you are welcome to stay on the boat, Mortimer," said Holmes. "You do not have the experience in this kind of venture that Watson and I have, or indeed that Sir Henry and Corporal Grier have. You are, for want of a better word, a civilian. No one would think any the less of you were you to sit this one out. In fact, I recommend it. We can manage perfectly well without you."

Mortimer remonstrated, but I could tell he was relieved. He lacked the physicality of the rest of us. As a rural physician, he had little need of it. He might prove a liability rather than an asset.

Presently, we heard the engine die down. This was the signal to go back up on deck. The plan was that Suarez and Ramón would leave us on the riverbank just around the corner from the mansion and would remain there with the steamboat, out of sight, while we made our approach on foot.

Outside, we were soaked to the skin within seconds. The rain was warm, but that was small consolation. There was no convenient landing place on the bank, so we had to clamber over the side of the boat and lower ourselves into the water. Submerged up to the thighs, we waded ashore. Then, dripping and squelching, the four of us strode through the forest, with Grier once again wielding Suarez's machete to hack out a path.

Even among the trees there was no relief from the rain. The foliage funnelled it down onto us like some sort of natural sluice mechanism. Meanwhile, lightning flickered overhead like snakes' tongues and thunder crackled.

We had some notion where the Garcia estate lay, and within half an hour we caught a glimpse of something large and off-white ahead of us. This proved to be a two-storey colonial mansion with a verandah running all the way around the lower floor and louvred shutters on the windows. It sat on a hillside, its front elevation supported by posts whose bases were driven into the earth.

The house might have been impressive once, even imposing, but time and neglect had left it in a sorry state. The apex of the roof sagged and many of the slates were missing. The paintwork was peeling and discoloured. Vines wreathed their tendrils over its walls. Several of the window shutters dangled off a single hinge, and a couple were missing completely.

The land surrounding this dilapidated edifice had likewise seen better days. Everything was shaggily overgrown. What man had carved out as his own, the forest had begun to reclaim. Still in evidence, however, were the remnants of an ornamental pond, thick with green slime, and a few flowerbeds and trellises. There was also, just visible, a series of steps cut into the earth and shored up with wooden risers. These led down to a jetty that jutted out perpendicular into the river, slumped drunkenly on its pilings.

Holmes commanded us to keep still and stay out of sight, and for a time we crouched, observing the mansion through the rain's rippling, gauzy screen.

Eventually I said, "There seems to be nobody home."

What with the hissing rain and the intermittent peals of thunder, I felt under no compunction to lower my voice.

"No. See there." Holmes pointed to one of the downstairs windows. "Twice I have spied a figure moving within."

"Are you sure? This wretched rain – it's hard to make out anything clearly."

"I am sure. I propose we split our party in half. Watson and I will approach the house from this side. Sir Henry and Grier will approach it from the other."

"A two-pronged assault," said Grier. "Good idea. That way, if one lot of us are seen, the other lot may not be."

"You have twenty minutes to circumvent the house, keeping to the trees. When you are at the far side and ready to proceed, give some sort of signal."

"I can do birdcalls. My impersonation of a whippoorwill is, I have been told, uncanny."

"How does it sound? Do it so that we can know, but softly."

Grier sheathed the machete in his belt, cupped his hands and hooted through them. The call sounded very much like the word "whippoorwill". "When I deliver it at full volume," he said, "you will be able to hear it clearly above the rain."

"Good," said Holmes. "A whippoorwill it is. Each pair of us will move in simultaneously. You and Sir Henry, Grier, take the verandah and try the front door. Watson and I will look for a rear entrance. Agreed?"

There were nods all round. Then Sir Henry and Grier crept off through the undergrowth.

"Now to see how this all plays out," said Holmes.

"Yesterday," I said, "when you spoke of a snake in our midst… I have been racking my brains, but I am still unsure to whom you were referring. I am wondering whether it is Sir Henry, and that is the reason why you have sent him off with Grier. You mistrust him and would rather he were not present when we have our confrontation with Mrs Stapleton."

"You and I are to go in early, then, Watson? Is that my plan? The two of us alone, without reinforcements?"

"Yes. Better that than have a traitor with us, ready to stab us in the back."

"There are few people in this world in whom I have implicit faith. You, it goes without saying, are one of them. Another is Sir Henry Baskerville."

"Really?" I said. "But Sir Henry attacked Grier with the hook block."

"Did he?"

"Did he not? You said as much."

"I said it was plausible. I did not go so far as to declare it a fact."

"So having Mortimer and me keep watch over Sir Henry – there was no real justification for it?"

"A feint, so that the enemy would think I had fallen for his trick."

"You could have told me that, Holmes," I said somewhat hotly. "If nothing else, all this time I have been thinking ill of Sir Henry, without good cause. Might you not have taken me into your confidence?"

"For the feint to work, it had to be convincing," said Holmes, "and for *that* to happen, you could not be a party to it. You are accomplished in many fields but dissimulation is not one of them."

I nodded, acknowledging the truth of this. Unlike Holmes with his natural bent for theatrics and disguises, I struggled with subterfuge and was apt to give the game away through some careless word or action. Thus he was at pains to leave me ignorant of his more intricate stratagems until they were revealed.

"Well then," I said, "by a process of elimination, the enemy must be Grier."

"What leads you to that conclusion? Did Grier not, after all, come to see me at Baker Street in order to engage my services right at the very start of this affair?"

"Yes, but think about it. Grier may have feared that Sir Henry would come to his senses and seek your aid. By doing so himself before Sir Henry could, he could give the impression of innocence. Moreover, having gained your confidence, he would then be able to monitor the investigation at first hand and perhaps even subtly misdirect you along the way."

"A bluff, in other words?" said Holmes. "If so, a spectacularly bold one."

"No less boldly, Grier inflicted that injury on himself with the hook block and planted the cufflink to cast the blame on Sir Henry."

"And the reason for this drastic measure?"

"He had some idea that you were on to him, and sought to mislead you."

"I am not certain I would be willing to put myself to that much trouble and discomfort just to allay suspicion. No, Watson, Grier is as pure as the driven snow. I trust him as much as I do you and Sir Henry. Our 'snake' is someone else."

I scratched my head. "I am very confused right now."

"Some might say that was the natural state of Dr John Watson."

"Too harsh."

"You are right. I apologise, old friend."

"Could the villain be Suarez?" I offered.

"Suarez? That affable old worthy?"

"He has hardly been exerting himself to help us fulfil our quest. I am convinced his launch can go faster than he has allowed it to, and if anyone would know how best to sabotage it, it is he."

"And he was even willing to sacrifice the boat altogether?" said Holmes.

"Why not? It might have gained him a few days' extra pay."

"Another drastic measure. You seem to think that there is nothing people will not resort to in the name of distracting or swindling others. For the record, the various acts of sabotage carried out on Suarez's launch could not have been by his own hand. They were simply too inept for that. Recall how Suarez repaired the engine when it faltered; how little time it took him. Whatever the mechanical fault was, it can hardly have been serious since it offered him so little challenge. The true saboteur, not being *au fait* with engines, made a very poor fist of it."

He paused while a rumble of thunder rose to a crescendo and dwindled.

"As for the leak," he went on, "I took the opportunity to examine the damage over Suarez's shoulder as he was mending it. From the looks of it, a screwdriver or chisel or similar implement was used, something from the launch's toolbox. It was done hastily and clumsily. Suarez would surely have been subtler. Then there is the matter of the footprints beside the tree to which he had tied the launch's painter. I identified two separate sets. One was Suarez's, from when he tied the painter to it. He is not a tall man and takes, by my estimation, a rather dainty size seven shoe. The other set were left by someone with larger feet, and can only have belonged to whoever untied the painter."

"So if it is not Sir Henry, and not Grier, and not Suarez, then that leaves…"

"Shh!" Holmes held up a hand. "Do you hear that?"

Dimly through the rattle of the rain I discerned the rhythmic throb of an engine. Moments later, the steamboat appeared from around the bend in the river. It was cruising slowly towards the jetty.

On deck I saw two figures, one behind the other. The one in front was Suarez. The one behind, Mortimer. Mortimer was holding something to the Costa Rican's throat – a slim, silvery object. Ramón was in the wheelhouse, steering, looking anxious.

"Beryl!" Mortimer called out as he caught sight of the mansion. "Beryl! It's me. James. Are you there? They are coming for you, Beryl. Be on your guard. Holmes, Watson, the others… They are here."

"There is our Judas, Watson," said Holmes with grim satisfaction. "There is Beryl Stapleton's aider and abettor and someone who has been a thorn in our side since this whole affair began. I give you Dr James Mortimer, showing his true colours at long last."

Chapter Thirty-Six

DUAL HOSTAGES

"**B**ut... But..."

I was lost for words.

"But Mortimer is our friend?" said Holmes. "He may have been during our investigation into the hound. Five years on, he is our friend no longer. He has thrown in his lot with Mrs Stapleton."

"But why?"

"The reason is, I suspect, the reason any man would commit heinous deeds on behalf of a woman. The oldest reason in the book. Love."

"Beryl!" Mortimer yelled once more, as Ramón reduced speed and guided the steamboat carefully in alongside the jetty. "Can you hear me?"

There was definite ardour in his voice. He seemed almost euphoric, indeed. I was fairly sure that the object he was holding at Suarez's throat in a white-knuckled grasp was a surgical scalpel.

Holmes stood erect and stepped out from the forest into Mortimer's eyeline.

"Mortimer." The word, though delivered in a loud, authoritative voice, was drowned by thunder, and he was obliged to repeat it. "That's enough. Let Suarez go. He is innocent in all of this."

"I need him as my hostage, Holmes," came the reply. "Without him, I would not have been able to convince Ramón to bring us to the house. Ramón would not have been nearly so compliant if he did not think that I was prepared to slit open Suarez's jugular vein. Is that not right, Ramón?"

The steamboat pilot nodded guiltily.

"Take me instead," Holmes said. "I offer myself as a substitute."

"Oh no, Holmes. That would not do at all. Suarez won't think me rude, I am sure, when I say that he poses little threat to me. Whereas you, sir, are a dangerous man. You can fight. You have keen wits. You would find some way of turning the tables."

"And if I were to promise to offer no resistance?"

"I would not believe you."

Holmes canted his head to one side. "You see through me. But what is your next move, Doctor? We are in mate, but do you have an endgame?"

"He may not," said a feminine voice from the verandah, "but I do."

It was Beryl Stapleton. She had emerged from the house, barefoot and wearing a white cotton dress with voluminous skirts. I was struck again by her beauty, but also by a wild, imperious look in her eyes that I did not remember from before. She was still breathtakingly lovely. Yet there was a difference about her, a coldness, a haughtiness, which seemed somehow epitomised by the streaks of silver that now shot through her lustrous black hair. She appeared to have aged far more than five years. Here was a woman, I thought, who had undergone suffering, a woman who had been sorely tested and was now crueller, harder, for it.

She made an ushering gesture towards the doorway behind her, and out stepped a boy. I had not seen him myself before, but this could only be Harry Baskerville. His dark hair matched his father's, as did his forthright eyebrows. His eyes were big and round, registering bewilderment.

He hesitated. Mrs Stapleton beckoned to him again, and timidly he went to her side, joining her at the top of the short flight of wooden steps that descended from the verandah to the rankly verdant garden.

"There's a good boy," she said, stroking his hair. The verandah roof, which projected partway over the steps, afforded some shelter from the storm. Whereas the rest of us were wet through, both Mrs Stapleton and Harry remained more or less dry.

By now, the steamboat was at a standstill and Mortimer was directing Suarez to disembark. No sooner was the Costa Rican on the jetty than Mortimer leapt down to join him. Suarez stiffened as the scalpel resumed its place at his throat. He craned his head as far away from its blade as he dared. I wondered whether Mortimer would have the mettle to inflict a fatal wound if required to. I rather suspected he might.

"Harry!"

This shout came from the far side of the mansion. Sir Henry burst from the forest. He raced towards the verandah, forging a wayward path through the tangle of weeds that choked the garden. Grier followed close behind.

"Daddy!" said Harry. All at once his worried little face became rapturous. He was beaming all over. He made to run towards his father, but Mrs Stapleton stayed him with a firm hand.

"Do not move, Harry."

"But that's my daddy."

"And I said do not move. You too, Henry. Stop right there."

A brief flash of lightning, and the concomitant roll of thunder, served to punctuate her command.

Sir Henry slowed his pace but did not halt. "Or what,

you witch? Give me back my son. Hand him over to me right now."

"I shall not warn you again."

So saying, Mrs Stapleton reached into a pocket of her dress and produced a glass specimen jar. Something squat, bristly and many-legged was contained within.

Swiftly she unscrewed the specimen jar's lid, leaving it loose but still in place. Clutching Harry to her side with one hand, she poised the jar next to him with the other.

"What *is* that?" Sir Henry said. He and Grier were now level with the verandah steps.

"It is something I will unleash on Harry," said Mrs Stapleton, "if you force me to."

"Daddy…" Harry moaned, quailing.

The thing in the jar wriggled and writhed, as if it sensed the child's fear and was eager to be released.

"Do as she says, Sir Henry," Holmes cautioned. "And you, Grier. You should avoid antagonising her too."

Grier had his hand around the haft of the machete and was poised to draw it. At Holmes's instruction, but with a show of great reluctance, he relinquished his grip on the weapon.

"Unless I miss my guess," Holmes continued, "what Mrs Stapleton is holding is a Brazilian wandering spider. Genus *Phoneutria*, family *Ctenidae*. It is perhaps the most dangerous spider in the world."

"You are right, Mr Holmes," said Mrs Stapleton. "A Brazilian wandering spider. Its bite can kill a child, or even a grown man. This one here, it is very sensitive to disturbance. It does not like to be shaken around in this jar and is showing clear signs of distress. That being so, it will attack any creature it sees as a threat. I do not need to tell you how easily it might think that a three-year-old, squirming the way Harry is now, is a danger to it."

"For the love of God, Beryl," said Sir Henry, "what has Harry ever done to you? He is just a child. Give him to me, and then let us talk about this."

"Just a child," she echoed. "True. It is not what Harry *is* that matters. It is what he represents."

"And what is that?"

Before she could answer, Harry tried to break away from her. Mrs Stapleton pulled him even closer to her.

"Now, now, Harry, we had an agreement," she said in a parody of the soft croon of a loving mother. "What did we say when we were leaving England? We said you must behave yourself at all times, or...?"

"Or," Harry finished, "I would never see my daddy again."

"Quite right. You promised your Mama Beryl, didn't you? It was a very solemn promise. You even crossed your heart."

"But Daddy is here now. I've behaved myself. Can I go to him? I don't like that spider. I don't want it to bite me."

Mrs Stapleton was having none of it. "Look how the lid

sits on this jar, Harry. So lightly. How easy it would be for it to fall off. If you nudge me, even the tiniest little bit, it *will* fall off. The spider will be out in a flash. You do not want that, do you?"

"No, Mama Beryl. No, I don't."

"Then you have to keep still, like I said. As still as you can."

"Yes, Mama Beryl."

By now, Mortimer and Suarez were halfway up the steps from the river, the one pushing the other ahead of him. It was a dire predicament. Our villainous duo had a hostage each and could kill either with just the slightest of gestures. Holmes, Sir Henry and Grier, for all their combined physical prowess, were rendered powerless. Nor could Ramón be counted on to become involved.

There was, however, one factor which our antagonists had so far neglected.

Me.

Chapter Thirty-Seven

ARCHITECTS OF MISERY

I was still lurking in the forest, as yet unnoticed by Mrs Stapleton. There had to be some way of using this to our advantage. I just could not think how.

I could try to shoot Mrs Stapleton, but Harry stood between her and me. There was no guarantee I would not hit him by mistake.

Much the same was true of Dr Mortimer and Suarez. The only way I could shorten the range between me and either of my targets would be to come out into the open, and not only would that lose me the element of surprise, it would diminish only slightly the risk of the bullet finding the wrong mark.

For that matter, once I fired the first shot – and assuming it incapacitated whomever I was aiming at, be it Mrs Stapleton or Dr Mortimer – I might not get the chance to fire the second before the other of the twain was able to kill his or her hostage. In other words, I would have to choose which out of Harry and Suarez to save and which to sacrifice. That was the sort of choice no man should ever have to make.

Even as I inwardly debated my options – and found them unenticing – the whole question was rendered moot by Mortimer.

"I see Holmes, I see Sir Henry, I see Grier," he said, nodding at each man in turn. "I do not see Watson. I can only assume he is loitering nearby, perhaps thinking how he might save the day. Watson! I know you're out there. I know you can hear me. I know, too, that you have a revolver. Show yourself. And when you do, make sure that you have your hands above your head and the revolver is in one of them. I want to see the gun held by the barrel between thumb and forefinger. If you fail to meet these conditions, you will live to regret it. By which I mean, Señor Suarez will *not*."

"Do not be concerned for me, Dr Watson," Suarez said gamely. "I would die rather than let these *canallas* win." From the way he spat out the Spanish word, I had no doubt that it meant something highly uncomplimentary.

"Even if the old man cares nothing for himself, Dr Watson," said Mrs Stapleton, "I have Harry. Do as James says, or the boy will die."

That left me with no alternative. I raised my hands,

revolver held as instructed, and stepped out from the forest, into the full force of the cascading rain.

"There he is, the last of our players," said Mortimer. Rainwater plastered his hair to his scalp, bedewed the lenses of his glasses, and poured down his gloating face. "Put the gun down now, Watson. On the ground. There's a good man."

I bent and laid the revolver at my feet. "You worthless wretch, Mortimer," I said as I straightened up. "What do you hope to gain from this?"

"He gains what I gain," said Mrs Stapleton. "Revenge." Again, lightning flashed. Again, thunder rumbled. Both phenomena, however, were markedly less intense now than before. The storm was starting to relent.

"Revenge for what?" I said. "Unless I am misremembering things badly, you were a woman living in terror of a domineering husband. You were even willing to pretend to be his sister in order to protect your and his assumed identities. That way, nobody in Devon would associate the siblings Jack and Beryl Stapleton with the married couple Jack and Beryl Vandeleur, a Yorkshire schoolmaster of ill renown and his wife."

"I also did it so that Jack could romance Laura Lyons without any questions being raised."

"While you, likewise, were seemingly free to be courted by Sir Henry, which would encourage him to come to Merripit House and thus afford greater opportunity for your husband to kill him with that terrible hound of his. Stapleton made you an accomplice to all his crimes, until the time came when you rebelled, whereupon he tied you up and locked you away in an upstairs room. If it had not been for Holmes, Sir Henry and myself, he would certainly have killed you. Instead, through our combined efforts, you were liberated from his tyranny and are alive today. You owe us a debt of gratitude. Where on earth does this desire for revenge stem from?"

"From here." Beryl Stapleton nodded in the direction of her belly, near which she held the specimen jar with its crawling, agitated occupant. "From the womb which held a child who never lived."

"A child?" I said. "But whose?"

My eye strayed to Sir Henry.

He shook his head adamantly. "Not mine. It cannot have been."

"No," said Mrs Stapleton. "My husband was the father. I fell pregnant around the time he began his campaign to claim his Baskerville birthright. I did not even know I was with child, not with any certainty, until two months after he died. It was during those same two months that Sir Henry and I became close."

"You never told me, Beryl," said Sir Henry. "You could have said something. I'm sure I would have understood."

"Would you?" she retorted. "Or would you have seen a

woman with a bad reputation? One whose 'condition' would only make life more complicated for you?"

"We could have come to some kind of accommodation."

"Fine words, but hollow, as all men's words are. Once I realised I was carrying Jack's baby, I knew I had no choice. To protect myself – and also you, Henry, for I still had favourable feelings towards you – I decided I must leave Devon. I fled to my homeland, with my manservant Antonio. Here in Costa Rica I was still Beryl Garcia, of the well-respected Garcias of San José. I was a woman of good breeding and good standing. I would be able to distance myself from Jack's crimes. I would have my baby, and in time I would find myself a new husband. This was my plan."

"But it did not come to pass," said Holmes.

"It did not." All at once, Mrs Stapleton looked forlorn. "While I was away in England, my family's fortunes fell. My father's business collapsed. My mother took ill. My brother, my only sibling, was killed in a knife fight after a drunken argument at a gambling den. My father sold our house in San José to help pay off his debts and moved with my mother to this place, our country residence, which was all he had left. I came to join them here, and together the three of us lived like poor people. It was hard, so hard. We could not afford servants other than Antonio – good old Antonio, loyal come what may – and we had no friends nearby to turn to. For weeks Papa and I tended to my sick mother, even as my belly grew. Then Mama died, but after all that, still we had hope. My child would bring joy. That was what we thought. But the child…"

She hesitated, then continued.

"It was not born as it should have been. It was a child conceived in anger and fear, and its body had all the signs of that. It lived for five minutes only. The midwife, a local wise woman, said it was a mercy when it stopped breathing. No child like that child could ever have had a happy, healthy life."

Her face had taken on a tragic cast as she recalled this profound sadness. I found myself almost feeling sorry for her, in spite of everything.

"That was the end for my father," she said. "The final heartbreak. We buried him over there, Antonio and I, near the river, beside my mother. I was lost. I had nothing any more. A year passed, two, three. And then Antonio was gone, too. My last link to my old life, dead. I was truly alone. Everything was ashes. There seemed little point in living, yet still I lived. I had time to think. I thought about what had happened in England. I thought about Jack, and I thought about you, Henry, and you, Mr Holmes and Dr Watson."

Her spine straightened, and the fierce glow of imperiousness returned to her eyes.

"And the more I thought about the three of you, the more I understood who was responsible for my misery. Jack was a cruel man, yes, and he should not have tried to seize the Baskerville legacy from Sir Charles and Henry in the way he did. But the title and the land should have been his nonetheless. Should have been *ours*. You three were the ones who denied us our due. You were the ones who ruined my future and left me with nothing – nothing but a mouldering mansion in the depths of the forest."

"And we were the ones," said Holmes, "who must be made to pay."

"Yes! Exactly!"

As Mrs Stapleton exclaimed these words, the specimen jar shook in her hand. The lid slipped a little to one side, leaving a narrow gap. The spider lifted an exploratory leg. The tip of its leg fitted through the gap but the spider could not seem to push the lid fully off. I estimated that the creature's body was five inches long from its head to the end of its abdomen, and its legs might span a good twelve inches from one side to the other when it was not bounded by the confines of the jar. It was a truly hideous-looking beast, one of nature's great aberrations.

"I scraped together what money I could," said Mrs Stapleton. "I sold my few remaining possessions. I did things that I am not proud of and that I will not talk about. Whatever I had to, in order to earn enough to buy passage back to England. I travelled with nothing but the clothes on my back and a thirst for vengeance. I made my way to Devon, and there I began laying my plans. By chance, one of the first people I encountered in Dartmoor was Dr Mortimer. He too, as it turned out, was nursing a grudge. We had much in common, and decided to join forces."

"What was it?" I said. "What shared cause can possibly have united the two of you?"

Before either she or Mortimer could answer, Holmes said, "This mansion of yours is a rather ramshackle place, isn't it, Mrs Stapleton?"

The remark seemed something of a non sequitur, and I was puzzled. Why was Holmes bothered about the state of the house when lives hung in the balance?

"You characterise it as 'mouldering'," he continued. "I would go further and call it 'crumbling'. There are parts that look ready to collapse at any moment. The pillars which support the verandah you are standing on, to take an example at random. A bird might land on one and it would give way. Not even a large bird, for that matter. Something as small and light as a whippoorwill, for instance."

"A whippoorwill?" said Beryl Stapleton contemptuously. "What are you talking about, Mr Holmes? That is a North American bird. There are no whippoorwills in Costa Rica. Have you gone mad?"

Dr Mortimer was as perplexed as she, and wary, too. "Watch out, Beryl, my dear. Holmes is a slippery one. He may seem to be talking in riddles, but he is up to something."

"I was merely making an observation," Holmes said,

with every appearance of nonchalance. "I do not genuinely think that a whippoorwill, or any bird, could bring one of those pillars down. It would take an entity much larger. A chimneysweep, perhaps."

I realised then what he meant by these insinuating comments.

More importantly, so did Benjamin Grier.

Chapter Thirty-Eight

HOIST WITH HER OWN PETARD

Grier moved with a speed that belied his enormous bulk. He bent his knees, then rammed his shoulder into the pillar beside which he and Sir Henry were standing. He hit it with every ounce of strength in his body.

The old, half-rotten length of timber gave way. With an almighty, splintering *crack* that was almost as loud as the thunderclap which coincided with it, the pillar split in two.

The floorboards of the verandah, suddenly deprived of one of their props, sagged. They did not give way entirely, but they dropped just enough to throw Mrs Stapleton off-balance. The specimen jar fell from her hand, landing with a loud *clunk*.

Little Harry staggered too. Having been released from his captor's grasp, he tumbled forward to the stairs. Sir Henry was off like a champion sprinter from the starting blocks.

He darted up the verandah steps, grabbed his son and scooped him up into his arms, before backing hurriedly away.

Mrs Stapleton let out a hoarse, terrible shriek and crumpled, as though in a swoon. This galvanised Dr Mortimer, who for several seconds had been left dumbfounded by the turn of events. He thrust Suarez aside and hastened towards the house. Concern was etched on his features. It seemed that he could think only of his Beryl, his confederate and paramour. He was oblivious to all else.

And "all else" included me. I snatched up my revolver. I thumbed back the hammer. I was no great marksman, but Mortimer was less than five yards away. I had a clear shot. Blinking the rain out of my eyes, I took aim. I squeezed the trigger. The gun bucked and roared in my hand, and Mortimer plunged headlong to the ground. He did not get up.

Sherlock Holmes nodded to me in approval. Grier had performed as he had hoped, and so had I. Holmes crossed over to Mortimer's side, stooped to examine him, then mounted the steps. Swiftly he scanned the floorboards until he found what he was looking for. Raising one leg, he brought his foot down hard, once, twice, three times, with an expression of disgust and loathing etched on his face. Each impact, loud enough to be audible above the rain, was as much a squelch as a thump. He studied the results and seemed satisfied.

"The Brazilian wandering spider wanders no more," he said.

Mrs Stapleton moaned. Holmes knelt beside her, then summoned me over.

"She has been bitten," he said. "When she dropped the specimen jar, the spider escaped. It sank its fangs into her foot."

The bite marks were just above her heel, perilously close to the posterior tibial vein. I envisaged the venom racing through her bloodstream towards her heart. She was starting to shudder and her breath was coming in ragged gasps.

I looked at Holmes. "I fear there is nothing I can do for her. If that species of spider is as deadly as you say…"

"It is."

Abruptly, Mrs Stapleton went into convulsions. Her eyes bulged. She started foaming at the mouth. Truly repulsive retching sounds emanated from her throat.

Her death throes lasted a full minute, until all at once she went limp. There was a rattle of escaping breath, and it was over.

I closed the lids over her sightless eyes.

"The poor woman," I said. "Even after all she has done, it would be a hard man who did not feel some level of compassion for her."

"Do not forget that she was willing to kill Harry in just the same manner as she herself has been killed. She was hoist with her own petard, and there can be no more fitting end for her than that."

"I do not mean how she died. I mean how she lived, at least during the last few years. Alone in this godforsaken spot, with faded grandeur all around. Dwelling on the past and the slights inflicted upon her, whether real or imagined. Her bitterness festering until it became a hatred so blindingly intense, it could only be sated by the suffering of others."

"My sympathies lie elsewhere," said Holmes. "Principally with young Harry there. Sir Henry, how is the lad?"

Sir Henry had Harry clutched to his chest. He looked like a man who would never let go of his son again. He fixed Holmes with a glistening gaze and nodded. "He is safe," he said softly. "He is safe, he is safe, he is safe."

At that moment, Dr Mortimer gave an agonised groan. He tried to sit up, but sank down again immediately.

A swift examination revealed that my bullet had entered his chest between the fifth and sixth ribs. To judge by the blood on his lips and the wheeziness of his breathing, it had nicked a lung.

"Can anything be done for *him*, Watson?" Holmes enquired.

"If we can get him to a hospital, then possibly."

"There is no hospital for miles around, *señor*," Suarez offered. "The nearest I know of is back at Puerto Limón. It is the same distance from here to there as it is from here to

San José, but we will go quicker if we travel with the river's current rather than against. But I have to ask, why not simply leave this man to perish? Is his life worth saving?"

"If it means he eventually faces justice in an English court of law," I said, "then yes."

"Where surely he will be sentenced to hang for his crimes," said Grier.

"I am not a judge. I do not get to decide who should live and who should die. I am a doctor, and if someone may be saved, I must save him."

"Even if it is someone who held power over my life?" said Suarez.

"Even if it is someone you yourself shot?" said Grier.

"Even then," I said.

"There are unresolved questions about this case," Holmes chimed in, "and Mortimer can supply the answers. For that reason alone, Watson should minister to him."

So it was decided. Grier carried Mortimer down to the jetty and onto the steamboat. Soon Ramón had built up steam and we were heading away from that accursed spot, downriver, while above us the storm's fury was abating yet further and a pale, watery sun had begun to shine through the clouds.

Chapter Thirty-Nine

MAKING A CLEAN BREAST OF THINGS

I had made Dr Mortimer as comfortable as possible. I had
bound up the bullet wound, and now he was propped up
in a sitting position in a curtained-off sleeping berth at the
aft end of the steamboat's cabin. While his torso remained
erect, blood would fill his lung less quickly.

His face was corpse white, aside from the crimson-
flecked lips. Every time he coughed, pink spittle sprayed.

He had agreed to talk to Holmes. I was against the idea,
arguing that he should rest and conserve his energy, but
Mortimer was sanguine.

"I am as well versed in medicine as you, Watson," said he.
"I know what sort of wound I have and what the prognosis
is. I am never going to reach hospital. I am going to drown
in my own blood within a matter of hours. Why not make
a clean breast of things while I still can?"

So the two men conversed while I looked on.

It was Mortimer, not Holmes, who asked the first question.

"When...?" He heaved a wet, sucking breath and tried again. "When did you know?"

"That you and Mrs Stapleton were co-conspirators?" said Holmes. "You may congratulate yourself, Mortimer, on the fact that you both had me hoodwinked right up until Harry's kidnap. Only then did I realise that Beryl Stapleton had been behind it all – the moth, the murder of Lady Audrey, the framing of Laura Lyons. I knew, too, that she had a male accomplice, thanks to the second set of footprints beside the hedge at Baskerville Hall. I let everyone think that I believed this colleague to be Antonio."

"But by the time Mrs Stapleton came back to England, Antonio was dead," I pointed out.

"We know that now, Watson, but it is of no consequence. It cannot have been Antonio at the hedge for one simple reason."

"Namely?"

"It was Mortimer."

"How could you be so sure?" said Mortimer.

"Your dog," said Holmes simply.

"Galen?"

"Harry was playing with Galen when all at once the dog became aware of the presence of someone behind the hedge."

"That was intentional. The plan was that Galen would come over, Harry would inevitably follow, and then we could grab the boy."

"Of course it was intentional," said Holmes. "In fact you summoned Galen to you, didn't you? Mrs Barrymore spoke of a sound which she took to be a twig snapping underfoot. Her exact words were: '*Crick-crack*, it went. Like that'. I myself had heard a similar sound beforehand, when you and I, Mortimer, met at Crookback Samuel. It was the double cluck of the tongue which you use to bring Galen to heel. One might easily mistake it for the snapping of a twig."

"Dear me. Yes." Mortimer coughed again, rackingly. The fit lasted a good twenty seconds. By the end, his lips were heavily bedewed with blood, which I wiped away with a handkerchief. "I thought that if I did it softly enough, Mrs Barrymore and Harry would not notice, while of course Galen, with his sharp ears, would."

"And if Mrs Barrymore went to investigate, as she did, Mrs Stapleton had a venomous centipede ready to put her out of action."

"Yes. Horrid thing, that centipede. Beryl purchased it from a dealer in exotic animals, a Mr Sherman of Pinchin Lane in Lambeth."

"He is known to us," said Holmes.

"You may have noticed that arthropods in general loomed large in her plans. A moth, a centipede…"

"And that spider with which she threatened Harry and which ultimately proved her undoing. I presume she had developed an affinity towards such creatures owing to her husband's interest in entomology. In that respect, they were a useful means of misdirection, intended to make us think that Jack Stapleton might still be alive."

"They were a kind of tribute to him, too. For all that he ill-used her, Beryl still loved Stapleton, in her way."

"And you loved her."

"I did," Mortimer said.

"Yet it is not love alone that drove you to do what you did," said Holmes.

"You know my true motivation?"

"I have a fair idea. But first, let us turn our attention to how the two of you met. Mrs Stapleton told us it was by chance."

"She may have thought so, but it was not. I spied her one morning in Coombe Tracey, outside an estate agents. This was very soon after she came back to Dartmoor, just last January. She had changed. The years had not been kind to her. Yet who could forget those soulful dark eyes, those long lashes, that proud face? I will admit to being somewhat taken with her back in 'eighty-nine, when she was passing herself off as Stapleton's sister. I even set my cap at her then, only for my approaches to be gently but firmly rebuffed. Now she was once more in my neighbourhood. I contrived to bump into her, as it were. We fell to talking. It turned out that she was looking for a place to live, somewhere off the beaten track. I was by then the tenant of Merripit House. I suggested she move in with me. She agreed. She made it plain that the arrangement would be a formal one only. I was not to get 'ideas'. She also said she would be spending most of her time indoors. If she went out at all, it would be at night. This, she told me, was so that nobody would know we were cohabiting, and thus any suspicion of impropriety could be avoided."

Mortimer paused, gathering his strength.

"I was content with that," he said. "I hoped proximity would lead to warmth being kindled between us. It did, to a certain extent. Beryl kept to herself, I went about my daily business, but gradually an intimacy flourished, as it almost inevitably will when a man and a woman are at close quarters for any period of time. I had been unable to establish why she had returned to Dartmoor. I had a hunch about it, but it wasn't until one evening in spring that the truth came out. She was in a dark, melancholy mood that day, and confessed all. What had happened in Costa Rica. Her various family tragedies. The loathing she now felt for Sir Henry and for you two gentlemen. It was Sir Henry whom she wished to suffer most of all. She would hurt him, she said. She would let him know the pain she had known."

"And you agreed to be her ally," said Holmes.

"Let us say that her needs and mine converged. Besides,

by then I was wholly infatuated with her. Even if I had not had a vested interest in her scheme, I would still have gone along with it."

"A vested interest?" I remarked. "Is this the 'true motivation' to which you referred a moment ago? So you had another reason for acting as accomplice to Beryl Stapleton besides merely wishing to curry favour with her."

"We shall come to that shortly, Watson," said Holmes. He fixed his attention back on Mortimer. "Your role, originally, was to help cover up Mrs Stapleton's crimes. You started this by volunteering to prepare Lady Audrey Baskerville's death certificate. Any sign that Lady Audrey had been subdued before her blood was drained – bruising around the nose and mouth, say, resulting from the application of a chloroform-soaked cloth – you could conveniently omit from your report. You also had access to a potential scapegoat in the shape of Mrs Laura Lyons. You were her physician. You were an habitual visitor to her lodgings. You even gave the impression to me that you were more than just her doctor; that you were an ardent admirer of hers."

"You yourself offered the suggestion, Mr Holmes. I merely went along with it. It was a spur-of-the-moment thing. I suppose my thinking was that you were better off believing my interest in her was amorous. It would excuse my some-what unprofessional overzealousness towards her."

"Whereas, in truth, you needed frequent access to her

because you and Mrs Stapleton knew that at some point you might well require a hapless third party to pin blame for your crimes on. I presume you had a key to the front door of the boarding house and also to the door to Mrs Lyons's rooms. You'd borrowed her set of keys one day, while she was in a laudanum-induced stupor, and had copies made. This enabled Mrs Stapleton to enter the house at night undetected, drug Mrs Lyons and kill her."

"You are right."

"With hindsight, Mortimer," I said, "your constant eagerness to become involved in the case does seem rather telling."

"Agreed," said Holmes. "At every turn, there you were, playing the role of concerned citizen, the troubled friend, the solicitous godfather."

Mortimer essayed a wry smile. "Why would you not think it was merely your old ally Dr Mortimer, acting out of concern for Sir Henry, as he had the last time?"

"Indeed I did at first," said Holmes. "And no doubt I was supposed to continue thinking that when you showed yourself so keen to accompany us on our expedition to Costa Rica. Naturally you would be anxious about Harry, your godson. By then, however, I was already certain that you and Mrs Stapleton were in cahoots."

"So why did you agree I should come with you? Why did you not simply denounce me then and there?"

"I felt it was better to have you by my side, where I could keep an eye on you. If all else failed, you could have been persuaded to give up Mrs Stapleton's whereabouts in Costa Rica, which you must have known. What I did not foresee – and this is a source of great regret to me – was that you would make an attempt on Grier's life and try to make Sir Henry seem culpable. This was to deflect attention away from yourself, was it not?"

"Sir Henry was a loose cannon. It was just about conceivable that he might have attacked Grier in some kind of inebriated fit of madness. And you, then, would be so preoccupied with that matter, you would be distracted, your focus diverted. You would think Sir Henry so deranged that he might be prepared to do anything, go to any extreme, even to the point of staging the kidnapping of his own son. Such was my logic, at any rate. It was not a well-thought-through plan, but it was the best I could manage in the circumstances."

"I was not fooled," Holmes said. "However, I still needed you compliant and acquiescent, so I played along with the charade. I did ensure that you were occupied for the rest of the voyage, charging you to look after Sir Henry along with Watson, so that you would have little opportunity to attempt another similar trick."

"I presume Watson was in on it."

"Oh no, he was none the wiser. I have a tendency to

keep Watson in the dark when it comes to my little ruses. It is safer that way. Honest fellow that he is, he is bad at keeping secrets."

"I am well accustomed to being your unsuspecting dupe," I said with a resigned sigh.

"Then, as we began the journey up the Rio Banano, you grew ever more desperate," said Holmes to Mortimer. "You sabotaged Suarez's launch twice, and finally, when that proved an ineffective deterrent, unmoored it."

"Again, though, you did not point the finger at me," said Mortimer.

"As long as we were making progress, there was no call for it. You may have inconvenienced us somewhat, but in the end we still got to where we wanted to be. I would rather you had not taken Suarez hostage at the Garcia mansion. That did somewhat complicate matters. Nevertheless, all was resolved."

"In hindsight, I would rather I had not taken him hostage either. It is the reason I am in this position now, with death's cold breath on my neck. I simply wanted to help Beryl in any way I could."

"And now we come to the heart of it," said Holmes, "why you joined forces with Mrs Stapleton in executing her plan of revenge. It is connected with who you really are."

"Who he really is?" I said, frowning. "You mean there isn't anyone called James Mortimer? He is a fraud?"

"No, Watson. The man you see before you is indeed a country medical officer by the name of James Mortimer. It just happens that he shares near-consanguinity with the greatest villain you or I have ever known."

Holmes gestured towards the occupant of the sleeping berth.

"You are looking, old friend," he said, "at the stepbrother of Professor James Moriarty."

Chapter Forty

DE MORTUIS NIL NISI BONUM

I stared at Dr Mortimer.

"How?" I said. "It is surely not possible. Absurd. Professor Moriarty's stepbrother?"

Mortimer gave a nod. The effort this demanded of him was enormous. It was plain, even to the inexpert eye, that he did not have long left. The life was visibly ebbing out of him.

"It is true," he said.

"But your connection to him was never mentioned when we first knew you."

"The subject never came up. Why would it? Five years ago, few people outside academic circles had ever heard of Professor Moriarty. As far as anyone was aware, he was nothing other than a scientist and philosopher who had suffered a fall from grace. He was not yet renowned as the 'Napoleon of crime', as you have dubbed him, Holmes.

He was not the notorious creature we all now know him to have been, the shadowy, unseen presence at the heart of the London criminal underworld, with a network of agents all across the country doing his bidding. Back then, even I had not the faintest idea of the truth about him. To me, he was always just James, my stepbrother."

"Moriarty's mother, I take it, remarried after his father died," said Holmes.

"That is correct. James was six years old when his father passed away. His mother then met my father, Stephen Mortimer, a widower whose first wife had died in childbirth, delivering me. They were wed and were a happy couple. The coincidence of each having a son named James was forever a source of amusement to them. James and I grew up together and were close, despite the disparity in our ages. We scarcely regarded ourselves as stepbrothers. We called ourselves 'the Brothers James' and were quite inseparable. Even when we were at separate schools, we wrote to each other constantly. James was a prodigy and always seemed destined for great things. He excelled in exams, whereas I was of average ability, scholastically speaking. His teachers often spoke of him in whispers, as though his extraordinary mental gifts merited hushed reverence. It was no surprise that he went into academia, nor that he should write his groundbreaking treatise on the binomial theorem at the tender age of twenty-one."

"I still don't understand," I said. "When did you find out that your stepbrother was not just a mathematical celebrity but something altogether worse?"

"This may seem hard to believe, Watson," replied Mortimer, "but it was around the same time that you did. Before then, I knew there had been some form of disgrace which had obliged him to resign his university chair and move to London to set up as an army coach. James, however, had me convinced that he had been the victim of malicious gossip, nothing more. Jealous rivals had forced him out. He was my beloved brother; who was I to doubt his version of events? When he died in 'ninety-one, like everyone else I accepted the official line that he had been killed in a climbing accident. He had disappeared near Meiringen in the Swiss Alps, so what else could one assume but that he had fallen to his death while attempting to scale some precipice?"

"That was the story my brother Mycroft worked hard to promulgate," said Holmes. "Likewise, for my protection and that of others such as Watson, he and I allowed the world to think that I was dead too."

"I grieved for James sorely and tried to get on with my life," said Mortimer. "However, I could not."

"Why not?" I said.

"For one thing, rumours had begun to swirl regarding James's involvement in certain nefarious enterprises. That was a bitter pill to swallow, discovering that the stepbrother whom I had loved and admired, who was my hero, was not so heroic after all. For another thing, James had always been a cerebral rather than a physical man. The most exercise he ever did was a gentle stroll. He was not the sort to sally forth to Switzerland and go up a mountain just for fun. I decided I could not let this incongruity lie. I went to Meiringen and started digging around. Gradually I unearthed the truth of James's final hours. The picture I pieced together was at odds with all I had been led to believe. I knew, now, that James and you, Holmes, had been mortal enemies and that he had died at your hand."

"It was then, late last year, that you wrote letters to the newspapers defending your stepbrother and casting aspersions on me," said Holmes.

"*You* wrote them, Mortimer?" I said. "Not Colonel James Moriarty?"

"There is no Colonel James Moriarty, Watson," said Holmes. "There never was. It was merely a pseudonym Mortimer used."

"I always thought it a bit rum," I admitted, "two brothers sharing the exact same name."

"I don't think Mortimer really thought it out. Did you, Mortimer?"

"Not really," said Mortimer. "The pseudonym made a kind of sense, I suppose. Colonel James Moriarty, former military man, now in the respected position of station master – the epitome of integrity. I changed my own name slightly, and there it was. It never even occurred to me that it might look strange. But then, I was angry. I was lashing out. Sherlock Holmes was no longer alive but that would not stop me from publicly setting the record straight."

"Which you did in a rather offensive manner, regardless of the fact that I was 'dead'," said Holmes. "Clearly the old adage about '*de mortuis nil nisi bonum*' means nothing to you."

"Those letters prompted me to retaliate in my own way," I said.

"Yes, by publishing your 'Final Problem'," said Mortimer. "That was when…"

He was seized by yet another coughing fit. This one left him choking and gasping, his mouth filled with so much blood that he was obliged to spit it out into a bucket.

"Not long left," he said, sounding more rueful than frightened. "Not long at all. There isn't much more to say, anyway. You returned to the world, Holmes, in April of this year. There you were, blithely going about your business again as if nothing had happened, as if my beloved stepbrother's blood were not on your hands. Imagine how badly I wished to settle scores with you."

"Even though you were fully aware of the extent of Moriarty's wrongdoing."

"Even so."

"And since Mrs Stapleton was all set to embark on her

own campaign of vengeance against Sir Henry, one which would almost inevitably draw Watson and myself into its ambit…"

"Why not merge our goals? If nothing else, it would cement the bond between me and her. A shared project would be the soil in which our love could blossom."

"A project to inflict misery and death," I said.

Mortimer shrugged, as if this made little difference to him.

"But how," Holmes said, "were you proposing to get even? Not by killing me, it would seem."

"By besting you," Mortimer replied simply. "By ensuring that you failed. I am not a murderer."

"You are an accessory to murder."

"True, but I could never have committed the actual deed myself. It is not in my nature. Beryl had that streak within her, that necessary lack of conscience, but not I."

"You seemed ready enough to kill Suarez with that scalpel not so long ago," I said.

"Did I? It was pure pretence. I am too squeamish ever to have delivered a fatal cut. No, all I wanted from this whole enterprise was the chance to prove that I was better than the vaunted Sherlock Holmes and, for that matter, than his doughty associate. I would be doing what my stepbrother had not done, and by that means I could lay James's ghost to rest. But it turns out that it was all in vain and I am the one who has been bested. I am the one who has failed. Perhaps I should have known that I could never be the equal of my stepbrother, let alone his superior. If even he could not win against Sherlock Holmes, then what earthly hope had I?"

"It was ambitious of you, certainly," said Holmes.

"How did you know that James and I were affiliated?" Mortimer asked. "What gave it away?"

"I had already verified that there was no such person as Colonel James Moriarty," my friend said. "Having learned of his 'existence' last year, while I was still allegedly dead and roaming the world in various disguises, I made some enquiries through the auspices of my brother Mycroft. It was a simple matter to ascertain that no railway station in the West Country, or indeed the entire country, had a station master by the name of James Moriarty. He was obviously a fake. I reasoned that the person responsible for the letters to the newspapers was merely some prankster and left it at that. Only when you and I became reacquainted, Mortimer, did I begin to notice certain things about you. Although you are not a blood relation of Professor Moriarty, you exhibit various traits which you must have picked up from him during your shared youth. A tendency to oscillate your head from side to side, for instance, when you are considering something. The frequent use of the phrase 'dear me', a habit of Moriarty's. Then there was the marked similarity between the name James Mortimer and that of the pseudonymous letter writer James Moriarty. Once I knew you were Mrs Stapleton's collaborator, I began to look for reasons why that might be – beyond any passionate feelings you harboured for her, that is. The connections began to mount up until I could no longer deny them."

"Dear me," said Mortimer, with knowing irony. "How transparent I have been, when I thought I was so artfully opaque."

More coughing left him fighting for breath and too weak to continue. Holmes withdrew. I ministered to the dying man for another three hours. His final moments were not pretty, and I shall not recount them here. The end came as a mercy, that is all I will say.

With some relief I joined Holmes, Sir Henry, Harry, Grier and Suarez up on the steamboat's deck. Ramón had the helm. Sir Henry stood at the prow with Harry, an arm around the boy's shoulder, Harry's head resting against his hip. Father and son were talking together in low tones. What confidences they were sharing, I do not know and would not repeat even if I did. They were the present and future of the Baskerville dynasty, and they were proving a comfort to each other, and that should be enough.

Grier, meanwhile, was in some discomfort from a sprained shoulder, a legacy of his Samsonian feat back at the mansion, but was putting a brave face on it. As I came up, I heard him say to Holmes, "My shoulder hurts like the blazes, but it's worth it to know that at last, after all this time, you called me Mr Chimneysweep."

"I referred to 'a chimneysweep', Grier," Holmes replied. "I did not prefix it with 'Mr'."

"Close enough. I said you would use the name in the end, Mr Scarecrow, and you did."

"Let us agree to disagree. Ah, Watson." Holmes turned to me, his eyes begging a question.

In answer, I solemnly shook my head.

"Then it is done," said he. "Any last words from Mortimer?"

"A request that someone should look after Galen for him once he was gone. That is all."

Holmes aimed a glance at Harry Baskerville. "I can think of a certain young shaver who would be more than willing."

"Willing?" I said. "He would be overjoyed."

"And then there would be a new Hound of the Baskervilles," said Holmes. "A far friendlier one than the last."

"It might even symbolise an end to the family curse."

"Who knows, Watson?" my friend mused, with the slimmest of smiles. "It might at that."

The river stretched before us, winding its way through the steaming forest, wide, brown and serene. The sun was at our backs, its heat and light rapidly diminishing. The trees were hung with shadows, and the darkness that lurked between their trunks was fearsome and impenetrable – as fearsome and impenetrable as the darkness that lurks within the hearts of some men.

James Lovegrove is the *New York Times* bestselling author of *The Age of Odin*. He was shortlisted for the Arthur C. Clarke Award in 1998 and for the John W. Campbell Memorial Award in 2004, and also reviews fiction for the *Financial Times*. He is the author of *Firefly: The Magnificent Nine* and of *Firefly: Big Damn Hero* with Nancy Holder and several Sherlock Holmes novels for Titan Books.